From a Laboratory High in the Swiss Alps

where Victor Frankenstein reassembles long-dead limbs and prepares the electrical equipment that will prove his theory that Man can triumph over Death;

To a Love That Would Not Die

as Frankenstein does what he vowed he would not do again—create another being, a woman, who is torn between her love for her creator and her undying bond with the Creature;

To a Blinding Blizzard on the Frozen Arctic Ice

where the final confrontation between Dr. Frankenstein and the Creature begins—a battle between father and son for the ultimate power over life and death and love . . .

Mary Shelley's Frankenstein

Mary Shelley's Frankenstein

by
Leonore Fleischer

**Based on a Screenplay
by Steph Lady and Frank Darabont
from Mary Shelley's Novel**

**With an Afterword
by Kenneth Branagh**

A SIGNET BOOK

SIGNET
Published by the Penguin Group
Penguin Books USA Inc., 375 Hudson Street,
New York, New York 10014, U.S.A.
Penguin Books Ltd, 27 Wrights Lane,
London W8 5TZ, England
Penguin Books Australia Ltd, Ringwood,
Victoria, Australia
Penguin Books Canada Ltd, 10 Alcorn Avenue,
Toronto, Ontario, Canada M4V 3B2
Penguin Books (N.Z.) Ltd, 182-190 Wairau Road,
Auckland 10, New Zealand

Penguin Books Ltd, Registered Offices:
Harmondsworth, Middlesex, England

First published by Signet, an imprint of Dutton Signet,
a division of Penguin Books USA Inc.

First Printing, October, 1994
10 9 8 7 6 5 4 3 2 1

Mary Shelley's
Frankenstein

Life

The newly created planet whirled in the cosmos for more than a billion years, a molten globe ripped again and again by explosions from its core, its surface oozing and erupting liquid fire. If flamed, then it burned, then it smoldered, but it was still hot enough to melt rock and vaporize water. Yet, eventually, in a million years, it would cool, and the toxic icy moisture that formed its atmosphere would melt as condensation on the surface, creating a vast ocean that covered most of the planet, broken only by scattered chains of still-erupting volcanoes.

Another half a billion years and more passed by in the history of the planet Earth. Because of the heavy cloud cover, only dim light from the sun broke through to the surface, which choked under a cloud cover of carbon dioxide, hydrogen sulfide, and methane. There was very little oxygen, and no life. How could life form in that stinking morass of poisonous chemical gases?

Yet is it not the essential nature of life to form, to live, to reproduce, to adapt . . . in short, to survive and prevail? Life is in the loving mother suckling her baby, but it is also in the small bits of coral that link to form great reefs under the sea. Life is in the strong, callused hand wielding the sculptor's chisel, but it is also the single-celled paramecium waving its cilia under a microscope. In the infinite scheme of things, the artist and the bacterium are first cousins.

The miracle does not lie in the incredible diversity of Earth's living species, in the differences between the human baby and the protozoa and the bird and the house cat and the lichen and the komodo dragon, between the kangaroo and the kangaroo rat, the algae and the humpback whale. No, where the miracle lies is in that first moment of creation of *something* out of *nothingness*. For there, close to five billion years ago in Earth's endless ocean, was floating a primordial soup of organic chemicals—organic, but not alive. Carbon, nitrogen, sulfur, hydrogen, separate chemicals.

And yet, the miracle actually happened. Something touched these disparate elements and they formed into compounds—carbohydrates, amino acids, nucleotides—the very building blocks of life. From these compounds would come the first single-celled organisms, near-invisible microscopic beings that ate, moved a little, excreted, divided themselves to multiply, and were, by any definition you can name, alive.

And out of those primitive single-celled bacteria would one day arise Alexander the Great, Homer and Virgil, Leonardo Da Vinci, Mozart, Madame Curie, William Shakespeare, Lao Tzu, Jane Austen, Amelia

Earhart, Emily Dickinson, Martin Luther King, Jr., Isaac Bashevis Singer, a cricketer named Grace, and a baseball player named Willie Mays. From the same simple protozoic organism would be born the painter Paul Gaugin who, when he was dying in Tahiti, would write upon his final masterwork the all-important, unanswerable questions: *"What are we? Where did we come from? Where will we go?"*

Unanswerable because: almost five billion years ago, something touched those loose chemical elements floating like microscopic dumplings in the primordial soup, touched them and made them *alive*. But what? Whose magical hand touched them? What caused that miraculous instant in time when life came into existence where it hadn't existed but a moment earlier?

Many would tell you with the greatest certainty that it must have been the hand of God. But to some others, scientists, the most reasonable answer is a simple one—a natural power source, crackling with energy, most likely radiation or lightning. Yes, common lightning. Picture the first strands of DNA forming under the impact of a strong energy field and little oxygen. Violent electrical storms raging over the surface of the new planet, bolts of lightning striking the ocean, causing chemical reactions, creating the first life. Life's first ingredients were already present in that vast ocean—all they needed was the magic touch of electricity.

This would be a much more comfortable theory if it could be proved empirically, reproduced in a laboratory. But so far, although many, many have tried over the centuries, nobody has yet succeeded in creating life in a test tube.

But suppose that somebody could!

To create life—surely that must be the highest

aspiration of scientific endeavor. What benefit to the human race could be greater than overcoming death? The scientist who finally ascends that unclimbed pinnacle by performing that miracle and cheating death must therefore be the most honored human in history. His name must be enshrined and blessed forevermore. He must be the happiest of men.

And yet . . . what terrible consequences might follow this most godlike of acts? To use the magic touch that makes life eternal? Should life be eternal? Is death not the inevitable last scene in the cycle of nature? Who dares to interrupt that cycle? What might follow such an interruption?

The gods do not take kindly to mortals who usurp their powers, not even for the benefit of humankind. What if, instead of being honored, the creator of life was instead punished as cruelly as the immortal Titan Prometheus?

Before the beginning of history, the greatest god of all, Father Zeus, hid the precious gift of fire away from early man. Prometheus, taking pity on the poor naked creatures trying to exist without heat or light, stole some fire away from the gods and gave it to humankind. For this benevolence he was punished most terribly. Zeus had him chained to a rock, and sent an eagle to devour Prometheus's liver by day. By night, the immortal liver would regenerate, only to be devoured again the next day, so that Prometheus's torment was an eternal sentencing.

And what of the human soul, Man's only immortal part? Can this, too, be recreated in the laboratory? And, if it can, will it be a redeemed soul or one damned, like Prometheus, to eternal perdition?

Much of what follows is taken from the pages, written in a large, flowing hand, of *The Journal of Victor Frankenstein*.

1 Ice

The Barent Sea, 1794

The large wooden ship pitched and yawed, her hull grinding through the thirty-foot swells, her canvas sails straining and flapping dangerously as they filled with the heavy, icy winds. Sailors dressed in slick oilskins clambered with enormous difficulty over the topdeck, trying vainly to keep the vessel under control, but a storm of inconceivable force and violence kept lifting the ship from the waves and dashing her down again, a raging animal worrying its helpless prey with razor-sharp teeth. The merciless ice-laden winds howled around the hapless vessel, whipping the sea into a frenzy to slam again and again at her hull.

Although the three-masted sailing ship the *Aleksandr Nevsky* was built heavy-hulled to withstand the harshness of the Arctic seas, she was hardly a match for such a sudden ferocious storm as this one, and the weight of her decking and timbers cut down sharply on her ability to maneuver. Beaten by the waves and the winds, the *Nevsky* groaned and shuddered as she plowed through the swells.

Visibility was close to zero; not only was the Arctic night inky dark, but a thick mist enveloped the scene, blotting out the constellations and making navigation close to impossible. The only illumination came from momentary bursts of heavy lightning, which cast an eerie glow over the ship, silhouetting the frightened sailors before plunging them back into the depths of night. Making progress in these storm-tossed waters was out of the question; it was all the *Nevsky* could do to keep herself afloat against all odds.

Out of the darkness and chaos the prow would appear and disappear into the raging sea, crashing upward through a swell and slamming back down again, plunging nose-first into the trough. She was still sailing under canvas; the shrouds on the mainmast and mizzenmast had been stowed, but the square-rigged yards on the foremast were still swelling in the howling winds, straining at the mast as the icy blasts from the frozen north tore through them.

Dark shouting figures could be glimpsed and half glimpsed as the crew emerged from the swell and were submerged again, clinging desperately to the lines, slipping and sliding in the sea water that washed over the deck, hampered by their heavy oilskin clothes flapping in the gale and in danger at any moment of being swept overboard into the frigid sea.

From belowdecks, the terrified howling of large, wolflike dogs rose to add their noise to the noise of the storm. Poor sailors even in the best of weather, the teams of sled dogs in the hold were now almost hysterical with fear because of the steep pitching and rolling of the ship. Their natural environment was the open tundra of clean fresh snow, not the foul-smelling convulsing confinement of a ship's hold in a winter storm.

At his station in the prow of the *Nevsky*, young Billy Jenkins, the lookout, heard a sharp cracking noise above him, felt an ominous shivering rippling through the bow, and peered up through streaming water. Dimly, he could see that the topsail brace on the foremast had splintered. The canvas yard had shredded in the wind, and was now hanging useless.

"Captain!" he called, but the raging winds snatched the word from his lips and carried it out to sea, unheard.

Joseph, the second mate, tried desperately to secure the shredded sail before it could come crashing perilously down on the deck. One hand was wrapped around the line, tying it off, and with the other he rang the ship's bell furiously, its clangor cutting through the noisy wind.

"All hands on deck!" he shouted, cords standing out on his neck. "All hands on deck!"

The first mate, a burly bearded Russian named Grigori, jumped down from the rigging and ran to grab hold of a loose line. He yelled hoarsely over to the lookout, "Billy, tell the captain the topsail's gone."

The boy nodded, and took off aft across the slippery deck toward the wheel. A huge wave hit him, knocking Billy off his feet. He went sliding along the deck, fetching up against the mizzenmast, where the bosun, Mick, was hanging onto the ropes while another crewman, David, struggled to lash down a heavy ice-sledge, which threatened to go overboard, taking David with it.

Struggling to his feet, buffeted by the winds and the rain, Billy Jenkins made a dash for the bridge. Ahead of him, he could see the dim form of a wild-eyed bearded man, clutching the wheel in a white-knuckled death grip, standing with his legs braced wide apart against the hammering force of wind and wave. This was Robert Walton, an Englishman and the captain of the *Aleksandr Nevsky*. Salt water was streaming off him in rivulets; salt and ice turned his black beard and eyebrows white, but this only added to the look of desperate ferocity that he wore as he struggled with all his strength to keep his ship from foundering in the storm.

The frightened lookout rushed to him, his face distorted by terror and the incredible cold of the seawater in which he was drenched, his teeth chattering as he gave his captain the news. "Captain, we're losing the topsail!"

Walton uttered a low, angry growl and pushed him away. "Get back to your post!" he snarled. "Lash the wheel," he yelled to the bosun, surrendering the tiller and moving toward the bow, his head bowed, his body almost doubled by the wind as he fought his way along the deck. His heavy oilskins weighed him down.

Grigori was hauling on a line at the mainmast. Walton joined his first mate just in time to hear a loud ripping sound, loud enough to be heard over the gale. *Riiiiippp!* The uppermost sail tore loose and the yardarm began its plummet down toward the deck.

"Move, Captain!" Grigori shouted, giving Walton a shove. All around them, crewmen dove aside for safety as the heavy yard smashed into the deck.

But Walton wasn't quite quick enough. He caught a glancing blow to the head and was slammed face-down onto the pitching deck. With a splintering of timber, the yardarm disappeared over the side in another huge wave.

The first mate scrambled to his captain's aid, but Walton shoved him off. A wide streak of lightning split the sky, revealing in one brilliantly illuminated instant the expression of pain and rage on Walton's face. Blood streamed down his forehead and into his beard from the cut on his scalp. The salt water on his face made the cut doubly painful. He craned his head back to look up at the mainsail, which was still intact, although it was straining hard against the ungoverned force of the wind.

But in the next instant the power of the gale in the foremast sails was too strong for its timbering. The lines would never hold. There was a huge crack, as of thunder from the heavens, but it wasn't thunder. The sailors peered up. The top of the mast was starting to give.

"Why didn't you listen!" Grigori growled, through the film of ice on his cracked lips. "I told you this wouldn't work!" This Englishman was quite mad; he seemed to be bent upon his own destruction, and would take his hapless crew with him down into Hell.

"Cut the damn rigging!" snarled Walton impatiently.

The first mate shook his head. "There's too much canvas up!" Above their heads, the remaining foremast sails—the fore top-gallant yard and the upper fore topsail-yard—still flapped explosively, filled with Arctic wind.

"Shut up!" the captain shouted back. "Cut the

rest of the damn rigging free before we lose the mast."

Walton grabbed a knife from Grigori's belt and pushed his way to the mast, followed by the crew. Together, their fingers almost numb with cold, they attacked a guy-rope with primal fury, trying to cut the sails free before they were dashed down to the deck, carrying with them the rest of the foremast.

Suddenly, a chilling cry came from the bow of the ship. It was the lookout, yelling in panic as he clung to his post. "Captain!!!"

Walton and the others spun around to look as the mist cleared momentarily.

What they saw struck them with dread, the nightmare of every sailor of the Arctic seas. A huge floating monster of snowy white, eerie and dazzling even in the darkness of the stormy night. Ice. An iceberg—massive and unexpected—loomed directly ahead off the port bow, like a ghostly white mountain. The *Aleksandr Nevsky* was heading straight for it and for the rapidly appearing pack ice beyond. Iceberg, the ruthless destroyer of ships, the mindless murderer of sailors. The men stood frozen in horror, barely able to breathe.

"Hard to starboard, Captain!" shrieked the lookout. The iceberg was almost upon them. The men all knew that, as huge as it was above the surface of the water, there was even more of the mammoth ice mountain lurking beneath the waves, ready to rip the wooden hull of the *Nevsky* to splinters and send ship and crew to the bottom of the frigid sea.

"It's going to ram us!" yelled Grigori hoarsely in the teeth of the gale.

"It wouldn't dare," Walton snarled furiously, irrationally. He was taking all this personally—the storm, the iceberg, the broken mast and shredded sails. They were all deliberate attacks on his ambitions, malevolent onslaughts by a pitiless nature on Robert Walton's scheme for life. Nature itself was his enemy, and he was not yet defeated, he would never allow defeat.

"Hard to starboard!" he yelled aft at the wheelman.

Mick the bosun and the second mate Joseph began to fight their way through the wind toward the wheel, but it was already too late.

With a sickening crash, the *Nevsky* lurched onto her port side as she slammed into the iceberg at the front. The screaming sailors were thrown across the deck onto the port side, scattered like leaves by an autumn wind as though they weighed nothing at all. Like a great wall of white, the iceberg rose up beside them as they got shakily to their feet, bruised, cut and badly shaken. The ship, rudderless, with no one at the wheel, rammed herself deeper into the ice.

And then the ship lurched again, this time over onto her starboard side, and all the men were once again hurled across the ship, sliding sideways, tumbling, screaming. Before they could get up, the prow of the *Nevsky* slammed into the pack ice up ahead of them. Now, everyone was thrown forward, like rag dolls hurled around by a child in a tantrum.

Walton and Grigori were flung toward the bow of the ship; with great difficulty both men hung on grimly to the lines and kept their feet. A loud noise above them made them start, and they turned and looked up in time to see the main top mast snap like a matchstick and begin to topple.

"Look out!" Walton yelled hoarsely into the wind. "Look out below!"

The top mast slammed to the deck with a crash like thunder. As it fell, it knocked a crewman over the rail on the starboard side. With a shriek of terror, the man plunged into the sea. Walton and his first mate raced to the starboard rail and peered over the side, searching for the sailor. They heard a long, strangled scream and saw with horror the unlucky crewman crushed to death by the ice, which closed around and over his broken body like a silent tomb.

And then, with growing fear, they watched helplessly as a massive ice floe jammed itself up against the *Nevsky*. She was rapidly being caught up in a net of ice. With a loud sickening crunching sound, the ice hit the starboard side. But it didn't stop there. With another burst of earsplitting noise, the ship's stern was also enclosed with a crash. Now the *Nevsky* came to rest, completely locked in ice.

Utter panic swept across the decks, gripping the men. Their faces were contorted into masklike grimaces of mortal terror. This must be their death, and they were staring into its implacable eyes. They would all perish right here, frozen corpses in the embrace of a coffin of ice.

And a madman had brought them to it, driven by his obsession into taking greater and greater risks, oblivious of their safety, oblivious, too, of his own. Walton, their captain, who even now was feeling more frustrated than afraid, Walton was the man obsessed by an impossible ambition. Even now, with death inevitable, it was plain that Robert Walton cared more about losing his ship and his God-cursed goal than his crew. Their lives were of no importance to him, compared with what he intended to achieve.

Grigori turned away in disgust and joined the rest of the crew, leaving the mad captain alone to stare around him at his trapped ship, his fists clenched in fury, raging in his heart against his old enemy, nature.

* * *

The storm's fury lessened in the early hours of the morning and finally passed, leaving the *Nevsky* intact but trapped in a wilderness of frozen white. That is, intact with the exception of half their mastage. They had been icelocked for an entire day, and now in the long, long Arctic twilight the crew was still working desperately with axes and picks to free the ship from the ice. They'd been laboring in the bitter cold for many hours, without food or respite, and by now they were worn to the bone, near total exhaustion. Then, too, with the approach of night, the mists were rising again.

Close by the ship the pack of dogs, huskies, and malamutes freed from the ship's hold, huddled in the snow, their weird blue eyes, so alien in the faces of dogs, reflecting like blue mirrors the looming dusk. Robert Walton bent to check them; this team of trained sled dogs was crucial to the success of the overland portion of his mission. The dogs growled and muttered softly; they were famished and restless, but otherwise they appeared not to have suffered injury from the terrible passage of last night's storm.

Satisfied that his animals were unharmed, Walton moved on to check on the crew as Grigori joined him. "Come on, men. Put your backs into it. Let's go."

"Captain, this is useless," pointed out Grigori. "The ice stretches for miles." The first mate had used up most of his reserve of strength and was close to dropping from fatigue. The crew had been chopping away at the ice for many hours, barely making a dent. The hull of the *Nevsky* was still tightly locked in on all sides. The men were freezing right through to the marrow, and hungry; most of all, they were dispirited, by their ordeal and by the cruel death of their shipmate, and they yearned to get back home to

Archangel, any way they could. Even if it meant an overland journey by dogsled over hundreds of miles of ice and snow.

But Walton just set his jaw grimly, determined. "I haven't come this far to give up now," he growled. "What are you suggesting, that we just surrender, lie down and die?"

"The men can't go on, sir. They're exhausted."

Walton shook his head wearily, and a scowl cut a deep groove between his bushy eyebrows. "They knew the risks when they signed on. We'll chop our way to the North Pole if we have to." He brandished his own pick for emphasis.

"Then you run the risk of mutiny," Grigori said stubbornly.

Freezing with his pick in midair, Walton whirled to face his first mate. "Did you say mutiny?" he demanded.

He knew the heavy import carried by that word, but stubbornly, Grigori met his captain's eyes. "Yes, sir."

Walton shot his first mate a look tinged with contempt. "We proceed north as planned," he said shortly, and turned and walked away.

"At the cost of how many more lives?" Grigori called after him. Even though he was an officer, his sympathies were with his fellow sailors.

Walton stopped and whirled around, glaring at the burly Russian. "As many as it takes." Grigori only dropped his eyes and nodded, but his lips were still set in a stubborn line. He knew how close the men were to rebellion. The men were worn to a thread. It wouldn't take much to set a mutiny off, like touching a lit match to gunpowder.

As he turned again to move on Walton was halted in his tracks. In the distance, from off in the mist, a long, chilling howl arose. It wasn't a human sound, nor yet quite an animal sound either. If a damned soul could give voice to its agony in hell, this might be its voice. It was like nothing human ears had ever heard, but it was terrible enough to freeze the blood in human veins.

At once, the lead husky jumped to his feet, the fur on the ridge of his spine up and bristling, howling and snarling at some unseen but dangerous thing in the distance. The other dogs in the pack moved restlessly, growling and baring their large sharp teeth. They raised their heads like wolves, sniffing the air which carried a mysterious message to their sensitive canine nostrils.

"There's something out there," Grigori said in a low voice. The rising mists were curling thickly around them, making it impossible to see. Whatever was out there, he didn't like it. It wasn't like anything in his long experience at sea. Nothing about this voyage was natural or right, he thought. Like all Russian peasants, Grigori appeared stolid on the outside, but his superstitious Russian soul was in touch with the mystic and inexplicable, and feared most greatly those things his hands couldn't touch or his eyes see.

Grabbing up their weapons, knives and clubs and rifles, and here and there a pistol, the crew ran to join their captain. The eerie howl sounded again, nearer this time.

"What the hell is that?" snapped Walton, his eyes wide.

The men stared into the misty opacity, seeing nothing. But if they could not see, in the icy silence, they could hear. Something was approaching them, coming nearer to the *Nevsky* with every moment. A dragging sound, heavy and slow. But making steady progress, coming closer and closer.

And then they saw it. An unearthly apparition loomed eerily out of the mist, freezing the sailors' blood in their veins. Hastily, Grigori crossed himself in the Russian style, from right to left. Other sailors blessed themselves or clutched at the lucky pieces they carried with them.

What they saw was a creature entirely covered in fur, with no feature visible. It moved with halting step across the ice pack toward the ship, and it came dragging behind it a weird sledge, like no sled ever seen. Where dogs would normally be used in a sled harness, there were no dogs, only the creature itself with the reins around his neck. Taking one slow step, dragging, another slow step, dragging, it inched forward toward the *Aleksandr Nevsky*.

The crew stood staring at the apparition for what seemed a heart-stopping eternity. Then one of the younger men broke down. Unable to take any more of the suspense, he cried out hysterically. "It's a demon!" he shrieked, shouldering his rifle and taking aim.

But before the seaman could fire, the strange figure reached up and threw back the hood of its long wolf-fur garment. A human face emerged, a man's face, bearded. Incredibly, the figure was human, just a mortal man hauling the weight of a sled behind him over the wastes of the ice. But what a strange vehicle! As out of the ordinary as the appearance of the stranger himself.

At the rear of the sled two poles stood up, over which was slung a huge billowing greatcoat, like a sail. The flapping coat made the sled, as it loomed out of the mist, appear like a giant and sinister bat.

Small wonder the first sight of it was enough to congeal the blood in a crewman's veins.

As the sled came ever nearer to the ship Walton noticed that also tacked to the poles and dangling in the wind was the livid carrion of dead dogs. This must be the man's traveling larder; he ate this dog-flesh to survive. Though obviously exhausted, weighted down by his burden, the stranger came on steadily, fiercely determined.

The figure scanned the icebound ship ahead of him, seeing the huge carved figurehead depicting a woman cradling a child, a large teardrop carved deeply in her cheek. He saw the ship's name on its bow—*Aleksandr Nevsky*. He saw the broken masts and the tattered sails, the frightened faces of the sailors staring at him, the dogs moving nervously on the ice. The ship was in grave trouble, yet these were the first humans this man had encountered in many weeks, and he was in desperate need of their help.

Stopping at last in front of Walton, he took off his hood. The man's hair and beard were white, and his cheeks were burned red by the fierce Arctic winds, crisscrossed by the lines of weather-beating. He appeared to be middle-aged or older, painfully thin and somewhat stooped by the weight of the sled he was dragging. But it was the stranger's eyes that were most arresting. They were terrible, deepset, burning holes in his face. These were eyes that had looked upon horror.

"Who is your captain?" he demanded.

"I am," retorted Robert Walton coldly. "What the devil are you?"

The stranger shook his head, and his eyes blazed brighter. "I haven't got time to talk. Bring your men and weapons, and follow me."

Walton and his crew merely stared astonished at this odd creature who dared to issue orders.

"NOW!"

There was such command in the stranger's voice, such a tone of authority, that instinctively the sailors began to follow him.

"Stay where you are," barked Walton. "I give the orders here." He curled his right hand around the wooden handle of the pistol in his belt and moved closer to the stranger. His eyes narrowed. "I don't know who the hell you are, but how on earth did you get here?"

Before the man could answer, another strange howl sounded in the distance. The sailors shrank back and muttered among themselves, and the dogs reacted with ferocious snaps and snarls. Maddened by his senses, the lead husky broke free and hurled itself snarling and barking into the mist. The other dogs instinctively followed their leader, and the pack raced over the ice, disappearing into the murkiness that obscured the men's vision.

"Get the dogs!" ordered Walton in a sharp command. He mustn't lose them; he couldn't proceed overland to the Pole without dogsleds.

"Leave them," the stranger said wearily, without expression. "They're already dead."

As though to underscore his words, yet another inhuman howl came to them from out of the mist. The howling was nearer now, much nearer. The sailors crowded together for safety in numbers, but they were trembling with more than the cold. Fear held them tightly in its merciless grip. This cursed trip was turning into the voyage to hell, and all of their souls might end up damned.

From closer than they expected they heard the fierce barking of their dogs as they found what they were hunting. Then the loud barking changed suddenly, to high-pitched yips and shrill squeals. Then followed screams, terrible, terrible screams.

Whatever demon was out there, it had the *Nevsky*'s dogs.

2   Out There

If only the sailors of the *Aleksandr Nevsky* could have pierced through the twilight mists and witnessed the unfolding fate of their dog team, the powerful dread that now gripped these men would have been increased tenfold, a hundredfold, overwhelming and blackening their minds until they fell unconscious. For nothing like this brutal scene of carnage had ever been viewed by human eyes, nor could it ever be imagined even by the most morbid and unhealthy human imagination. The sailors were blessed that they could not see what was taking place out there in the misty twilight.

The malamutes and huskies of the *Nevsky's* dog team went rushing forward, barking loudly, to confront and overcome whatever was out there howling so strangely. These were healthy animals in their prime, heavy with muscle, as close to feral wolves as domesticated dogs can come. They were strong, ferocious, courageous, quick to act, to react, to attack when threatened. Their primal instincts had told them something unseen was waiting out there, and the something was threatening, dangerous, a wild beast of some kind.

The only beast these sled dogs feared was the giant polar bear, which could stand as high as twelve feet, with claws and fangs in proportion, but whatever this was didn't smell or growl like a bear. It didn't smell or sound like any animal with which they were familiar. Nevertheless, they went loping onward fearlessly to the attack, slavering like the wolves they so closely resembled.

Something was moving slowly toward them out of the mist, a massively amorphous form that was almost human, yet not quite human. It moved quickly but awkwardly, like a man, and yet not like a man at all. It was wearing a loose, flapping garment like a ragged greatcoat, so that the shape of the body inside was obscured. Yet it was roughly man-shaped.

An arm, scarred and powerful, whipped out suddenly, and a husky rose in the air to sink its teeth into it. A huge hand grabbed the dog by the throat, its thick fingers crushing the fur and the flesh and the windpipe, as the dog flailed and thrashed its suffocating body in the air, trying in vain to breathe. When the animal was almost still, the powerful arm hurled it away toward the ground.

But the dog was not yet quite dead. As it hit the ice floe the same large hand grabbed the hairy scruff of the husky's neck, while the other hand clutched at its hind legs and thrust the dog hard down onto the ice as if to break all its bones. There was a sickening crunch and a long, loud shriek from the dog. Thick red blood spurted from the animal's mouth.

Then, a grisly sound of rending and ripping, a final choking scream, and a severed husky hind leg was thrown across the ice floe. Blood splattered over the ice as it landed.

Maddened by the ripe scent of fresh blood, the rest of the team rose barking to the attack, surrounding the bizarre figure. A malamute leaped high and bit into its arm, but the arm jerked powerfully, sending the dog hurtling through the air to fall hard to the ground.

The Creature—whatever it was—was not finished with the dog. Its large hand flexed and squeezed tightly, throttling the struggling malamute, cutting off its high scream. The dog's eyes started out of its head; it bit through its tongue, blood poured from between its jaws and from its eye sockets. Only when it was dead did the choking hand finally release it.

At last, fear struck the rest of the pack, and they sensed a very great peril, much greater than they could deal with. They began to yip and squeal, uncertain whether to attack or to run away with their tails tucked under their bellies. They chose to attack, but it was already too late for choices; their doom was sealed.

Everything happened now in a red-hazed frenzy. A pair of hands ripped the head of one husky from its body. The headless body, blood gushing from its ragged neck like a spouting geyser, shivered in its death-throes. Another husky bravely assaulted a massive foot bound in rags, but the foot kicked the dog off viciously, and tamped down hard onto another dog's head. The head exploded like a ripe cantaloupe under the blows of a hammer, and its blood and brains froze to the ice floe in clots of scarlet and gray.

The few dogs still remaining were screaming now

as the malevolent Creature, apparently maddened by blood-lust, ended their lives one by one, kicking, punching, choking and tearing. Those hapless animals, which attempted escape, were hauled back with enormous strength and swiftly dismembered. Grabbing one dog's front legs, the Creature ripped them apart, tearing the malamute's chest in half so that its heart was rent in several places, its arteries severed so that its blood flew everywhere. The Creature discarded the lifeless dog like an empty orange peel, tossing it down hard onto the ice.

At last the beastly Creature, panting with exertion, stood alone. Every dog was dead. Body parts, severed limbs, torn fur, bones, and blood were splattered over the ice floe around the bizarre figure. Only one being had stood defending itself against eight strong attacking dogs, and yet it had turned out to be an unequal contest of a very different kind from what one would have expected.

What kind of Creature could possess enough strength and power to kill eight wolf-dogs in their prime, ripping through fur, flesh, muscle, sinew, and bone as though they were just so much tissue paper? What kind of Creature might have the heart and stomach for such grisly work? And where did this Creature come from? From the hand of what sort of Creator?

Back on the ice around the trapped *Nevsky*, the sailors jittered nervously, staying close together, filled with terror at the sound of the dogs' death-screams. They could not begin to imagine the animals' gory fate, but they knew that it must be hideous—so much frightening noise! Walton kept his eye on the stranger; his intuition was telling him that this man who had turned up apparently out of nowhere must be connected intimately with the loss of his precious dogs.

The stranger's eyes were tightly shut, but his face contorted in agony as he heard the choking screams. Walton was right; he *did* know what was happening out there in the murky mists. In his own pain he forgot that he was not alone, that Captain Walton was within earshot, and whispered to himself, "I know you're there. I'll find you."

At last the piteous yelping stopped, and there was silence on the ice floe. It was over. The stranger, who was the only man among them who could accurately picture what must have happened, wore a look of suffering.

The seamen's tense muscles began to relax and Grigori's hold on his gun slackened. At once, the stranger made a grab for it and began to run off in the direction the dogs had taken. Moving quickly, Robert Walton pulled him back by the shoulder and punched him in the face to subdue him. The man rocked backward as the crew came to their captain's aid, falling on the struggling but weakened stranger.

"Get him to the ship. To the ship!" commanded Walton.

Obeying, the sailors dragged the man away as Walton cast a last look back. At that moment, the wind picked up, and the mists parted—just a little. But enough to show Robert Walton a hideous sight. Bits and pieces of torn animal flesh and fur congealing to the floe. Dismembered limbs. A dog's head without a body. And blood everywhere, already freezing to scarlet ice. Walton flinched, scarcely believing his eyes. Of what had caused this incredible carnage there was no visible sign. Only a shadow, massive hulking. Mercifully, the mists closed again, like curtains, blotting out the gruesome sight.

But something was definitely still out there, a Creature with huge hands reddened by gore, thickly veined, yellow skin. Something resting on a rock, tired from its labors, making the air around it noisy with heavy rasps of its breath. Something watching the crew scatter back to the *Nevsky*. Something watching the stranger.

The Creature rose from the rock and began pounding across the ice, with the *Aleksandr Nevsky* as its destination. Short, powerful steaming jets of the thing's breath made smoky puffs in the cold air. The legs, oddly bandaged, took long loping strides, covering the distance to the ship with astonishing swiftness.

Whatever this Creature might be, it was terrifyingly powerful.

The crew hadn't bargained for anything like this when they'd signed on the *Nevsky* back in Archangel. When they'd returned to the *Nevsky*, the sailors gathered on the upper deck of the frozen ship to talk over their suspicions and speculations in muffled voices. The captain was below with his strange visitor; God alone knew what *they* might be talking about!

The sailors had recognized even before they weighed anchor that they would be in for a difficult voyage—the pay Walton offered was too generous for a mere pleasure trip—and they also knew that the Englishman was obsessed and most likely demented, but they never expected to encounter things that they couldn't explain, things from hell.

Storms, yes, ripped sails and broken masts, icebergs—those were familiar, even expected perils of any voyage into the frozen north. They could be seen, touched, comprehended. They were of this world.

But this eerie stranger, traveling alone across the ice like a damned spirit out of Hades, and those bone-chilling unnatural howling cries that had materialized from the mist! The terrible screams of the dogs! Whatever had happened out there on the floe wasn't normal, it was supernatural. And it wasn't over yet! Not as long as that man was on this ship! If in fact he *was* a human man! No sailor's wages no matter how generous could ever cover dangers like these! They hadn't signed on to meet the Devil! The men crowded around Grigori as he made his way along the deck towards Walton's cabin.

"What's out there?" asked Davey, his eyes round and wide. "Does the captain know what's out there?"

The Irishman Mulligan glanced uneasily behind him, as though whatever it was had reached the ship and was already prowling the decks. "That's like nothing I've seen before. It's a bloody animal! A polar bear, maybe!"

Morrell shook his grizzled head dourly. "Bears don't kill like that. Nothing does."

"Maybe it wants the man with the captain . . ." put in Billy Jenkins slowly.

"Or it wants the captain . . ." added Davey.

Morrell, one of the ratings, nodded agreement. "The captain's the Devil's man . . . he cursed the voyage."

Billy Jenkins drew in his breath, and lowered his voice to a whisper. "It's the Devil come for the captain." He believed it with all his soul.

The other members of the crew nodded their heads and muttered among themselves. The word spread quickly. "Aye . . . it's the Devil . . . the Devil . . . Old Nick has come for the captain, maybe even for us . . . for our very souls. . . ."

* * *

The stranger sat huddled on the narrow bunk in the captain's cabin belowdecks, where the sailors had flung him on their commanding officer's orders. Robert Walton stood above him, his pistol primed and the hammer cocked back, holding the man at gunpoint.

Once they were indoors, by the light of the hanging lantern in his cabin Captain Walton could see that his first impression of this man was a mistaken one. The stranger was not old at all; in fact, he was surprisingly young, surely less than thirty years old. The white in his hair and beard was merely rime; when the film of ice melted away, Walton could see that the stranger's hair and beard were fair; the hair thick, blond, and wavy, the beard of a deep, ruddy tone. His face beneath the weathering and windburn was youthful and firm, his starved body, emaciated and suffering from the ravages of the elements, was nonetheless the physique of a young man.

But the stranger's eyes—ah, those eyes were old indeed, as old as time, darkened blue pools of ineffable sadness which reflected, from their hollowed sockets, the many terrible things they must have been forced to witness. The eyes were the soul of this man; and it seemed to be a soul that did not expect to see Heaven.

With an effort, the young man attempted to stand, but Walton waved his pistol at him, in a threatening gesture meant to keep him in his place.

"Why can't you understand? Please!" begged the stranger. He was desperate to get out of here, get off the *Nevsky*, and return again to his strange personal quest.

Walton shook his head firmly. "Sit back down. You're not going anywhere."

"I haven't got much time," pleaded the other. He sounded truly at his wit's end, as though he might easily go mad.

"Then I suggest you talk quickly."

The stranger shook his head impatiently, exasperated. Why couldn't this Englishman believe him? "For the last time, I made my way from Saint Petersburg to Archangel on foot. From there I took a whaling ship north. When we hit the ice I used the dogs . . ."

Before he could speak another word, his narrative was interrupted by another unearthly howl from outside the ship, very nearby. The two men exchanged horrified looks.

"What's out there?" Walton demanded hoarsely. "What are you chasing?" Although he was a courageous man who had never yet quailed in the face of difficulties or adversity, even Robert Walton felt a thrill of fear run through him at the unnatural events on the floe.

The stranger rose quickly and rushed over to the cabin's porthole. Thanks to the chilly winds, the mists had parted for the moment, and there was some visibility. He peered out into the twilight, his eyes straining to see, half expectant, half fearful.

Yes. It was out there—that unbearable nightmare that he dreaded most and hated most and yet was tracking night and day at the risk of everything. What any other man would flee from, this man was pursuing. Yes, it was out there—the massive outline of a monstrous, spectral figure standing hunched on the ice, waiting, watching, haunting the ship. Haunting the man who shrank back in horror when he caught sight of it.

This was becoming too much for Walton. First the storm, which had cost the *Nevsky* precious masts and sails, then the masses of floating ice, which had trapped the ship like a fly caught in amber, and now this . . . this whatever it was. Moving to the porthole, he took hold of the stranger, turning him away from the glass. He spoke coldly to the young man, in a threatening tone.

"Listen to me, I've spent eight years planning this. My entire fortune. I will not be stopped by you or by some phantom."

The stranger looked keenly at the captain. Despite the gray hairs in his black hair and beard, Walton was also relatively young, a strongly built man in his mid thirties. His eyes were the green color of a warm ocean, and there was a fierce light in them that the other man recognized.

"Do you share my madness?" he asked.

Walton shook his head strongly. "No, not madness," he denied intensely. "There *is* a passage to the North Pole. And I *will* find it!"

Ah, thought the stranger. The Northeast Passage, of course. I should have guessed that the *Nevsky* must be on a voyage of exploration. What else would bring the ship this far north into a white, uninhabited wilderness?

Ever since the Danish explorer Vitus Bering discovered the Bering Strait between Asia and North America in 1728, there had developed among adventurers of many nations a raging Northeast Passage fever, the determination to get to the top of the world, to the North Pole.

In 1733 the Russians had set out on what they called the Great Nordic Expedition; not only were they looking for the northeastern sea passage, but they were hunting valuable fur otters besides. Eight years later Russian pioneers in Siberia set out for North America in small boats from Kamchatka. On that voyage, Alexei Ilich Tschirikov and Vitus Jonasson Bering discovered the coast of Alaska and the Aleutian Islands. But on the return voyage, Vitus Bering perished, dying of hunger and cold and almost certainly of scurvy as well.

Up to now, 1794, no explorer had as yet discovered the fabled Northeast Passage. It remained elusive, almost mythical. So *this* was Robert Walton's dream, to which he had dedicated his life, his youth, and all his material resources. More than a dream, it had become an obsession.

The stranger knew obsession well. They were old companions. It was obsession that gripped his own soul, which drove him onward, traveling alone over ice and snow in a climate that would long ago have killed a weaker man, that was probably killing him, too.

Suddenly, the muffled figure out on the floe disappeared from view, but not before the crew of the *Nevsky* had caught one long terrified glimpse of it. They had been frightened before, and were made further unnerved by the sickening screaming of the dogs, but that was as nothing to the horror they felt at the actual sight of a shadowy Creature they could not recognize either as human or as beast.

And what in God's name were those gobbets of bloody flesh and fur strewn over the ice like clumps of refuse? Could those be the remains of the dogs? What evil power could work such desecrations? The sailors shivered in their clothes. There was only one such power they could give a name to.

"It's the Devil himself, old Satan." The word spread like a fire through the near-mutinous crew.

Only the first mate Grigori remained outwardly firm, although inwardly he, too, was trembling. But he knew that it would do the men no good to allow

Mary Shelley's Frankenstein   35

themselves to be overwhelmed by hysteria. "Hold your tongues," he commanded.

But the lookout, who was little more than a boy, lost control and flung himself on Grigori. "The Devil's amongst us . . ." he babbled tearfully, "he's amongst us."

Grigori and other members of the crew grabbed hold of the lookout, pushing him against the side of the ship to calm him.

"Easy boy, easy," said the first mate in a gruff, kindly voice. But the young lookout continued to blubber and would not let himself be comforted, while his abject fear did nothing to allay the terrors of his shipmates.

What nobody on the *Nevsky* saw was the hideous hand with blood dripping from it working its way along the hull of the ship. It clung to the hull like a deadly spider. The Creature made no sound except for the rasp of its breath in the icy air.

The first mate Grigori and the crew huddled around the lookout, trying to calm young Billy Jenkins.

"It's the captain's fault," said Morrell.

"It's the same for all of us, Billy," put in Dave.

"Ah, the lad's terrified," Mulligan said pityingly in his rich Donegal brogue.

"We're all going home, Billy. We're all going home," said Grigori.

Suddenly, they heard a noise and fell silent, looking around them uneasily. Billy began feverishly to recite the 23rd Psalm, as the rest of the crew moved along the deck, trying to discover where the unfamiliar noise was coming from. Only Grigori remained behind with young Jenkins.

"Yea, though I walk through the valley of the shadow of death," whispered Billy, *"I will fear no evil: for thou art with me: thy rod and thy staff shall comfort me. Thou preparest a table before me in the presence of mine enemies: thou anointest my head with oil: my cup runneth over. Surely goodness and mercy shall follow me all the days of my life: and I will dwell in the house of the Lord forever."*

"Amen," whispered the first mate. But there was precious little comfort in the words.

So this young English captain was searching for the Northeast Passage to the Pole. "And you'd persist in this ambition at the cost of your own life and the lives of your crew?" asked the stranger.

Robert Walton nodded fiercely, and his green eyes blazed like emeralds. He spoke with passion. "Yes! Lives come and go. If we succeed, our names will live forever. I will be hailed as the benefactor of our species."

The benefactor of our species. Where had he heard *those* words before? A bitter smile touched the corners of the stranger's cracked lips. "No, Captain, you're wrong," he said gently. "I of all men know that."

The man turned back to the porthole, looking out across the ice. But there was no sign of the Creature. As he looked out the porthole he noticed that the *Nevsky* had sunk so far into the ice that his face was almost level with the surface of the ice. He turned away, not knowing that, just out of his sight, a massive foot, clad in dirty wrappings, was out on the *Nevsky*'s hull, clinging close to the porthole.

The stranger sighed deeply. The road that still lay ahead of him was perilous and exhausting, and his strength was already waning, mostly depleted. Yet he must go on; he must see his dangerous quest to its end, no matter if it cost him his life. That was the central fact of his life.

In their hearts, these two driven men might be brothers. For the first time, Robert Walton looked upon this stranger not as an unwelcome intruder, but as a man with a unique story to tell. Surely he wouldn't have come this far and suffered so many obvious privations if he weren't on a mission that was worth hearing about, something no doubt connected with that almost-supernatural figure out on the ice. Walton's hand relaxed on the butt of the pistol. "Who are you?" he asked suddenly, not with hostility but with normal human curiosity.

At the question, tears sprung to the stranger's eyes. He recognized that the captain was speaking to him man to man, and he was touched by the other man's humanity. He answered slowly, the words sounding unfamiliar even to him.

"My . . . name is . . . Victor . . . Frankenstein," he began.

3   Victor

In these pages you will follow the incredible story exactly as revealed to Captain Robert Walton of the *Aleksandr Nevsky* by Victor Frankenstein, a stranger who found himself on a crippled ship locked frozen into an ice floe in the Barent Sea, a stranger who was pursuing a quest so unique and unnatural, so perilous that he stood an excellent chance of not surviving it. Listening to the young man's narration, the hairs on the nape of Walton's neck prickled and stood up.

As the stranger's bizarre tale unfolded, through episodes of great beauty and revelations of unbelievably grisly details, the captain was fascinated, then astounded, then horrified and, finally, greatly moved. He knew that Victor's story must be true—everything in the young man's demeanor bespoke honesty and courage—but he also knew that this was a tale that others, who had not heard it from the lips of Victor Frankenstein himself, could not possibly believe. What rational man could give credit to this hair-raising narration of such grotesque horrors? Only someone as obsessed as Walton himself might understand how and why these bizarre things happened, and sympathize with its anguished protagonist.

"My name is Victor Frankenstein," the young man began slowly.

Victor Frankenstein was born twenty-five years earlier, Anno Domini 1769. His environment was a world of peace, prosperity, and love. He spent his childhood in his father's large, bright mansion house in Geneva, Switzerland, not far from the banks of beautiful Lake Geneva. The house stood on an impressive acreage of land, approached through an avenue of stately chestnut trees lining a gravel path. Around it stretched colorful flower beds and green lawns on which grew stands of ancient trees, oak and ash and birch. Especially majestic was one old oak tree, close to sixty feet high, which had flourished there for more than two centuries, spreading its broad, sheltering branches over generations of children who played beneath it in comfort and security.

The working animals, such as the thick-legged cart horses and the oxen that pulled the plows on the estate, were stabled way from the house, near the cultivated fields. Behind the house were large brick stables in which sleek and lively horses, spirited mounts for the saddle and heavier, dependable horses for the carriages, were sheltered and fed. There was also a carriage house in which stood ready a number of equipages, from the stately coach with the Frankenstein coat of arms painted on the door, to the sporty open brougham with room for only four merrymakers, to the one-seat gig to the high-sided brightly painted pony car in which the small child Victor was taken for joyful outings.

As to the mansion itself—tall windows draped in fine brocades looked out onto well-kept gardens with their thick lilac trees whose fragrance perfumed the spring, and fine old rosebushes whose fragrance perfumed the summer. In the orchard, the boughs of well-grown pear and plum trees were heavy with pale pink blossoms in May and with sweet ripe fruit in August. Every winter, the evergreen trees—tall pines, firs, balsams, and cedars—added their fresh, pungent scent to the crispness of the air.

Apart from the lake, the most prominent geographical features of Geneva—in fact, of all of Switzerland—were undoubtedly the Alps, which stand guard over the small country like undefeated armies. These magnificent mountains ringed the city, often wreathed in clouds, their summits capped in white by heavy snows even in summer. The contrast between the sheer, rocky heights above and the prosperous red-roofed city built around the lake shore below was a dramatic one; many painters had tried to capture that drama on canvas, but only a few had succeeded.

From the windows of his large nursery, the child Victor could see the Alpine ridge, and the awe-inspiring majesty of Mont Blanc, the highest mountain near Geneva. He grew up loving that mountain, watching the moving clouds conceal and reveal its summit like a flirtatious mistress, seeing the stars crowning it at night and the moon illuminating its slopes.

The Frankenstein mansion had been built a hundred years earlier, by Victor's grandfather's grandfather, a man who appreciated his comforts and who had a great sense of style. No expense had been spared to achieve both comfort and style. The property contained every convenience for pleasant—even luxurious—living.

The house boasted several huge drawing rooms in which guests would sit at their ease, making pleasant conversation, sipping port and Madeira and nibbling dainties from a silver platter offered by a liveried servant. There was a long dining room, with a high, baronial marble fireplace at one end, and a polished mahogany table draped in Brussels lace that was often piled high with game and fresh fish and roasted meats and teamed puddings. A music room held a large gilded harp, a spinet, a violincello, and several violins.

Upstairs, reached by a broad, sweeping staircase, was the pride of the mansion, a huge ballroom with large, magnificent crystal chandeliers and beautiful blue brocaded fabric wall paneling; the ballroom took up most of an entire floor. At one end of the room stood a gilded harpsichord used to beat out the lively rhythms of schottiches and varsoviennes, of mazurkas, minuets, or the very new dance, the waltz, for the enjoyment of the Frankensteins' guests.

On the story above the ballroom were many large, well-furnished bedrooms, each with a tall fireplace to warm it, each with a wide feather bed canopied by embroidered bed-curtains. Above the master bedrooms were the servants' rooms, and the nursery, which consisted of Victor's bedroom, his playroom, a small schoolroom with battered old desks, and a bedroom for his nanny. Up under the high roof was a spacious and deserted attic, into which nobody penetrated.

In the cool darkness of the cellar hundreds of

bottles of fine wines lay in dusty bins, while large wooden casks held quantities of sherry and brandy. No guest of the Frankensteins ever went hungry or thirsty. In addition to all these creature comforts, the mansion held food for the mind as well. Victor's great-grandfather, grandfather, and father, avid readers and collectors, had built up an enviable library, a large bright room in which were shelved thousands of classic leather-bound volumes, many of them in Latin and Greek, the rest in French, German, Italian, and English. There were books of philosophy, literature, poetry, mathematics, physics, and the natural sciences, travel and exploration, essays on ethics and religion. A private chapel was attached to the house, where family prayers were held and religious holidays celebrated.

Victor's father, Dr. Karl Peter Frankenstein, was a man of importance in Geneva, held in high regard, like his father and his father's father before him. He was an excellent physician, who cared as much for his penniless patients as he did for his aristocratic ones. The Frankenstein family had for generations held public office as prominent counselors and magistrates for the city of Geneva. Victor's father continued this tradition, giving selflessly of his time and talents in projects for the public good.

The family wealth was based mostly on land. The Frankensteins had long owned many acres of prime timber, and close to a dozen large dairy farms that were worked by tenant farmers. The cows on these farms gave milk that was almost bright yellow, there was so much heavy cream in it, and many pounds of rich butter and soft cheeses were sent to market in carts bearing the Frankenstein name.

Victor's father married relatively late in life. As a busy doctor, magistrate, and sometime gentleman farmer, his days were full and the demands on his time and energies many, leaving little time for a personal life. From time to time the thought troubled him that, unmarried, he might turn out to be the last of his direct line, and that the large and valuable estates which ought to pass to sons of his might one day be inherited by distant cousins.

But destiny held other plans for the Frankensteins. Only a few days after he passed the age of forty-five, he learned that a childhood friend of his, a man named Beaufort, was ill and destitute in a nearby city, Lucerne. Immediately, Karl Peter Frankenstein mounted his gelding and rode to his old friend's aid, but he arrived just hours too late to find his friend Beaufort alive.

What he found was his friend's daughter weeping at the side of her father's deathbed. Caroline, a beautiful and sensitive motherless girl of fifteen, courageous, selfless, and virtuous, had nursed her father night and day, and was now alone in the world with no money and no hope. Without hesitation, after paying for a decent Christian burial for his old friend, Dr. Frankenstein swept Caroline Beaufort up and brought her home on the pommel of his saddle.

A man of the highest respectability and moral character, Frankenstein saw to it that Caroline was placed in an excellent boarding school for young women, where she flourished. Her gratitude toward her benefactor soon turned to something deeper, romantic love for this special man. Visiting her at her school, over the years Dr. Karl Frankenstein watched the girl blossom into a ravishing and educated young woman. Her virtues and her strong yet sweet nature made the deepest impression on him. At last—how could he help it? He, too, fell deeply in love and, when Caroline was eighteen years old, they were married.

The doctor brought his young bride home to his large empty mansion, which she soon filled with love and merriment, with flowers and music, with friends who came to dine and make conversation and dance contra-dances, mazurkas, and minuets in the high-ceilinged ballroom under the glitter of a hundred wax candles burning brightly in the chandeliers.

Not many years after the marriage, a bright-faced, blue-eyed baby boy was born to the Frankensteins. Now the mansion was at last a home. Soon there would be many children to inherit the Frankenstein name and fortune.

But that did not come to pass. For years, there were no other children born to Caroline and Karl Peter Frankenstein. There was only Victor, but no child was ever loved better by his parents. He was their hope, their future. To his father, the intelligent young boy was a source of pride, but to his mother, he was her heart's darling.

A home is not libraries or wine cellars, ballrooms, or drawing rooms, not dining or music rooms, not maids or cooks or coachmen, footmen, grooms, stable hands, gardeners, or valets, not even rosebushes and pine trees. A home is life, and love, and laughter. It is safety and kindness and affection, and all of these young Victor Frankenstein enjoyed. He was a bright, happy, intelligent, and curious boy, a loved and wanted only son. His childhood passed happily, secure as he was of the affections of both his indulgent parents. Looking back on those earliest years, Victor had the impression that it was always high summer then, and that the sun always shone warmly down on the roof of his father's house.

From his father, the young boy learned a strong

sense of public responsibility, moral rectitude, and ethics. His father taught him to ride and shoot, to pursue his scientific curiosity by taking notes on natural phenomena. From his mother Victor learned to dance and to love music and poetry, Homer and Bach, Vivaldi and Virgil. By the time he was seven, Victor could speak, read, and write not only the native French and German of his native Switzerland, but he was also fluent in English and with the help of his tutor he was beginning to navigate through the labyrinths of Greek and Latin.

From both his father and his mother, Victor learned: the importance of kindness to all living things, a respect for life that extended to all God's creatures, from the fat bumblebees that flew around the garden to the old gray-striped cat who dozed before the kitchen fire, to the pony in the stable and the hounds who ran barking around the stable yard. All life is sacred to Heaven, Caroline would tell her son, and the boy would always nod gravely.

The Frankensteins were always openhanded to others less fortunate than themselves. Many francs were donated to orphanages and charity hospitals; many hours were spent in selfless acts. Their kindness and charity made their name a blessed one, and their lives progressed from one day to the next in a glow of happiness.

Of the childhood days that stood out clearly in Victor's memory, the most clear was the day that Elizabeth Lavenza came to live in the Frankenstein home.

Victor was seven years old, and looking back later he would always remember the brisk tinkling melodies of the harpsichord together with the rustling sound of his mother's silken gown, the smell of his mother's perfumed hair, and the shine of the bright brass buttons on his own knee breeches and on his striped satin waistcoat. He was in the ballroom with his mother, enduring yet another lesson in how to dance with a partner, while the housekeeper, a cultivated woman named Mrs. Moritz, beat out the rapid measures on the keyboard.

Ever after, Victor would subconsciously associate the tinkling of harpsichord music and the rustle of silk with Elizabeth.

He remembered quite clearly stumbling in the dance, and hearing his mother say, with love in her voice, "Failure has no pride, Victor. You must try again."

"Yes, ma'am."

They whirled around again, a bit faster this time. His mother's eyes were bright and her cheeks flushed red; she was such a beautiful woman, and Victor adored her. Mother and son were virtually inseparable; each of them was the center of the other's universe. Seated at the harpsichord, Mrs. Moritz set a livelier pace. Beside her sat her baby daughter Justine, who was only four years old. Justine kept her eyes fixed on Victor, whom she perceived as some kind of bright godling and who was the object of her babyish worship.

As they turned and dipped across the polished ballroom floor, Caroline, laughing, singsonged to the rhythm of the dance.

"My wonderful Victor, you are the handsomest, brightest, cleverest, most wonderfulest boy in the whole world." She grabbed him up tightly in a hug, making him lose his balance. Victor tripped and clutched at his mother until she tripped with him, and both of them tipped over onto the polished floor, shrieking with laughter.

It was at that moment that the enormous door

of the ballroom swung open. Mrs. Moritz stopped playing. As his father entered the room, Victor scrambled to his feet and Caroline stood up with quiet grace.

The boy was surprised to see that his father was not alone. He was ushering in a somber and beautiful little girl, no more than six years old, dressed all in black, wearing somewhat shabby mourning clothes.

Victor stared. The child had an arresting face, with a very red mouth and a square chin. Her thick hair curled naturally over an unusually broad brow. But it was her eyes that fixed Victor's attention. He had never before seen eyes like this little girl's; under thick black eyebrows they were very large and very round and as black as her dress, sad velvet eyes, yet with the fire of passion and pride burning in them. As young as she was, and as frightened as she was, the little girl carried herself like a gypsy princess. The only sign of timidity about her was the tight grip with which her tiny fingers clung to Dr. Frankenstein's hand.

Recognizing that the family now needed their privacy, Mrs. Moritz stood up from the instrument, and bowed. "Doctor. Madame. Come along, Justine." Taking her little daughter by the hand, she left the ballroom. As usual, Justine was reluctant to leave Victor's shining presence; she gazed back over her shoulder at the other two children as her mother whisked her off.

Caroline leaned down until her face was close to her son's. "Victor, this is Elizabeth," she told him in her melodious voice. "She's coming to live with us."

"She has lost both her mother and father to the scarlet fever," explained Dr. Frankenstein. "She's an orphan now."

Victor's mother smiled gently. "You must think of

her as your own sister, she said softly, mindful of her own past as a penniless orphan and the great benevolence that had been shown to her. "You must look after her. And be kind to her. Always. Go on." She gave him a little push.

Slowly, Victor walked toward Elizabeth, who stood watching him gravely with those remarkable eyes. Then Dr. Frankenstein gave the girl a gentle prodding and she took a few steps forward. They met in the middle of the room.

"Always? Does that mean you won't die?" Elizabeth spoke so low that only Victor could hear her. Her eyes searched his face with serious anxiety.

The boy nodded. "I won't if you won't," he promised.

She held out her little hand, Victor accepted it with proper formality, and they shook hands solemnly on their agreement. Blue eyes looked deeply into black ones. Then Victor felt a sudden shock, an actual physical sensation rippling all along his nerves. He had the sudden sense that something of monumental significance had just taken place, more important than a seven-year-old could possibly understand, but something that would change the direction of his life. It was a feeling he was never to forget.

Within the next few months, Victor Frankenstein came to accept and love Elizabeth completely as his sister, and it was soon as if she had always lived with them. Sad and fragile at first, devastated by the loss of her parents, Elizabeth was still only a little girl and eager for affection and security, so she soon began to forget the sorrows of the past, and accept her full share of the happiness of the present.

Mrs. Moritz continued to play the harpsichord for Victor's dancing lessons, and they still took place in the grand blue-walled ballroom, but his partner from now on was not to be Caroline, but Elizabeth. Both Dr. Frankenstein and his wife were present on the occasion of this momentous first dance lesson. As Mrs. Moritz sat down at the keyboard for their first dance together, Justine as always was beside her, with her doll in her arms and her eyes fixed worshipfully on Victor, and enviously on Elizabeth.

"You must begin, Victor," the housekeeper said sternly. "But remember: as it is in the dance, so it is in life. The lady is your partner."

"Yes, Mrs. Moritz." He bowed with grave politeness to Elizabeth, meanwhile crossing his eyes at her behind Mrs. Moritz's back. Elizabeth curtsied back, but she wrinkled up her nose and stuck her tongue out at him where Mrs. Moritz couldn't see. Their parents, observing the lesson, smiled to each other in amusement. How exactly like an older brother and a younger sister!

"Mama, can I dance with Victor?" begged Justine.

"Nonsense, Justine," her mother answered harshly. Mrs. Moritz had very little patience with her needful small daughter. Only the Frankensteins interested her, with their wealth and prominence they impressed her deeply. Her attention was always focused on Victor. The young master was for Mrs. Moritz, as for everyone in the family, the center of the household and of the universe. "Hush. Now join hands together. Back to back. And one, two . . ."

The two children started off, taking a couple of false steps, then gamely working their way across the vast room, tripping on each other's toes. Soon they became accustomed to each other, and the dancing became a bit easier. Watching them fondly, Caroline and Dr. Frankenstein, whose toes were already tapping, couldn't help but join in, and the two couples began to swoop joyously across the highly polished floor.

The tempo of the music quickened as Mrs. Moritz's fingers fairly flew over the keys.

"Gallop. . . . Change partners," she called out. The four dancers began to alternate partners as they swept across the room, little Elizabeth with tall Dr. Frankenstein, and Victor with his beautiful mother. Everyone was laughing.

"Twirl . . . twirl your partner," commanded Mrs. Moritz. Her face was bright red, and the curls under her starched and ruffled cap bounced as she played vigorously. "Join together all . . . and twirl round . . . now forward gallop!"

The figures of the dance grew more complicated and athletic. Everyone was out of breath, and having a wonderful time. The scene was celebratory, making Elizabeth feel as though she had always lived here, joyful, happy, a part of everything, and Victor's sister.

Three months after she became a part of the Frankenstein family, Caroline took away Elizabeth's mourning clothes of black and burned them. She had always wanted a daughter of her own, to love her, dress her like a doll in exquisite clothing, and to braid silk ribbons into her hair. Now she had one. Elizabeth was decked out in bright frocks and cheerful pinafores, in lace-edged petticoats and silken slippers, finery that made her black eyes dance with pleasure. Her thick black hair curled riotously, escaping from its ribbons, and her pale cheeks were soon as rosy as Victor's.

The two children spent many hours in each other's company. They went everywhere together, riding in the pony cart, sharing the nursery playroom on rainy days, falling asleep side by side in front of the drawing room fire at the end of a long and eventful day.

Because Victor was the elder by a year, he was the leader in everything. Elizabeth looked up to him and adored him, but it was not with the same blind devotion that Justine had for him. Elizabeth had a mind of her own. In their play-fantasies, Victor built the castles and fought the dragons, but Elizabeth was rarely content only to be the maiden rescued. She wanted her own make-believe sword and shield. Victor might tell her what books would form her mind, but Elizabeth had her own ideas about what she read.

Yet the girl possessed the same feminine tenderness and the same moral strength that Victor saw in his mother, and he loved Elizabeth for it, even while he sometimes bullied her, which seemed to him only right as the elder brother.

So the boy and girl grew up together, as though they were brother and sister. They shared everything—the love of their parents Karl Peter and Caroline Frankenstein, the same toys and books, the same tutor who taught both of them history and mathematics, Latin, and literature.

They were different, those two. Victor loved learning, and drank his lessons down in large, thirsty gulps, eager for more and more knowledge. From his earliest years he possessed a true scientific curiosity, and although he would happily pursue physical activities out of doors, he would also happily spend hours at a time shut away in the schoolroom by himself, working out mathematics problems or setting up one of his boyish scientific experiments.

Elizabeth, on the other hand, chafed under her lessons. Science and mathematics bored her. She wanted to be out in the fresh air, climbing the large oak tree or chasing after the stable hounds. The only subject she really enjoyed—besides drawing, in which she excelled—was poetry, especially the poetry of William Shakespeare. She could read the sonnets and the plays in French and German translations, and even a bit in English, which she was struggling to grasp. Although she didn't always understand their meaning, the sound of the words thrilled her with their beauty.

Victor's fingers were usually covered in ink, and Elizabeth's knees were usually covered in scratches. Yet these were superficial differences. They shared a great deal, and they saw life in much the same way, thanks to the high moral precepts instilled in them by their father and mother. The same things made them both laugh, and they both loved to play harmless little practical jokes, on the servants, the dogs, the kitchen cat, and Justine.

But, while Victor, strong and clear-eyed, courageous and quick to act, tended to be rather nervous and obsessive, the gypsy princess Elizabeth, whose temper flared easily, was actually as steady as a rock inside, with reserves of strength it was impossible to fathom.

Who could have imagined almost twenty years ago, in those sunny, playful days when the large house echoed with laughter, that the time would someday come when Elizabeth would need every ounce of that strength and Victor every fiber of that courage?

4 Loss

The ten years following Elizabeth's arrival brought with them an increase in the family's happiness. She matured from a lovely child into a blooming and very beautiful young woman, for whom every person in the household—from the stable grooms to the parlor maids—felt affection. She was a loving sister and playmate to Victor, a precious daughter to Dr. Frankenstein to spoil and indulge, but most of all a great comfort and confidante to Caroline, who had begun to harbor secret hopes that her adopted daughter would one day be much more than a sister to her son Victor.

It was a secret hope that Elizabeth herself shared. Although she still loved him as a sister—how could she not, she who had been his childhood companion?—since the age of thirteen, when her body had begun to ripen, Elizabeth had considered marriage with Victor as the only one that could guarantee her lifelong happiness.

Victor himself, grown into a handsome young man standing poised on the threshold of his life, seemed to be fulfilling his youthful promise. He was a great source of satisfaction to his parents, especially to his father, who saw in the boy the realization of all his fond dreams of passing his medical practice along to his son. It had been decided long ago that Victor would follow his father into medicine. His teachers at the technical school he attended all agreed. Victor had what it took to become a brilliant physician. Caring and benevolent in nature, he had an abiding love for science, and excelled in his studies.

At the same time, Victor was an active and vigorous young man, fond of riding and hunting and every form of athletics. Most especially, he enjoyed rock and mountain climbing, and was often on the steeper slopes of the nearby Alpine ridge, pitting his own strength against the mountains' might.

But Victor was far from complacent. There was more to Victor than just the well-rounded and outstanding young student looking forward to medical school and to a well-ordered and predictably prosperous life as a doctor. Like an iceberg, much of his nature was hidden below the surface and went very deep. Yes, he would go into medicine, and yes, he loved the pursuit of science, but somehow he couldn't picture himself in the act of setting broken legs, purging fevers, lancing boils, or laying poultices on catarrhal chests. He possessed a deep, thoughtful intelligence and an insatiable curiosity on the subject of life and death. Research beckoned to him strongly. Victor was very attracted by the notion of venturing into a realm of learning where nobody had ventured before, and discovering some important benefit for humankind.

By the age of seventeen, he had already read a great many of the volumes in the extensive Frankenstein library, but it was the ancient books of the alchemists that most fascinated him and fired up his youthful imagination. These medieval natural philosophers combined the teachings of the Pythagoreans and later Greeks, of the Egyptians and the Arabs, with mysticism, astrology, and an exploration of the properties of metals, which they believed to have great magical and curative powers.

The alchemists looked at natural world in a mystical way. They were continually searching for what they called "the Elixir of Life," which existed somewhere in space and time and was supposed to confer immortality on anyone who could discover it, and for the Philosopher's Stone, another near-unattainable guarantee of immortality that could be used to transmute base metals into precious gold.

The Elixir of Life! The Philosopher's Stone! What thrilling concepts! Realistically they were impossibilities, just myth, of course, but even so . . . what if through modern techniques something like them could be proved genuine? After all, what did the ancients really know of the modern science of electromagnetism, which was the magic of today? Victor's eyes brightened at the thought, and he dived back eagerly into his alchemical texts. The mystical quality of these studies, so much at variance with the practical matters his schoolteachers had imparted, appealed greatly to that part of his nature which believed that medicine should be more than merely setting broken bones. Perhaps it would take someone like Victor Frankenstein to reconcile the ancient ar-

cane with the mysterious new and unite the alchemists' wisdom and the scientists' techniques.

Night after night he stayed up late in his room,
reading avidly until his candles were burned down
into stubs and shed no more light on the pages. Then
Victor would lay his head on the pillow, his brain still
spinning with the strange and tempting concepts
offered by these arcane books. Life and death and
the mysteries of both fascinated him endlessly.
Where did life come from? Where does it go when
the heart stops beating? What is the essential nature
of life? Is it biological? Chemical? Electrical? He
longed to know with certainty.

Victor began his alchemical studies with a rare
manuscript of the philosophical-religious works *Her-
metica*, essays on alchemy, magic, and occultism by
"Hermes Trismegistus," supposedly based on ancient Greek and Egyptian mystic beliefs. From there
he went on to read Albertus Magnus, who died in
1230, a German scholastic philosopher and church-
man, whose works included paraphrases of Aristot-
le's works. Greek-influenced though he was, Albertus was very advanced for his day in experimental
science; Thomas Aquinas was one of his students.
Then Victor read *The Occult Philosophy* by Heinrich
Cornelius Agrippa, born in 1486, who pursued alchemy and occult studies in his youth, although he
turned away from them in later years.

Finally, Victor immersed himself in the collected
works of the physician and alchemist Philippus Aure-
olus Paracelsus, who was born in Switzerland in the
15th century as Theophrastus Bombast von Hohen-
heim. As a doctor, Paracelsus introduced tincture of
opium, which he named laudanum, into medicine
around the year 1520, thus helping to conquer that
bitter enemy of mankind, unbearable pain. Here was

one practical application of mystical alchemy—
surely, thought Victor, there must be others, equally
valuable!

Paracelsus's 1530 manuscript *Paragranum* argued
that the practice of medicine should be based on
nature and its physical laws; it was Paracelsus who
first suggested the use of chemical substances, such
as compounds of mercury and antimony, as reme-
dies. Moreover, he claimed to have found the Philosopher's Stone and thus he would live forever. But
Paracelsus didn't live forever; his immortality came to
an abrupt end in 1541, when he died in a fall—
possibly a drunken fall, since he was a notorious
toper. So his alleged possession of the Philosopher's
Stone didn't go far in saving Paracelsus's nack.
Maybe it just doesn't work on drunkards.

Excited as he was by occult ideations, Victor knew
better than to mention his private study sessions to
his pragmatic father. He understood that Dr. Frankenstein would be horrified and vastly disappointed
to know that Victor's extracurricular readings pointed
his son in directions away from the mere practice of
day-to-day medicine. Although he didn't . . . well,
not exactly . . . believe in the existence of a Philosopher's Stone or the Elixir of Life, enticing concepts
though they were, Victor still hoped that there must
something . . . beyond . . . simply prescribing pills
and applying leeches to cure an inflamed liver, something that touched upon the infinite questions and
attempted to answer them.

Could there not be a higher, a nobler calling
waiting for him, one in which great secrets would
be unfolded, and Victor Frankenstein would stand
initiated into the sacred knowledge of the ancient
sages? Perhaps he might even become the modern
Prometheus, although without, Heaven help him,

suffering Prometheus's wretched fate. It was a lovely dream.

When Victor was seventeen and Elizabeth sixteen years of age, something unexpected occurred in the Frankenstein household. Caroline became pregnant, which caught everyone, including Caroline herself, by surprise.

She was more than thirty-seven years old now, and had long ago given up hope of having any more children. She was happy with her son and her adopted daughter, fulfilled as a wife and mother. But the thought of bringing a new life into the world, of having a baby at her breast again, made her the happiest of women.

Dr. Frankenstein's feelings on the subject were mixed. He, too, rejoiced in the thought of the life to come, and it gladdened him to see his beloved wife so happy, but as a doctor, he was afraid for her. Thirty-seven was perhaps too old for bearing a child, especially after so many years of barrenness. There were dangers in a pregnancy like this. Concerned, Dr. Karl watched over his Caroline like a bird guarding its nest, looking for the first signs of trouble.

Yet, as Caroline Frankenstein entered her ninth month of pregnancy in good spirits and excellent condition, a mood of cheerful anticipation filled all of them, and even the good doctor relaxed somewhat. None of the dire complications he had feared had so far surfaced. His wife was blooming; her cheeks sparkled and her eyes were bright; her appetite was good, her energy level high, her temperament optimistic. With God's help, there would be no danger and all would be well.

The Frankenstein family still kept a hospitable table, still entertained their visitors, and still danced in their ballroom as they were doing today, two happy couples, the doctor and his wife, Victor and Elizabeth. The only difference between today and ten years earlier was that it was Justine, now fourteen, who sat at the harpsichord. Mrs. Moritz was still conducting the lessons, beating out the time by clapping her hands but it was Justine's nimble fingers that played the dance melodies.

Whenever Victor danced with Elizabeth, even though the steps often kept them at arm's length from each other, he nevertheless felt an electrical movement in the palm of his hand where her hand rested, and a warmth pulsing through his fingers whenever they touched her shoulder or waist while dancing. There was a palpable physical connection between them always; he was certain that she was as aware of it as he was, although feminine modesty prevented her from showing it or alluding to it in any way. But there was a softness in the depths of her velvet black eyes whenever they looked into his that told him she had some idea of what he was feeling.

As the two couples danced energetically around the room, Caroline stopped suddenly, all the color draining from her face, and pressed her hand to her great swelling belly. At once, her husband was at her side.

"You mustn't exert yourself, my dearest Caroline," he scolded her gently, but his face wore a look of anxiety, as his early misgivings came flooding back.

Caroline smiled, but her face was still very pale. "I'll be fine, Karl, don't worry. Just a little out of breath, that's all. Please don't make a fuss."

"Even so, you had better sit down." With her arm tucked into his, and her weight leaning on him, the doctor led his wife to a large gilded chair standing by the piano, and lovingly settled her into it.

Reassured, Victor and Elizabeth danced on, watched by the others. They made a handsome picture, the young man so fair, the young woman so dark. Because they'd been partnered for years, by now their steps matched perfectly.

"Excellent!" Mrs. Moritz called out. "You'll be the envy of all the young ladies and gentlemen!"

They were certainly the envy of Justine, who gazed longingly at Victor as he swept Elizabeth into his arms with a flourish. Watching him, she stopped concentrating on her music, and fumbled on the keyboard. Her mother threw her a harsh look of reproval. "Justine!"

Flustered, the girl turned her attention back to the harpsichord. But Victor had noticed Justine's discomfiture. Her mother was often too hard on her, poor thing. "Mrs. Moritz, that's all right." Letting go of Elizabeth's hand, Victor reached out to Justine. "May I have this dance, Justine?"

Blushing, the girl stood up and her mother took her place at the keyboard. Victor put one hand on her waist and they were just about to set off in a mazurka when Caroline suddenly uttered a low moan and crumpled to the floor in a faint.

"Mother!" cried Victor, as all of them rushed to her.

"No!" Dr. Frankenstein commanded. "Give her room to breathe." He lifted his wife up in his arms and headed for the staircase. "Victor and Elizabeth, you remain here. Under no circumstances are you to come upstairs unless I summon you. Mrs. Moritz and Justine, come with me."

Elizabeth and Victor exchanged frightened glances, and sank down into ballroom chairs. For several minutes they said nothing but sat mutely, wanting desperately to know what was going on upstairs. The vast empty ballroom had suddenly become an ominous space in which they were trapped.

Then the screaming began—loud, long, protracted. Never had either one of them heard such screaming; it was as though a living animal was being torn apart. Instinctively, Elizabeth clapped her hands to her ears and moaned miserably. Victor leaped to his feet and began to pace around the huge room like a panther in a cage.

The screaming continued, hoarse and loud, with the shrieks coming closer and closer together. Dear God, what was happening? Why wasn't his father doing something? Give her something for the pain, *anything*! Distracted, Victor leaped up and took several agonized steps toward the door, but Elizabeth put out her hand in a preventive gesture and shook her head. Their father had forbidden them. Uttering a deep groan, the boy sank back down into his seat and dropped his face into his hands.

Outside there was a sudden crack of lightning and a deep boom of thunder. The winds rose, banging tree branches against the windows. It began to rain heavily.

Upstairs, in the candlelit chamber, things were not going well. Caroline Frankenstein, fastened into the birthing chair in her bedroom, lay writhing in anguish. Her swollen body glistened with sweat. She screamed and screamed, clutching at Mrs. Moritz's hands. Between her legs, which were held apart by leather restraints, her husband tried vainly to stanch the flow of bright red blood that poured out of her body. The baby would not come.

Justine and her mother exchanged frightened

looks, and Mrs. Moritz couldn't help it. She shook her head from side to side. Fortunately, neither Dr. Frankenstein nor his wife saw the negative gesture.

This was the most difficult labor Dr. Frankenstein had ever attended. By custom only women were usually present at a confinement and delivery, midwives and friends of the birthing mother, who'd been through many childbeds of their own and knew what to do. Physicians were called in only in extreme situations, so Caroline's husband had seen his share of only difficult cases. But this was by far the worst in his experience.

The infant was so twisted in its mother's womb that it was blocking the cervix with its back and shoulders. Forceps would be of no value here, because the head was not coming out in a way that could be grasped and eased through the birth canal. Nor could Dr. Frankenstein relieve his wife's agonies with morphia. Anesthesia such as ether or chloroform were discoveries that would not be made for another fifty years. But even if he possessed such anesthetics, Dr. Frankenstein couldn't use them. Caroline had to be awake throughout, so that she would continue to labor, and perhaps her exertions might move the infant from its disastrous position.

Yet, as hard as she labored and as much as she endured, it wasn't working; it seemed hopeless. The only way this baby would be born alive was by cutting its mother's belly open and releasing it. But an emergency Caesarean in these conditions—with no assistance, no sophisticated instruments, no proper operating table, no laudanum! Impossible! Caroline would never survive such a procedure.

Justine wrung a linen cloth out in cool water, and laid it gently on Mrs. Frankenstein's face, sponging her sweaty brow, cheeks, and neck. But Caroline could only moan and push the girl's hands away.

The housekeeper gave her mistress her hands to cling to, and Caroline grasped them so tightly hands that they ached. "That's it, I've got you," Mrs. Moritz whispered into the laboring woman's ear. "You lie back. That's it, I've got you. Hold tight."

"Breathe! Try to breathe!" urged Dr. Frankenstein desperately.

But Caroline could not breathe, except to scream. The screams were not even hers, really; they were torn from her chest by something standing outside herself, by the dark torturer who was ripping her life away. Outside the bedroom window, lightning suddenly split the sky, brightening the room as with a thousand candles. Mrs. Moritz gasped. So much blood! She hadn't realized there was so much blood! Urgently, she spoke in an undertone to Dr. Frankenstein.

"Sir. Sir," she whispered urgently. "This cannot continue. You must make a decision."

Paralyzed, anxious, the doctor was torn by hesitation. He knew Mrs. Moritz was right. Caroline must be close to death; how much blood could a body lose, how much agony could a frail body endure? Yet he loved her as he loved his own life. He couldn't bear to lose her.

"How can I? The baby is in the wrong position. I can't proceed . . . unless . . ." Dr. Frankenstein broke down, unable to continue. He couldn't give words to the terrible thought that seemed to be the only solution.

But Caroline could give it words. She fought back the pain in order to speak, and her voice was weak and hoarse from screaming. "Cut me. . . . Save the baby."

An endless moment passed, in which husband and wife exchanged long anguished looks. Both of them knew what would inevitably happen. In their looks, they bade each other loving farewell; she gave him her forgiveness and he agreed to let her go.

At last, Dr. Frankenstein nodded. Mrs. Moritz handed him a scalpel. With a small whimper of misery, he lifted the hem of his wife's bloody nightgown and inserted the knife. Lightning flashed again, very close to the window, striking the oak tree outside the house. It was a crackling report that resonated throughout the mansion. But the alarming noise couldn't mask that last drawn-out scream of agony.

Downstairs, as the storm raged and heavy drops of rain drummed the window glass, Caroline's screams echoed through the ballroom. Elizabeth winced and her hands made unconscious wringing motions. Unable to sit still, Victor had jumped to his feet to watch the thunderstorm. He stood looking out of a window, waiting for the next bolt of lightning. Elizabeth ran to his side.

"Please, Victor, let us sit back down."

He nodded without looking at her, and she led him to the window seat, where he kept his eyes on the raging outside, while his thoughts remained fixed on the raging going on upstairs.

Elizabeth squeezed Victor's arm, trying to reassure him. "She'll be all right," she told him in a shaky voice. "Father's the finest doctor in Geneva."

But when Caroline screamed again, even more loudly this time, Elizabeth shivered and moved closer to Victor. Tears welled up in her large black eyes and rolled slowly down her cheeks. Her brother stroked her hand absently, less to comfort her than to comfort

himself. Every one of his mother's agonized shrieks
tore through him like a sword of fire. He had never
felt so helpless or useless in his life. He who would
do anything for his beloved mother could now only
stand by and do nothing. Nothing!

A wave of anguished frustration washed over
Victor, and he pulled away from Elizabeth, clenching
his fists so hard that his fingernails cut into the palms
of his hands.

Suddenly, a massive bolt of lightning hammered
down from the heavens, slamming into the large oak
tree that had stood for centuries on the lawn in front
of the mansion. A trail of fire followed the bolt and
split the fine old tree down the middle. The tree top
came crashing to the ground, and the broad stump
began to burn to a smoldering ruin. The noise was
deafening; a crash-sound as if the world was coming
to an end.

Elizabeth and Victor jumped to their feet and
ran to the ballroom window, where they stared out
disbelieving at the ruins of the wonderful old tree
under which they had passed so many happy playful
hours. The rain streamed down the window glass,
making wide rivulets, and poured onto the fallen
tree, putting the fire out with a hiss of damp smoke.

Death was striking hard at the very soul of the
house. At the same moment that the oak tree perished, Caroline Frankenstein's death-agonies came to
a merciful end.

A footstep on the stairs made them both turn, to
see Dr. Frankenstein coming slowly down the staircase from the bedroom, dragging his feet down one
step at a time. He looked ghastly; his face was completely drained of color, and his hair, usually brushed
into neatness by a pair of military brushes with

monogrammed silver backs, stood up in tufts of gray all over his head. He seemed like a very old man.

"Father!" cried Victor, and he and Elizabeth tore across the ballroom. They went racing up the great staircase. Dr. Frankenstein was coming down in a daze, and for the first time Elizabeth noticed that there was blood on his hands. She gasped. As Victor pushed past him, she paused, horrified. Her mouth opened in an unspoken question.

Dr. Frankenstein shook his head numbly. "I did . . . everything . . . I could," he said brokenly, his eyes vacant, barely seeing Elizabeth.

Uttering a small moan, Elizabeth gathered up her skirts and followed Victor up the stairs. Father sank down onto the steps, staring emptily at the blood on his hands.

Victor reached the bedroom first, and pushed open the door. He gasped in horror as he saw his mother hanging limply in the birthing chair, a lifeless heap. His bright, gay, beautiful mother! No longer an animate human being, but a bundle of bloody rags. The shock of it sent tears streaming down his face.

"Bring her back. Please bring her back," he wept, like a little boy, pleading with a greater power that turned a deaf ear to his beseeching.

Suddenly, a loud booming clap of thunder, and then he heard a baby begin to cry. Victor turned. Mrs. Moritz was cradling his newborn baby brother. Justine stood next to her mother, looking forlornly at Victor. The rain howled and rattled at the windows, like a lost ghostly soul announcing a death.

Caroline Frankenstein's funeral was held in their private family chapel. Dozens of mourners, their faces sad and their eyes downcast, gathered to pay their final respects to a good wife, a good mother, and a good Christian.

The altar was draped in black, like a bier, and before it stood Caroline's coffin, a surprisingly small white-and-gold box, also draped in black, with a sheaf of white lilies resting on top of it. Tall vases of lilies stood around the chapel; their smell was overpoweringly sweet, like death itself. Victor flinched from the heavy perfume; his head throbbed with pain, and the sickening lily scent was only making it worse.

He and Elizabeth stood apart from the other mourners, watching numbly as the holy words were spoken over the casket, words that held out promises of redemption and eternal bliss. To Victor, empty words, false promises. The only true thing in this large chapel was the rotting corpse of his mother, who would never again see the sky, never again dance in the blue ballroom, never again fondly touch the golden hair of her precious son. For Caroline, the only future was the grave.

Victor's father slowly made his way up the aisle to the coffin. He looked suddenly twenty years older, with his white hair and stooped shoulders. Victor realized with a sudden shock that Dr. Frankenstein *was* an old man; only his marriage had made him youthful. The joy his wife had brought to him had invigorated him. Now bereft, he would begin to die. Oh, he might live on for ten or fifteen years or even longer, but it would be as a dying man.

Mrs. Moritz stood near the coffin, holding in her ample arms the tiny baby, who had not yet been christened. Her own children, her son Claude and daughter Justine, were with her. Dr. Frankenstein reached the coffin, and stood for a moment weeping over it.

"Goodbye, Caroline," he whispered. "I love you."

"Why her? Why?" Victor asked softly, more to himself than to Elizabeth. He could not cry; it seemed to him that he had shed the last tear he would ever weep. He was truly unable to comprehend the loss of his mother. Nothing in any of his readings, not alchemy, not natural philosophy, not even religion, had prepared him for a loss such as this—sudden, final, devastating.

His mother, so bright, so beautiful, and above all, so kind and affectionate—how could she just die in the space of a couple of hours? Without warning? Why couldn't a being so beloved by everybody live forever? If, as religion taught, the soul was immortal, then why shouldn't the body have a share in its immortality as well? Why was it so much less worthy? What was the value of the very concept of immortality if it could not be applied to a person like Caroline Frankenstein?

All I know is that we must accept it," Elizabeth said quietly. Her small body was draped in black from head to toe, and her skin shone palely from under its veil of black. Her large eyes were as dark as her mourning garb.

But Victor could not, would not accept it. Nothing would reconcile him to the picture of his beautiful mother turning to dust in her coffin as the death-worms gluttonously feasted on her loveliness.

"Why?!" he cried out loudly, so loudly that the other mourners stirred at the noise, and turned their hands slightly. But as prosperous Swiss they were too discreet, or too embarrassed, to make a point of noticing the son's public outburst.

"Because it's the only thing we can do," said Elizabeth firmly.

"No." Victor refused all comfort. He had seen the face of the enemy, and it was a grinning death's-head, laughing at him. Caroline's death had changed him profoundly. His existence from now on would take a new and determined direction. On this dark day of his beloved mother's funeral the seventeen-year-old Victor Frankenstein dedicated his life to only one goal. To conquer the enemy death, and bring him to his knees.

"Victor." Elizabeth laid her soft hand on his black-clothed shoulder. "It's up to us now to hold this family together. Think of Father. He needs you. I need you. Think of your studies, you could be a great doctor. We have a baby brother now, and we have to take care of him. We have to take care of each other."

Yes. He needed her. He needed Elizabeth more than ever before in his life. Victor turned to her and hugged her tightly. And the tears he'd believed could not be shed stung his eyes and rolled down his cheeks.

"We will . . . we will . . . I'm sorry . . ." he wept.

5   Elizabeth

Less than a week after his mother's funeral, the newborn was christened William Karl Peter Christian Frankenstein, but from his earliest days he was known only as Willie. In all his features little Willie looked so much like his late mother that it seemed to everybody that Caroline had been reborn in the body of her infant son. He resembled her greatly in personality as well—sweet-natured, gentle, trusting, and very affectionate. Sometimes it pained his father to see so much of his mother in him, but nobody could remain immune to Willie's charms and virtues for very long. He soon became everybody's favorite, not only because he was a baby, but because he made everyone feel better by his easy smiles and sunny disposition. Willie was in love with the whole wide world, and the whole wide world loved him back.

So the years drifted past—1786, 1787, 1788,

1790—and the deep wound inflicted on the family by the death of Caroline began slowly to heal. With Mrs. Moritz's invaluable help, Elizabeth took over the management of the household, as Caroline had prepared her, and was running both the home and the family efficiently. Willie grew from infant to baby to toddler to little man of four. He adored Elizabeth as the only mother he ever knew, thought of Justine as his older sister, and simply worshiped his big brother Victor. Dr. Frankenstein grew older and much more quiet, given to long silences and bouts of melancholy. He missed his wife sorely. Yet he still practiced both medicine and philanthropy because he knew that Caroline would have wanted him to go on living.

Victor was graduated from secondary school, the *gymnasium*, and spent the next three years in completing a course of scientific studies at Geneva University, in preparation for three years of medical school. At twenty-one, he was a serious man, deeply absorbed in his own experiments, still searching for knowledge not taught at the university. He had set up the nearest thing he could manage to a laboratory upstairs, and spent many hours behind a closed door duplicating some of this century's famous experiments with electricity and electromagnetism.

But on this brilliant summer's day the mansion was bathed in a warm, golden light. Estate workers were getting ready for the harvests, working in field and orchard, hauling bales and baskets to and fro. It was too blissful a day for anyone to be cooped up indoors; Elizabeth determined to rouse Victor out of his stuffy lair and carry him into the sunshine. He was working much too hard, she thought, and would turn old before his time if he didn't take some recreation. All work and no play was making Victor a very dull boy.

With her characteristic determination, she mounted the steps to his private laboratory. The door was firmly shut, but Elizabeth didn't care. Bending over, she peeped through the keyhole. She saw a candle arrangement which drove a wheel, which in turn drove the strings of a puppet dog, which danced a little jig. It was a simple experiment in heat conversion to kinetic energy, but to Elizabeth the dancing dog was merely a toy. What was so scientific about a puppet?

"Victor!" she called through the door. "Come on out!"

"No, go away. I'm busy." He didn't bother to look up from his workbench, but kept his eyes on the new experiment he was setting up. Victor had turned his old nursery schoolroom into his laboratory, off limits to everyone except himself. He was twenty-one years old, and a man in the eyes of the law and society, and he deserved to be treated like a man, and accorded the privilege of complete privacy.

But Elizabeth was not to be discouraged. Now that he had completed his university studies and would enter medical school in the autumn, her brother had become impossibly self-important. What he needed was to stop fooling around with puppets, get out of that "laboratory" of his and get into the fresh air.

"Please come outside, Victor. It's such a beautiful day!" She made her voice cajoling, but her knuckles rapped impatiently at the wooden door. Elizabeth hated being left out of anything, and she missed Victor, who was shutting himself away for longer and longer hours.

Victor paid her no attention, but continued to

adjust a metal rod. His new experiments with electricity were more engrossing than anything going on outside today. The rapping on his door grew louder.

"Go away, Elizabeth," he called impatiently. "Don't bother me now. I told you, I'm busy."

Defiantly, Elizabeth pushed the door opened and came inside. Victor was sitting hunched over his workbench, fiddling with a lot of equipment, including strange-looking glass bottles and jars, which she'd never seen before and didn't recognize. Next to him, on the floor, stood a large vat in which live eels were wriggling. She moved closer and picked up a long metal instrument.

"What's this?"

Reaching down into the vat, Victor pulled out one of the eels, which thrashed about in his fingers. He gave the object in Elizabeth's hand only a cursory glance.

"It's for spraying down the electric eels."

Elizabeth gave it a shake and pressed the tip. A small jet of water came spritzing out and sprayed Victor in the face, making him jump. Uttering a squeal of delight, she laughed out loud at the indignant expression on Victor's dripping-wet face. Tossing his eel back in the tank, he leaped to his feet and began to chase her around the room. Elizabeth dodged him nimbly as she continued to spray the water at him. This was a great game.

Victor was fast, but Elizabeth was lighter on her feet and continued to elude him. "Come back!" he yelled at her, but he was no longer really serious. Her playfulness was infectious, and he was enjoying this game. "Leave that alone, it's not funny," he scolded, but it was in truth very funny, and he couldn't help it—he had to laugh.

They continued to chase each other around the

room, laughing hysterically. "This is a good experiment," crowed Elizabeth. "Let me have a couple of those eels."

"All right, all right, you win," Victor conceded finally, almost out of breath. "I'll come outside with you. Just give me a few minutes to put on a dry shirt. Go and pack us a lunch. A big one. We'll take Willie and Justine along with us."

As Elizabeth had promised, it was indeed a beautiful day, although hot and still. Elizabeth wanted to fly her kite, but there was no breeze, so they decided to head for the mountains. As Swiss who knew and loved the Alps, they were all fairly good climbers; even Victor's four-year-old brother Willie could churn his chubby little legs up a sloping cliff face if it wasn't too steep. Victor carried the picnic basket, which was surprisingly heavy, and Justine took some blankets since Elizabeth was burdened with the kite.

When they reached the top of the low ridge, they were met by mountain breezes and the delightful perfume of Alpine wildflowers in summer. Above them on the higher slopes of the mountains they could see a herd of goats pasturing; the males bounded from crag to crag, while the little spring newborns stayed close to their nursing mothers. Clouds like tufts of white lambs wool drifted across a sky the color of the deep blue Canton china in the Frankenstein dining room.

Victor strode in front of them, their undisputed leader. Justine and Willie ran along the top of the ridge, trying to keep up. Elizabeth scampered ahead, attempting to get her kite into the air. Her long dark hair, unbound, streamed out behind her like a sable flag and her full stiff skirts looked like ballooning sails. She picked up speed, then looked over her shoulder. Willie and Justine were getting left behind.

"Willie!" called Elizabeth.

"Come on!" Victor shouted to his little brother.

"Yes, come on!" Elizabeth echoed. "After all, we should be grateful to Victor for abandoning his experiments for one afternoon." She cast a playfully mocking look at him.

"Who says I have?" Victor said with a grin.

"What do you mean?" Elizabeth raised a curious eyebrow.

"Look." Victor turned and pointed to the distance. They could see a black storm cloud, bristling with lightning, heading straight for them. It was massive and menacing. The smiles on the girls' faces vanished.

"You knew this was going to happen!" Elizabeth said accusingly.

Shrugging slightly, Victor grinned. "Not for certain, but I had hoped the conditions would be right. They're quite common up here at this time of the year. I've never seen one quite as large as this, though. Isn't it wonderful?"

Wonderful? It was terrifying! Justine shuddered in panic. "We're all going to die!" she whimpered.

"Victor, you shouldn't have done this!" cried Elizabeth. "We must find shelter. A tree!"

"No!" Victor said urgently. "That's just the wrong thing to do. A tree is potentially a much larger conductor of electricity than we are."

Justine was looking desperate. "What about Willie?"

"What are we to do?" cried Elizabeth.

"Come on," Victor said decisively. As the black storm cloud came nearer and nearer, with lightning streaking from it into the blue sky around it, he led them to an Alpine meadow, a flat stretch of ground where the soil was soft and the grass grew thinly.

Setting down the picnic basket, he opened it, revealing, along with the lunch Elizabeth had packed, some lighting conductor equipment he had slipped inside. No wonder the basket had been so heavy! Victor took out a folded metal rod, extended it and fitted it on the lightning conductor, spreading out the metal fingers. Then he told them all what to do.

Following his instructions, Elizabeth opened up the shooting stick and pushed it into the ground. The metal rod slotted through the handle of the shooting stick and also into the ground. Victor intended this to be a somewhat cruder duplication of one of Benjamin Franklin's famous experiments in conductivity. He had wished for a long time to duplicate Franklin's experiment, and had been waiting for a cloud exactly like this one.

Justine and Willie laid out the blankets on the grass in a star shape around the picnic basket and conductor. Victor looked up to see the lightning-cloud almost upon them.

"Lie down," he ordered. "And stay down. Don't get up or even raise your heads, no matter what happens. I'll tell you when to move."

They took their positions on the blankets, lying flat on their stomachs around the lightning rod, close to one another but not touching. They stayed down so as not to attract the lightning, which always looks for something tall to strike. Victor stared up into the heavens, watching the cloud's swift approach. When it was close to overhead, he too laid his head down on the blanket. They waited: Victor with anticipation, the other three in fear.

"Victor?" Elizabeth whispered, as though the storm cloud could hear her.

"Wait," said Victor calmly.

Then the cloud was right above them and they

heard a loud crack and saw a blinding flash. A bolt of lightning struck the conductor, which glowed blue and rattled madly. The electricity crackled as it traveled down the rod and entered the ground, where it became earthed and harmless. A strong odor of ozone filled the air, making them all feel a little giddy.

"One, two, three, *now!*" called Victor. He got to his knees, smiling. They were all unharmed. Elizabeth followed. She looked at her hands in wonder. What on earth . . .? Tiny, livid snakes of electricity were dancing all over her hands. She put her fingers together, and a spark leaped across. There was no pain at all, no burning, just this inexplicable feeling of tremendous energy, and she was right at the focus of it. Elizabeth looked over at Victor, then at Justine and Willie. They, too, were surrounded by dancing fields of energy, residual sparks left by the lightning.

At the same moment, Elizabeth and Victor both stretched their index fingers out toward each other, and a spark leapt across from point to point, making a crack and a tiny shock. Then they put their faces close together, and a spark leapt between their noses. What a sensation! They laughed with delight.

"How do you feel, Elizabeth?" whispered Victor.

"Alive," she whispered back.

Hearing a sizzling noise, they both looked down into the picnic basket. The food was charred and smoking into ashes.

"And hungry," she added, laughing.

Justine and Willie scrambled to their feet, staring in wonder at the sparks surrounding them like auras.

"Look at the sparks, Willie, they're dancing," giggled Justine.

"Dancing?" said Elizabeth and Victor at the same

time. Both of them loved to dance, especially with each other. They sprang to their feet.

"What an excellent idea." Elizabeth smiled.

"My dear, will you do me the honor?" Victor smiled back.

"It would be my pleasure." Elizabeth dropped a small curtsy. Victor made a mock formal bow and both struck a pose and as they began to dance, while Justine, who as usual had hoped to dance with Victor herself and who as usual had been disappointed, picked up little Willie and began to swing him around as her partner. Then the four of them danced off across the ridge, their laughter echoing across the mountains.

The chimes of the great rosewood grandfather clock in the library sounded the hours one after another. More years ticked past, busy and prosperous years. Happy and productive years: 1791, 1792, 1793. Victor completed the course at the Geneva medical college. He was now twenty-four, Elizabeth twenty-three, and Willie a well-grown lad of seven.

If medical school had given Victor anything, it was the conviction that he wasn't destined to become a general practitioner following in his father's footsteps. In the last three years he had learned all about the circulation of the blood, the nature of diseases, how bones knit together, which medicines to prescribe for which illnesses. Now he was an expert on the circulatory system, on the nerves that connected the body to the brain, on the skeleton underneath that held the human mass together. Medical school had taught him all that, and more. But what it didn't offer him were any of the answers to the unanswerable questions Victor was always posing.

Where does life come from? What is the absolute

pinpoint moment of its creation, and how is it formed? By what combination of elements, powered by what energy or dynamic? Why do people ever have to die? Why was no scientific effort being put forth to discover a way to cheat death? Here they were, living in the eighteenth century, an age of enormous technological advancement—discoveries in steam power, gases, electricity, the discovery and isolation of elements, yet virtually nothing had been accomplished in what was surely the most important field of all—the infinite prolongation of human life.

This had become Victor's own mission; he was convinced that the only satisfaction he would ever achieve in his work would come from there. He knew that he was taking on a monumental task, and he wasn't even certain where to begin. But he had the fixed idea that by creating life in a laboratory, by re-animating dead tissue, he must learn secrets that would inevitably lead to the secret of immortality.

So, upon his graduation, instead of entering his father's medical practice, he applied to the great University at Ingolstadt for research and postgraduate studies. Many celebrated doctors taught there, and many young and fiery students went there to learn what ordinary medical schools did not or could not teach.

His path lay in research, and Victor Frankenstein intended to follow that path wherever it might lead. He looked forward to leaving for Ingolstadt, yet at the same time, he bitterly regretted having to leave his home, and most of all having to leave Elizabeth. Not seeing her virtually every day, not sharing confidence with her, would leave an enormous void in his life, and as the day grew nearer for their parting, Victor began to realize exactly how deep a void it would be. Like the pole star, his Elizabeth had become the lodestone of his life, attracting him by her brilliance and beauty.

On the eve of his departure for Ingolstadt, Dr. Frankenstein held a large farewell party in the ballroom of the mansion. He invited all their old family friends, and many young people, playfellows and schoolmates of Victor's, and gaily dressed young women who were friends of Elizabeth's, and who dearly loved any occasion for a dress-up ball.

For ten days beforehand, an army of maids and footmen scrubbed at the mansion, washing windows inside and out, taking down old curtains and putting up newer and costlier ones, making every doorknob shine and sweeping the cobwebs out from behind every corner. An orchestra was hired for the evening, and hundreds of candles were set into the massive ballroom crystal chandeliers, which had been rinsed in vinegar-and-water solution until they sparkled like diamonds.

Then the evening of the ball came at last. The guests began arriving in their carriages, with their footmen perched up behind on the rear box. Horses' hooves crunched the gravel drive underfoot. Women in beautiful wide-skirted gowns and fine shawls from Kashmir, their necks, fingers, bosoms, and ears decked out in elegant jewelry, and men in powdered wigs, wearing chamois knee breeches with polished silver buttons, ruffled shirts under silk brocade waistcoats, and wonderfully fitted fine wool tailcoats, all crowded up the stairs, as the musicians tuned up their instruments.

Mrs. Moritz's son Claude, who last year had been promoted to majordomo, stood on the stairs to usher the guests into the large blue ballroom. He clapped his hands twice, and the orchestra began to play vigorously.

Victor, Elizabeth, Justine, and Willie were magically transformed by their magnificent evening dress. They felt self-conscious, but they were conscious, too, of their youthful radiance. Victor was in the prime of young manhood. Elizabeth, womanly now, radiated poise and intelligence. As they moved gracefully around the ballroom floor together, they were, as Mrs. Moritz had predicted, the envy of all eyes, and they were not unaware of how handsome a couple they made.

Justine had also grown into an attractive woman, although somewhat nervous and intense. She, the daughter of the family housekeeper and something like a big sister/governess to Willie, was here as a guest, on an equal footing with other guests. This overjoyed her, but it also overawed her, and thus far she had danced only with Willie, who was looking charmingly formal in a miniature gold-buttoned red satin waistcoat embroidered all over with bright blue forget-me-nots and big shiny buckles on his new dancing pumps.

The spirited dance came to an end with a great flourish. Victor lifting Elizabeth into the air in a *volta*. The guests applauded the musicians and themselves. Victor lowered Elizabeth back to the floor. Flushed and happy, she fanned herself with a lace-embroidered fan from Spain.

"You dance so beautifully together," Justine said with a longing look at Victor.

"And you look lovely," said Elizabeth warmly. The two girls shared a sisterly hug and a radiant smile. The lush music started up again. "Victor? Dance with me?" Justine asked hopefully and awkwardly.

Victor hesitated, wishing to dance again with his sister, but Elizabeth caught his eye. A smile and a small nodding gesture of her lovely head plainly signaled "Go on, ask her."

"Please," she added out loud. "I'm quite out of breath. Besides, I am promised to Willie." Elizabeth curtsied to the ecstatic Willie and danced off with him. Victor gallantly offered Justine his arm. She took it, her whole being lighting up with happiness as they began to dance. She was absolutely glowing; this was a big moment for her. But they had hardly begun when Claude, from the stairs, interrupted.

"Ladies and Gentlemen," he announced. The dancers stopped. The orchestra fell silent. Justine tried to hide her disappointment as the guests gathered around to listen to Dr. Frankenstein.

"Dear friends," he began, a little shyly, "tomorrow my dear son, Victor, whom some of you may know . . ."—he stopped as a burst of warm laughter filled the room—". . . leaves me to pursue what I'm sure will be an illustrious career in a profession with which I myself am not altogether unconnected." He paused, expecting his audience to laugh, and they obliged. "In his three years in the Geneva Medical School, he has acquitted himself admirably."

All the guests broke into a polite round of applause.

"And I feel if he fares as well in his research at the University of Ingolstadt then he may well turn out to be . . . insufferable." More laughter followed.

Then Dr. Frankenstein's voice dropped, and shook a little as he continued. "My one regret is that his mother . . . my late wife . . . is not here to share the pride which . . . our son fills me with tonight. . . ."

Claude now passed Victor's father a handsome leather-bound journal, which the old man accepted with trembling hands, close to tears. "Oh yes, she

wanted you to have this, Victor, on your graduation."
He opened the cover of the book. "In it she has
written, 'This is the journal of Victor Frankenstein.'
The rest of its leaves are blank, waiting to be filled
with the deeds of a noble life."

Dr. Frankenstein's voice cracked, and he appeared to be on the verge of breaking down. The
thought of Caroline's absence, especially on this
night of nights when most of Geneva had come to
honor her son, was almost more than he could bear.
How she would have loved to see so many friends
enjoying their hospitality! She, to whom music and
dancing was food and drink!

Victor stepped forward and wordlessly accepted
the beautiful leather journal, putting his arm around
his father's shoulders in an affectionate hug. He,
too, missed Caroline, especially on this wonderful
evening. She should have been here, he thought. She
ought never to have died.

Suddenly, the sound of the harpsichord started
up. The guests all turned to look. Seated at the
keyboard, Elizabeth began to sing in a clear, sweet
voice, a simple, beautiful melody, quietly smiling.
The pretty air broke the tension in the room, and gave
Dr. Frankenstein a chance to recover his self-control.

So, we'll go no more a roving
So late into the night,
Though the heart be still as loving,
And the moon be still as bright.

Though the night was made for loving,
And the day returns too soon,
Yet we'll go no more a roving
By the light of the moon.

The gravel path crunched under their waltzing feet. Behind them, inside the house, the shadows of guests appeared and disappeared like silhouetted puppets dancing past the ballroom windows. The orchestra could be heard, faintly, but Elizabeth and Victor were really waltzing to an interior music they heard mostly with their hearts, not their ears. They danced by the light of the overhead stars, and the tall pitch pine torches that stood flickering in brackets outside the front entrance, to light the guests' way in and out.

"We'd better go in before they miss us," Elizabeth said at last, reluctantly. The night was clear, with many thousands of stars glittering an unimaginable distance away in the heavens. She wore a satin dress cut low in the bosom, with a wide, full skirt, and a lovely antique lace scarf over her thick curling black hair, and tiny diamonds glittered in the lace, echoing the sky and the pinpoints of light in her night-dark eyes. He had never seen her looking so beautiful.

"Just a little while longer, please," begged Victor. "I don't know when we'll be alone together again." He seemed agitated.

"Oh dear, Victor," Elizabeth laughed gently at the forlorn tone of his voice.

Her soft sympathy set Victor also to laughing. "I shall miss you laughing at me."

"I'll miss you making me laugh."

Indoors, the waltz came to an end, the music stopped, and now Elizabeth and Victor drew apart. He looked sadly and intently into her eyes. In the seventeen years since Victor had known Elizabeth, they had seldom been far apart, and never for very long. Even when he left their nursery tutor to attend school outside the home, all Victor's education had taken place in Geneva. His *gymnasium*, his university, even medical school were here, only a few miles on horseback from home. Now, for the first time, he would be traveling a long distance, hundreds of miles away to Ingolstadt. When would he be seeing Elizabeth again? The question had been uppermost in his mind these past few weeks.

"So . . . how do brothers and sisters say goodbye?" Victor asked with a crooked smile.

"Perhaps they never have to," Elizabeth answered slowly.

Now Victor remembered that first time he laid eyes on her, a sad-faced little girl of seven mourning the death of her parents. He recalled the bargain they'd made that day—never to die.

"I won't if you won't," he repeated those words now.

Elizabeth, too, remembered, and the teasing smile left her face. At last, she held out her hand and Victor reached his out to shake it, to renew their old bargain.

But as soon as his hand touched hers, Victor pulled Elizabeth toward him, holding her close. Their eyes searched each other's faces, seeing there reflections of the passion each of them felt. Then, for the first time, he kissed her on her full red mouth—a long, hungry, hot kiss.

Flooded by happiness, dizzy with emotion, she leaned into him, returning his feeling, as their bodies pressed tightly together.

At last, with reluctance, Elizabeth ended the kiss and they pulled apart. "I can't leave you!" cried Victor, anguished.

"I don't want you to go!" Elizabeth was equally agonized, trembling with fervor, and her breath came shallow. Her virginal body was burning for his touch, which both aroused and frightened her.

"I love you so much," breathed Victor.

Elizabeth pulled back to smile with tender certainty into Victor's face. "I love you, too. I have loved you all my life, it seems."

When did Victor first fall in love with Elizabeth? He had no idea. Probably also on first sight. But it had only been in the past year, with Ingolstadt and the separation that it meant hanging over his head, that he realized that he had fallen in love with this wonderful, beautiful girl, and acknowledged the importance of her in his life.

They kissed again, and her kiss was as hungry and intense as his own. Now it was Victor who finally broke off the kiss, holding her at arm's length, looking deeply into her eyes.

"Are you my sister?" he asked hoarsely.

Elizabeth was close to swooning under the onslaught of her emotions. "Sister, friend, lover . . ." she murmured breathlessly.

Victor fell to his knees before her. "Wife?" His voice was low, husky, heavy with feeling.

Elizabeth looked lovingly at him. Wife, oh, yes, she would be his wife. This was what she'd dreamed of for years, she and Victor joined by God for life. For her, there never could be another man.

"Yes," she answered simply but fervently.

She understood! She shared his feelings! Overjoyed, Victor lifted Elizabeth's hand to his lips, kissing it warmly. Then, impetuously, he begged, "Then come with me to Ingolstadt. Marry me now."

Elizabeth took a step backward in surprise. She found it hard to catch her breath. "No, Victor!"

He stood up. "Then I'll stay here," he declared.

Touched by his ardor, she still had to laugh at his boyish rashness. "And give up your work? You'd give up saving the world for me?"

"Yes. Even with you laughing at me."

Elizabeth's small face grew serious and her brows drew together. "I want more than anything else in the world to be your wife . . . but as long as you are away I belong here. I want to be here for Father and William. And I have work to do. I want to make this house live again. I want this to be a great home for our children. And now you must go and do the great things you need to do."

Her words inspired him, but they also inflamed him. Just the thought of having children with Elizabeth, of sharing her bed as her husband, of knowing her perfect body as well as he knew his own, made him shiver. "I want you so much," Victor whispered with tender passion.

He pulled her close to him again, pressing his ardent body tightly against hers again, savoring the moment, not wanting it to end. Her skin was so soft . . . how he burned to kiss her all over . . . her neck, her bare shoulders, her breasts, the rounded tops of which peeped enchantingly from the décolletage of the low-cut ball gown she was wearing.

Elizabeth sensed Victor's passion and shared it, but she, who had waited years for this moment, knew that it was only right to wait a bit longer. A love as soul-filled and enduring as theirs did not need to be rushed to its fulfillment like some shameful backstairs lust between a parlor maid and a groom.

"I will be here when you come back," she told him with a catch in her voice, "each holiday, every visit . . . and then on our wedding night . . ."

Their wedding night. Just imagining it was the sweetest torture, the expectation of passion deferred, exquisitely painful to both. But Victor knew that Elizabeth was right. They had to wait. To indulge themselves now would be to rob themselves of their virgin wedding, the lawful mating of their spirits. Yet it would happen. Some day soon they would be married, and Victor would possess her, making Elizabeth his own into eternity. Already they were mated; even though their flesh hadn't yet joined their spirits were already one.

But now Victor had to have another kiss, just one more, and so did Elizabeth. This time her lips parted under his, and his tongue sought hers, setting them both on fire. They were so young, and the fever in their blood was running hot with the depth of the emotion they felt for each other. They longed to go on touching forever.

At last they pulled apart, both of them breathing hard. "Until our wedding night," Victor assented.

Elizabeth closed her eyes, and a glittering tear, like the diamonds she wore in her hair, formed on her jet lashes. It was a tear of pure joy. "I give you my heart, Victor. I love you," she breathed.

Early the next morning Victor Frankenstein mounted his chestnut gelding and set off northward, up the Alpine road towards Ingolstadt. He had ahead of him a ride of more than five hundred miles, through northern Switzerland and southern Germany. He would cover mountain roads and ride through valleys, past cities like Bern, then crossing the Rhine, then through the large German center of Munschen, and finally, on to Ingolstadt.

This was now late August, and he expected to be in Ingolstadt in mid-September. Even if the roads were dry, staying in the saddle for most of every day, and stopping at wayside inns only to eat and sleep, would make it an arduous journey.

It was a brisk, chilly morning, perfect for riding, and the shoulder-capes of Victor's woolen greatcoat fluttered behind him in the wind. One hand held the reins in a light grip, the other held a small bouquet of Alpine flowers.

High on a ridge overlooking the Alps a marble monument had been erected. The figure of a woman stood on a pedestal base, one arm upraised in greeting, or more likely, thought Victor, in a blessing. On the base was a short, simple inscription.

Victor rode up to the monument and dismounted. As his horse grazed on the stubbly mountain grass, the reins loose around his neck, Victor knelt and placed his sprig of flowers at the statue's base, below the inscribed legend reading

Beloved Wife and Mother

CAROLINE
Beaufort
FRANKENSTEIN.

He rose to his feet and gazed longingly at the statue. His heart was very heavy with this final leave-taking. "Oh, Mother," he whispered with tears in his eyes, "you should never have died. No one need ever die. I will stop this. I *will* stop this. I promise you."

He bent over to pick up the chestnut's dangling reins. Then, swiftly mounting his horse, Victor Frankenstein rode north into his future without a backward look.

6   Ingolstadt

In the very early morning of a day in mid-September, Victor sat astride his horse on the slope of a green hill, looking down for the first time on the walled town of Ingolstadt. The surrounding hills were windy and cold, and he was glad of his warm great-coat, a long gray woolen garment that covered him from neck to heels and spread out behind him on the gelding's flanks. The picturesque city, famous for its churches as well as its university, lay nestled in a Danube valley, protected by hills on three sides.

From where he sat, Victor could see the far-off rooftops and tall church steeples of the city below. Finally at the end of his long journey, he felt a stab of anticipation. What secrets would the famous University of Ingolstadt unlock to his eager mind?

The city was only just opening its gates for the day as Victor steered his horse through them and into the main square, which stood at the heart of the old medieval city. Just as in classical times the *agora*, the open-air market, was the center of ancient Athens, this square and its outdoor market were the center of Ingolstadt. Seething with city life, surrounded by shops and businesses, even as it was still being set up the market was already busy. Housewives and cooks were elbowing one another out of the way to get at the best cuts of meat and the freshest fish, which lay displayed on open wooden stalls.

As his horse's hooves clip-clopped over the old cobblestones of the market square, Victor saw mounds of red and white potatoes, huge green cabbages, and purple-and-white turnips so large they looked like babies' heads wearing colorful caps. There was a baker with a stall filled with fresh-baked loaves and meat pies, a sausage maker vending eighteen different kinds of *wurst*, a poultry market for eggs, chickens, ducks, and fat geese, a knife grinder with his sharpening wheel, a dairy table piled high with wheels of rich cheese and big slabs of tempting yellow butter, and pens where live animals, lambs and calves, were being sold or traded. It seemed that nobody in Ingolstadt was about to go hungry today.

Riding through the narrow streets that surrounded the square, Victor found Frau Brach's boardinghouse without too much trouble. It had been recommended as respectable, clean, and inexpensive and situated not too far from the university. The house was large and old, characterized by the wedding cake baroque stone ornamentation of the previous century. Frau Brach herself, respectable and clean, had the plump, creamy look of a German pastry, which was not a coincidence, because it was mainly her indulgence in cakes and pastry that had made her so plump.

Now she trudged heavily up a long, steep, narrow flight of stairs, followed by her large and friendly sheepdog, Putzi. Victor followed along behind.

"I'm rather surprised at your request, as I hardly ever come up here. I'm afraid there are a lot of stairs," she wheezed, already out of breath. "They're only attic rooms—"

The boardinghouse attic was unappealing with its set of tiny rooms, a claustrophobic bedroom, a small sitting room, both of them plainly furnished. With the dog sniffing at his heels, Victor followed Frau Brach into a narrow corridor and then on into the dark, cheerless bedroom. Frau Brach kept chattering away.

"As I said, there's no real rooms left. All we've got is attic space. No one seems to want the attic space. Putzi likes you."

Victor, barely listening, moved off into the attic proper, an immensely long empty room stretching the entire length of the house. He drew his breath in as he saw massive vaulted beams and small, grimy dormer windows that dimly filtered in the light; at intervals in the ceiling a procession of skylights. At one end of the room there stood a dusty upright piano. The space and the privacy spoke eloquently to him; as living quarters, the garret might have some drawbacks, but as a laboratory for his intended experiments its possibilities were endless. He turned toward her, smiling broadly. "This will be perfect."

The landlady smiled back in happy surprise. She had never expected to earn a pfennig on this place. Seeing her mistress so pleased, Putzi wagged her shaggy tail. So with the dog's approval, the bargain was struck. Victor Frankenstein was to have the entire attic, including the long vacant room, for his exclusive use.

As soon as he settled in, Victor prepared to attend classes and lectures. Far and wide was the University of Ingolstadt known. The latest techniques and advances in medicine were taught here by a world-renowned faculty; graduate medicos such as Victor Frankenstein, mingling with undergraduate medical students, thronged in to fill up the lecture halls and operating theaters.

The permanent residents of Ingolstadt had mixed feelings about their celebrated university. On the one hand, its presence lent the city much prestige; on the other hand, many of the townsfolk still had the closed minds of the Middle Ages, and were suspicious of what was going on behind the university gates, and what sort of sinister witchcraft might be practiced there, especially in that mysterious medical school. They whispered that human bodies were cut up there, and the pieces used in unholy rituals.

Further irritating the "town versus gown" state of mind was the fact that many of the university students were rowdy. Working hard all day, they liked to enjoy themselves at night, and they often roistered through the narrow cobbled streets, looking for pretty girls and thick beer. Perhaps if the young men had been wealthy, with deep and overflowing pockets, the town's attitude toward them might have been friendlier. But students are notoriously poor, and generally have almost nothing to spend in the town, so the people of Ingolstadt had little reason to be gracious to their scholarly guests. Instead, they would cast them dirty looks and mutter insults whenever a group of students passed them on the streets.

The gates of the university were a single monumental stone structure. Deeply inscribed into its

arches was the legend KNOWLEDGE IS POWER ONLY
THROUGH GOD. A bell tolled the classroom hours.
Walking through the gates for the first time, Victor
Frankenstein felt a thrill of elation. Surely, here was
the place he would finally learn everything he wanted
to know!

Professor Krempe, a squat little man dressed in a
long academic gown, with a curly wig, a peruke,
sitting atop the fringe of wiry white hair around the
base of his bald head, was the chief of the medical
college. His popular lectures on human physiology
were invariably delivered to packed galleries of eager
young students who laughed, whistled, stomped,
and applauded. As he lectured, Krempe would pace
nervously back and forth, crackling like a lightning
rod with energy and sarcasm.

Victor arrived early at the lecture hall, snagging a
place at the front of one of the upper galleries. The
hall was built like a theater, with a round floor below,
and tiers of seats arranged in a rising semicircle
above, so that the maximum number of students
could see clearly the lecturer and the demonstration
below. Professor Krempe had such a reputation as an
expert on human muscles, nerves, joints, and ten-
dons that the young doctor was eager to hear him.

"The mistakes of the lawyer are left dangling in
the air, the doctor may at least bury his." Krempe
paused, expectant. This jest earned him a big laugh
every semester, and this term was no different. The
laughter lasted almost a minute. "But perhaps the
greatest mistake that all students make during their
time here is to suppose they will ever have an original
or creative thought. We have all imagined that in
our time."

As though to punctuate those remarks, he threw
a significant look toward the door of the lecture hall.

A tall, lean, dark-bearded man was watching silently from the doorway. The stranger's mute and expressionless face showed no reaction to Krempe's thinly veiled insult. This was another member of the faculty, Professor Jacob Heinrich Waldman, the famous—and notorious—specialist in the human brain.

"Gentlemen, you have come here not to think for yourselves," continued Krempe, pacing, "but to learn how to think for your patients. You will, therefore, first learn to submit yourselves to the established laws of physical reality."

Krempe's words took Victor by surprise. Not think for himself? But that was the very reason he had come all this way, to pursue his own researches using the new sharp tool of a deeper education by Ingolstadt's faculty. He raised his hand, leaned forward over the gallery railing, and spoke.

"But surely, Professor, you don't intend for us to disregard more . . . philosophical . . . approaches."

Professor Krempe looked startled. "Philosophical?" he echoed, scowling. The word sounded strange on his tongue, as though he were tasting it for the first time and didn't like the flavor.

"Those which stir the imagination a well as the intellect. As in Paracelsus, for example," Victor replied eagerly.

The reference was lost on all but a few other students. But, up among the others in the gallery opposite, a curly haired young man leaned forward and shot an amused look in Victor's direction.

Krempe's scowl deepened. "Paracelsus. An arrogant and foolish Swiss," he snorted.

"Albertus Magnus," Victor continued.

Irritation made Krempe's whiskers tremble. "His nonsense was exploded five hundred years ago!"

"Cornelius Agrippa." Victor was persistent.

"A sorcerer. An occultist," sneered the professor. "What is your name?"

"Victor Frankenstein, sir. Of Geneva."

Krempe smiled sourly. "Ah, another Swiss." His raspy voice dripped sarcasm. "Well, gentlemen, for those of you who are unfamiliar with Mr. Frankenstein of Geneva's reading list, which thankfully will be most of you, you would be well advised to avoid it. Here, at the University of Ingolstadt, we teach and indeed attempt to advance, the study of medicine, chemistry, biology, physics. We study hard science—"

Victor shook his head in protest. "But surely, Professor, the greatest possible advances lie in combining—"

The professor's sour smile disappeared and he interrupted sharply. "We do not study the ravings of lunatics and alchemists hundreds of years in their graves! Because their kind of amateur, fanatical, fantastical speculations do not heal bodies or save lives! Only science can do that. Now, have we your permission to continue?"

Victor's cheeks flushed; he'd been thoroughly humiliated. He would have liked to say more, but wisely he swallowed his anger. As a mere student, he could hardly prevail in public against the likes of Professor Krempe. But he couldn't bear to stay here any longer. Standing up, he left the lecture hall.

He strode through the university gates, his fists clenched, eyes blazing with anger. His greatcoat whipped around his ankles as he marched on. He didn't notice a few townsfolk hanging around, sullen, resentful, viewing with contempt the "young gentleman." Nor did he notice that he was being followed, at a trot, by the young student who'd watched him back in the lecture hall.

"Nice coat," remarked the stranger, a little out of breath as he caught up with Victor.

"Thank you," Victor replied grimly, without looking.

"Don't take it too hard," the young man said sympathetically. "It's just that Krempe doesn't approve of public humiliation."

Victor stopped and turned, eyeing this stranger for the first time. He saw a young man of about his own age, with a head of black curly hair, a friendly, plain face and an air of cheerfulness about him.

"I am not crazy, you know," he said grimly.

"My dear fellow, of course you're not." The young man smiled, showing very white teeth with a space between the two front ones. His small blue eyes disappeared into jolly slits. "In fact that's just the sort of thing I'd expect a perfectly rational person to say to a complete stranger."

Victor couldn't help but smile at the young man's sarcasm. The fellow put out his right hand. "Henry Clerval, by the way, and *I'm* completely crazy."

Victor shook the hand, laughing. "Victor Frankenstein."

"Of Geneva. . . ."

"Yes, of Geneva."

"I noticed—" But at that moment a very tall and broad young man, at least six feet four in height, came crashing into them.

"Why don't you look where I'm going?" he demanded, pushing through Henry and Victor as though they were nothing. Victor stared after him.

"That's Schiller, ornament of the playing field," Henry informed him. "He's new as well. You can tell because he goes around looking at things with his mouth open." Clerval sized up Victor curiously. "What are you here for?"

"Research."

"Oh, very grand," said Henry, in a heavily ironic tone. "I'm here to become a mere doctor. I'm told that has something to do with healing the sick. Which is a pity, really, because I find sick people rather revolting."

The pair walked on together in a friendly manner, but Victor stopped as he saw the shadowy figure of the man from the lecture hall moving away to his coach. That saturnine personage interested him; he felt a pull toward him, as though the man was going to be somehow significant in his life.

"Still, I'll have a good time, get my degree, if I can stop failing anatomy," Henry babbled on. "And then settle down to relieve rich old ladies of their imaginary ailments and then relieve their very real and beautiful daughters."

The coach drove off. "Who was that?" asked Victor, curious. "He was at the lecture." Henry, in his second year of medical school, already appeared to know everybody at Ingolstadt.

"Ah. That's Waldman."

Victor looked impressed. "So that's Waldman." Professor Jacob Heinrich Waldman, the greatest living expert on the human brain.

"Interesting case," Henry continued blithely. "They say in his youth he could break into heaven and lecture God on science. Ran into trouble with the authorities a few years back. Something to do with illegal experiments."

Now Victor was truly intrigued. "What kind of experiments, I wonder?" he murmured, mostly to himself. Then he caught Henry eyeing him strangely, and he recovered himself. "So, what was it you were saying? Rich old ladies and their daughters?"

Clerval put on a martyred face and gazed heavenward, sighing. "It's a life of sacrifice, I know, but someone's got to do it."

Victor burst out laughing and Henry joined in. Professor Waldman's coach passed them, driving out of the city. Victor turned to watch it go.

With diligent ferocity, Victor Frankenstein threw himself into his university studies. He would sit attentively in the classrooms, listening hard, setting down page after page of lecture notes, his quill pen rushing across the ruled page, nib splaying and scratching, scattering drops of ink from the inkwell that was sunk into his stained wooden desk. His hand was always raised, as he posed questions and challenges to all his professors, most of them unanswerable. Krempe had already despaired of him, recognizing Victor's abilities, but unable to get him to concentrate only on what he called "hard science." That boy's head was in the clouds somewhere, with his metaphysicists.

In particular, Professor Waldman's anatomy lectures and laboratory sessions inspired Victor's enthusiasm. The taciturn, shadowy, cadaverous Waldman had an air of mystery about him that fired Victor's imagination. It seemed as though Waldman was possessed of secret knowledge he dared not pass along. Victor longed to know his secrets.

In the university autopsy room, Victor shone. Nothing that Professor Waldman could tell his pupils about the myriad interior connections of the human body, particularly the marvelous mechanism of the brain and its neuronic pathways, was alien or unpleasant to him. Where other students turned away queasily from the dissection of pickled human corpses, stinking of formaldehyde, Frankenstein always picked up his scalpel willingly, eager to explore yet one more mystery of life and death, to answer yet another of his innumerable questions.

". . . And that is *why* the central nervous system and its crowning achievement, the brain, are as complicated and mysterious a set of organs as you are ever likely to encounter. Mr. Frankenstein, the incision is yours."

Waldman handed a scalpel over to Victor. The other students crowded to the front of the galleries around the autopsy room to get the best view of the dissecting table on which lay a naked-sheeted corpse, its face a waxy yellow, its jaw gaping open. Taking the sharp surgical knife, Victor cut deftly into the scalp around the hairline, making a deep circular incision all around the body's skull.

The professor's deep-set eyes narrowed, and he gave a grunt of satisfaction. "Excellent," he said, impressed. "Mr. Clerval, you may remove the cranial lid." Henry took one faltering step forward; a tiny whimper escaped his lips and his round blue eyes rolled up in their sockets. Then he crumpled to the floor in a dead faint.

Smiling and shaking his head, Victor looked down at his unconscious friend. Poor Henry! It appeared that in choosing medicine he had selected a very odd occupation for a man with a delicate stomach.

He took little or no part in the carousing life of the other students at the university. At night, while bands of half-drunk roistering students would stumble over the cobblestoned streets of Ingolstadt, in search of a beer or a barmaid, Victor would sit reading hour after hour. The university's medical curriculum and its required reading lists were insufficient to slake Victor's incessant thirst for more and more knowledge. Several times a week he would haunt the large university library, swallowing with a passion every recent scientific book or treatise available.

What a glorious century was this they were living in! Truly the eighteenth century must be an age of enlightenment that could spawn such brilliant scientific minds as Priestley, Lavoisier, Galvani, Linnaeus, Buffon, Swedenborg, Diderot, Voltaire, Watt, Volta, Helvetius, von Haller, and so many others, all laboring to increase the scope of human knowledge, all determined to expand the borders of empirical science until they might touch the infinite.

Again and again he promised himself that some day he, Victor Frankenstein, would be one of them; he would stand shoulder to shoulder with these scientific giants. He would take their practical modern work and expand on it, combining it with the knowledge of the ancients. The great secrets in the mysterious book of life would be open to him, and he would overcome death. There could be no greater gift to humankind; even Prometheus's bestowal on man of divine fire, a benevolence punished mercilessly by the gods, could compare with this, life everlasting. For this he had been born; for this he had been chosen; Victor believed this with all his heart.

The blood racing through his veins, the young Victor Frankenstein would bend his head over the borrowed volumes. In Latin, French, German, and English he read thrilling accounts of biological and electrical experimentation, the candle on his garret table growing shorter in its pewter holder until at last it sputtered out. Then, left to itself in the dark, Victor's mind would rove over what he had read, picturing each discovery so clearly it was though he himself had been there in the laboratory, working with some brilliant discoverer.

In his imagination the young man was standing at the elbow of Abraham Trembley, like Victor a Genevan, watching in fascination as Trembley operated on a tiny living creature, the primitive animal form hydra, which he had proved—oh, what a significant proof!—could regenerate amputated parts of itself. Victor imagined he could see there, beneath Trembley's skilled hands, the first permanent graft of living animal tissue in the making. Two hydra grafted together, forming one single individual. And the creation survived! Just the thought of the experiment's success took the young man's breath away. Life had been grafted onto life, and a new kind of existence was created in the laboratory.

Embryology, at the very beginnings of life, fascinated the young doctor. To think, that out of undifferentiated and generalized tissue, could grow such specialized and complicated organisms as the various component tissues of the eye, breast tissue, the human tongue and ear, hair and genitals and fingers! Nature was really ingenious, so why not man? Why couldn't man be equally as resourceful at developing such living tissues in his laboratory?

Victor's hands trembled with excitement as he turned the pages of Albrecht von Haller's 1766 experiments. Von Haller, another Swiss like himself, demonstrated that even the slightest stimulus to muscles would provoke a sharp contraction in reaction, and that an even smaller stimulus to a nerve would also provoke a contraction in the muscle to which that nerve was attached. It was nervous stimulation, then, which controlled the movement of muscles, nervous impulses, emanating from the brain or the spinal cord. Nerves all led to the brain, and carried sensations from the brain down their pathways to all the other parts of the body. Stimulate the brain, even in the slightest degree, and a part of the body would correspondingly move. The thought of that intricate neural network and its potential for research sent Victor Frankenstein's pulses racing.

Many nights, as he read through the precious volumes, absorbed in the dispassionate narration of some genius's seminal experiments, there would come a rattle of pebbles at his garret window. At first, Victor would not hear the summons, but it would grow more frequent and insistent until, reluctantly, he would put the book aside and come to the window.

"Frankenstein! Victor!" a familiar voice would bawl from the street. Standing with his legs apart and his hands thrust deep into his greatcoat pockets, Henry Clerval would grin up at him. As he did this evening.

"What do you want, Henry?"

"Come down and have supper with us. A few of us are going to the Boar tavern. Frau Schultze is cooking us her famous schnitzel. Hurry up! I'm starving!"

But Victor was not to be tempted, even by the celebrated Schultze schnitzel. Food was not what he craved, but knowledge. To abandon a scientific treatise for a veal cutlet? Infamous! "Go on without me, Clerval," he called down. "I'm not hungry. I have some cheese here, and a piece of bread."

Henry shook his curly dark head and uttered a loud, theatrical sigh. "Very well then, eat your mouse's dinner if that's what you want. But mark me, one of these days you're going to grow a long, skinny tail!"

Relieved that the interruption was over, Victor would dive back into his studies, soon to become lost in the wonder of expanding knowledge. How far the study of biology had come in this great century!

But biology combined with electricity! Here indeed was the true Promethean fire, the irresistible force of nature, the genuine spark of life! To Victor it seemed that the science of electricity must hold the answers he was seeking.

When the Italian anatomist Luigi Galvani accidentally discovered the electrical nature of nervous impulse—that a charge of electricity could cause the dead muscles of a dissected frog to twitch as though they were alive, he had opened the door to a great mystery. Perhaps here lay the beginning to conquering death! Dead flesh, reanimated by a controlled lightning flash in the laboratory! Perhaps, under the right circumstances, and with the correct materials, true reanimation might be accomplished. Instead of feigning life, perhaps the frog could live again to hop away.

Reanimation! To bring new life to dead human tissues! In short, to raise the dead. Yes, maybe it did seem a dream, but armed with the techniques of the new sciences, what might not be attained?

7   Waldman

Little by little, Victor began to resemble the equipment for his laboratory in the attic, carrying up the steep flights of stairs his wheels, rods, flasks, glass jars, insulators, conductors, preserving solution for dissections, and other necessities. One by one, in the utter privacy of the garret, he began setting up experiments that would duplicate and perhaps even carry further those which filled his imagination from his readings.

What great pioneering work had progressed toward solving the mysteries of electricity in the last few decades alone! Just as the alchemists of the Middle Ages had searched for lost mystical knowledge, which would purify base metals into precious ones, so the scientists of Victor Frankenstein's day, the men of enlightenment, sought to identify and define this divine spark of powerful energy, to capture it, store it, reproduce it, control it, and channel its use for the benefit of humankind.

In his readings Victor learned of Francis Hauksbee's discovery in 1706 that he could build up an intense electrical charge in a glass sphere turned by a crank. Two years later, a Dr. Wall first stated the connection between electricity and lightning. Less than twenty years after that, another Englishman, Stephen Gray, used a long glass tube to capture electricity. Electricity, posited Gray, was a fluid. And he found a way to keep the magic energy moving through a piece of twine 800 feet in length, concluding through experimentation that electricity could either be transported through "conductive" materials, or could be kept confined, using nonconductive materials Gray called "insulators."

Picturing Stephen Gray's laboratory, Victor could imagine clearly the fluid electricity traveling along the thread. In his mind's eye he witnessed Gray's excitement as he watched the current moving in a split second down its conductive path. Here, in Gray's laboratory, the godly power of lightning was tamed, and compelled to flow or stop flowing or remain confined at the researcher's bidding.

Research on electricity went further, as scientists continued to experiment. In 1733, a French physicist, Charles-François de Cisternay du Fay, discovered the attractive and repulsive aspects of electricity. And, in 1746, two men made Hauksbee's famous glass sphere obsolete.

The Dutch physicist and mathematician Pieter van Musschenbroek, working at the University of Leyden independently from the German Ewald Jurgen von Kleist working in Pomerania, invented a storage container for static electricity, the Leyden jar, also called the Kleistian jar, a vital element in the development of the electrical conduit. Two great minds had invented the capacitor at the same time, without reference to each other. In his experimentation with the jar, van Musschenbroek's lab assistant received a shock that sent him—and science—reeling, proving that the power of stored electricity was similar to that of lightning.

The jar was filled partly with water, and corked, while a nail projected out from the cork, and it was found to retain charges of static electricity generated by a spark-making device, glass rods revolving between pieces of rubbing cloth. Like the magic lamp of Aladdin, the Leyden jar held captive a genie of terrifying power.

The connection between electricity and lightning continued to absorb scientists. In 1752 Benjamin Franklin flew a kite in a thunderstorm to prove that lightning was indeed electrical in nature, that lightning and electricity were one and the same. The kite had a wire conductor, a metal key at the end of its wet kite twine, and a silk insulator that Franklin kept dry by standing in a doorway. By means of the lightning that was conducted by the wet string and the metal key, Franklin was able to charge a Leyden jar as easily as if he'd been warm and dry in a lab.

These proofs that lightning was in fact electricity Victor had proved again to his own satisfaction, beginning with that picnic on the Alps four years ago. But the experiments in Galvanic action, in the nerve response to electrical stimulation, these were what he was working on now at night in his laboratory. For a few *pfennigs* each he obtained live frogs for the experiments from the local children, who scoured the ponds to keep him supplied.

Although Victor spent long days at the university and long nights in his attic laboratory, although he fell into a deep exhausted sleep late every night, his precious Elizabeth was never far from his thoughts.

It seemed to him that everything he had accomplished or would accomplish was dedicated only to her, his dearest love. Whenever he thought of her he could picture every detail of her beautiful body and face; her soft, white breasts and narrow waist, her fragrant neck, those red lips, that creamy skin, the darkness of her hair and the way it curled into rebellious little tendrils on her forehead and, above all, her deep brown eyes, as he remembered them gazing at his face with passion the night before he left.

Victor's entire world was encompassed in the depths of those dark eyes. His entire life lay within the palms of her small white hands. With Elizabeth to love and encourage him, to ensure his future happiness, what could he not achieve! With her standing at his side, into what hidden realms would he not dare to travel?

All his life Victor had heard the expression "falling in love"; now that his own turn had come Victor realized that there was nothing of the "falling" about it. He *rose* to love, his soul soaring upward into realms of ethereal light where it joined and mingled with Elizabeth's. If there was a Heaven, it must be in her arms.

A letter from Victor was always a great event in the Frankenstein home. Elizabeth would read them aloud, with all the household—family and staff—gathered round her bedside the great fireplace in the drawing room as she broke the seal and opened the paper. Every least detail of Victor's exciting life at the university was taken in eagerly by them all. They missed him very much.

" 'Henry has now fully recovered and continues his struggle to pass anatomy,' " read Elizabeth.

"I was always terrible at anatomy," put in Victor's father.

" 'Professor Waldman is very tolerant of him and of myself. I am learning a great deal. Professor Waldman is remarkable—' "

"So is Victor," Justine interrupted.

" 'God bless you, all my love, Victor.' "

"That's very nice," remarked Mrs. Moritz.

" 'P.S.,' " continued Elizabeth. " 'I've fallen in love . . . ' "

"I beg your pardon?" Claude exclaimed, surprised.

" 'She's dark, sleek, and beautiful and always wags her tail whenever she sees me. Her name is Putzi and she's the friendliest sheepdog I've ever known.' " Everyone laughed, picturing their Victor's new inamorata with her affectionate wagging tail.

But the last paragraph of the letter she read silently to herself with blushing cheeks. "P.P.S. Elizabeth—I dream of how your hair shines in the moonlight, of how your lips taste. I dream of your arms, and of your breasts . . . and of the time, on our wedding night—"

"What else does it say?" demanded Willie, grabbing the letter. He could tell there was more by the trembling smile on Elizabeth's face. Quickly, embarrassed, Elizabeth snatched the letter away from him.

"It says, 'I am working very hard and making lots of new friends.' More coffee, anyone?"

But she kept Victor's precious letter pressed to her breast. Tonight, in bed, Elizabeth would read it again, especially the last part, which she would read over and over until her eyes were weary. Then she would fall asleep to dream of her Victor and of their wedding night.

* * *

The university lecture hall was overcrowded as it always was these days, with graduate and undergraduate students stuffed into the galleries above the round theater, hanging on the railings. Ever since Victor Frankenstein had arrived at Ingolstadt to take up the cudgels with Professor Krempe classes had become entertainment, more like a Roman circus than a lecture on human physiology. Victor might be cast as the Christian and Krempe as the lion, but the Christian kept putting up a pretty good fight and had not been devoured yet.

A half-dissected body lay on the table between Victor and Professor Krempe. Today, Krempe had been allowed to reach almost the midpoint of his lecture before Victor opened his mouth for another of his perpetually irritating questions about the potential "cure" for death. The professor rose to the bait, and the two started to go at it hammer and tongs, to the delight of the onlookers.

By now Krempe was nearly purple with fury. Droplets of enraged perspiration dripped from the naked skull under the curled peruke and ran down his plump cheeks. "Once and for all, Frankenstein, life is life, death is death. These things are real, they are absolute!"

At once, Victor became as hot under the collar as his professor. All circumspection was abandoned, as he was no longer capable of choosing his words tactfully. "Now that is rubbish! And you know it. That premise has been repeatedly challenged by members of your own staff."

Everyone in the lecture hall knew the man he meant. It was Waldman, with his mysterious past and his forbidden experiments, whatever they were. As soon as attention was called to him, the enigmatic figure of Waldman, who had been standing at the back of the hall, quickly and silently left.

"We don't know where life ends or death begins," Victor continued passionately. His cheeks glowed with the force of his argument. "Hair continues to grow after what we choose to call death. So do fingernails—"

"These are trivial examples," Krempe interrupted scornfully. "The reasons for which are known. It is not the fingernails and hair that grow, it is the decomposing skin that shrinks away from them—"

But Victor wouldn't be stopped. "We know that a man's brain may die but that his heart and lungs may continue to pump and breathe."

Now Professor Krempe could not help exploding. He could tell the direction in which Frankenstein was trying to take this debate. Toward those "experiments" he wanted the university to do to find what he called "the prime constituent." Krempe's face turned an even darker red and his stout little body swelled up like a puffer fish. He shook his finger angrily. "Mr. Frankenstein of Geneva, I warn you that what you are suggesting is not only illegal it is immoral!"

It was an argument that would never be settled between them; Krempe and Frankenstein were at opposite ends of the scientific spectrum. But it was Krempe who held the power at the University of Ingolstadt, and so Victor could never win out. Just as an explorer who wants to break new ground can never win out over a closed mind.

That evening, Henry and Victor left the university together, and headed down back streets in search of some supper. As they walked, Victor kept writing in his thick, well-worn leather journal, the journal his mother had bought for him just before she died. Even in the dim twilight he scribbled, barely glancing at the words he was putting down.

Henry Clerval peered over Victor's shoulder as they walked, pretending to read out of his friend's diary in a mocking tone, " 'Dear Diary, why does no one understand me? P.S. I am not mad.' "

Suddenly, out of nowhere, a hand grabbed Victor roughly by the shoulder and hurled him backward against a wall. He found himself looking into a narrow-jawed saturnine face whose black eyes snapped like electric sparks.

"Explain yourself," growled Professor Waldman. He was much taller than Victor, well over six feet high, and leaned forward so that the two were almost nose to nose.

Although he was thrown into confusion by the suddenness of the confrontation, Victor knew that this was perhaps the opening he had hoped for. "I came here, Professor, to learn all about the new science. Galvanism, Franklin's experiments. The combination of modern disciplines with ancient knowledge in an attempt to create—"

"To create what?" demanded Waldman intensely. His dark-rimmed eyes bored like drills into Victor's face, and his voice was low and harsh.

"Sir, we're on the verge of undreamt of discoveries. If only we ask the right questions."

Waldman straightened up and his eyes were hooded, his expression distant. "I have come across men like you before," he said guardedly. He turned to go, but a barely imperceptible nod of his head informed Victor that Waldman was beckoning him to follow him.

Seized by a sudden excitement, Victor immediately started to follow, but Henry stopped him. Putting one hand on his friend's sleeve, "Victor," he said in a warning tone.

But Victor had waited too long for this moment to be detained. "Come on, Henry," he called impatiently. Clerval thought for a moment, then shrugged and made up his mind to follow.

Professor Waldman's rooms were in an old house in a narrow crooked street about ten minutes' walk from the university. His front door was so low that he had to duck his head to get inside. The two students waited in the dark doorway until Waldman lit some candles. Then they came in and gazed around themselves curiously.

The large parlor room appeared to be an artist's studio. Paintings stood everywhere—on easels, stacked on the floor against the walls, some hanging. Most of the paintings were nude figures of men and women, with their musculature clearly showing. An artist! This was an unexpected side to Waldman that took Victor by surprise. Victor was no authority on art, but it seemed to him that the paintings had been done by a very sure hand; the figures in them seemed alive, about to leap from the canvas.

But the professor made no reference to the paintings; he led them instead to the far wall and over a high sill through a partially hidden door into a cramped but fully equipped laboratory. The room's walls were lined with bookcases crammed with old leather-bound volumes, including rare anatomy books by Vesalius and Galen, and medical books in Greek, Latin, and Sanskrit.

Victor looked around, fascinated and delighted. His eager eyes drank in every detail. On the wall hung strange anatomical charts, including a copy of Leonardo da Vinci's famous fully detailed study, *The Proportion of the Human Body After Vesalius*, more commonly called *The Study of Man* showing a perfect male, spread-eagled in a circle representing the classical concept of perfection, the Golden Mean. Another hanging, painted on silk and lettered in Chinese characters, depicted a human with long needles sticking out of various parts of his body. On the long laboratory table was a mound of something concealed by a green cloth.

Victor studied the laboratory equipment, recognizing most but not all of it. A great deal of it was devoted, he saw with satisfaction, to electrical experimentation—he saw the same capacitors, a dead frog hooked up to Galvanic batteries, Leyden jars, insulators that he himself had in his garret, and the same kind of wheel to generate electricity. Some of the connections were different, new to Victor, but yes, he was right! As he'd suspected, both he and Waldman were experimenting in the same direction. But he had no idea what was in the beakers and retorts that stood on Waldman's lab table, and he hoped that explanations would be made.

"Lock the door," Waldman said brusquely to Henry.

As Henry turned the key in the lock, Waldman addressed Victor. "Now, for thousands of years the Chinese have based their medical science on the belief that the human body is a chemical engine run by energy streams."

He broke off as he noticed Henry glancing into a heavy book filled with hand-written notes that he had taken from one of the bookcases. *"Don't touch that!"* he said harshly.

Henry jumped, quickly closed the book and shelved it, nervously moving away from the bookcase. Waldman resumed. "Their doctors treat patients by inserting needles like this into the flesh at various key points to manipulate these electric streams." Entranced, Victor listened carefully, determined not to miss a word.

Handing over a long silver acupuncture needle for the young man to examine, Waldman directed Victor's attention to the ancient Chinese silk painting on the wall. It depicted the human body from front and side angles. The acupuncture points were clearly marked on the diagram.

"I see," murmured Victor. All of this was new to him, new and infinitely exciting.

"Now, look at this." Waldman pulled off the green cloth from the hidden mound, to reveal the severed arm of a chimpanzee. Henry took a couple of hopping steps back, away from the arm, and his eyes were wide and round.

The ape's arm was pricked by acupuncture needles from which copper mounting pins trailed a number of wires to a small panel of switches. The switches, in turn, were connected to a series of Galvanic batteries. Waldman clipped the connectors up. Suddenly, the arm twitched. Henry let out a shriek, and Victor took a step backward.

"Go on, touch it," Waldman said to Henry.

Clerval stepped forward and placed one nervous finger on the back of the hand. "It feels warm," he said in a wondering voice. As he continued to touch the hand, Waldman tried another connector. A sudden spark in the equipment, and the ape's hand turned over and grabbed Henry's.

"Yes, well." Henry grinned. "How do you do?" He shook the simian hand politely, and pulled away. But the hand wouldn't let go. It kept increasing its grip on Clerval's hand, pulling Henry down onto his knees. Henry's voice shook with genuine panic. "Turn it off!"

"I can't," said Waldman, his dark face troubled. "It's not working."

The mood now changed to one of tension and fear. Henry Clerval was in genuine trouble. Victor attacked the situation with a sort of controlled frenzy.

"Try to stay calm, Henry," he said very clearly. "It's simply a matter of reducing the polarity between your body and the arm. A monkey's arm is basically the same as a human's."

"No arm is this strong!" retorted Henry through clenched teeth.

Victor was already busy trying the connectors. "These feed the annular ligaments, I assume, Professor?"

"Yes," said Waldman. "But they depend on the Galvanic flux."

"It's crushing my hand!" yelled Henry. His face was contorted in pain.

"Then this must work," said Victor confidently. He clipped on a last connector. A spark crackled brightly. The chimpanzee's hand opened its fingers and released Henry. Professor Waldman cast an admiring glance at Victor Frankenstein. This was an ingenious and talented young man.

"This is what I should be learning," Victor said in a hushed voice. "It is utterly fantastic."

"It is a perilous direction to explore," Waldman answered darkly. He was still slightly shaken.

"Perilous and thrilling," Victor replied, his eyes shining. "Let me help you, Professor."

Waldman eyed him speculatively. Victor, a helper? Perhaps. He'd never had an assistant before, had never shared his secrets. It was an intriguing possibility. But the professor had guarded his hidden researches for so long that all he said was, "You shall of course tell no one."

"They wouldn't believe you anyway," muttered Henry under his breath, rubbing away at his sore hand.

A sudden small movement caught their attention, and the three men turned at the same time to see. Astonished looks spread over their faces. The electrical current was switched off, yet the chimpanzee's arm was now gently pulsating of its own accord. It appeared in every way to be . . . alive.

In Geneva, life went on peacefully as before. The household revolved around Victor's letters; just hearing Elizabeth read aloud his few words—for the letters were becoming shorter and further apart—lifted everybody's spirits. Their own lives seemed so uneventful, even dull, compared with his. What news did they have to report? Willie now had a tutor. Dr. Frankenstein acquired a new mare when his old one went lame. A family dinner at which a neighbor or two had attended and asked after Victor. Justine, now twenty-two, had received a proposal of marriage from the butcher's son and had rejected it.

Whereas, Victor's letters were bursting with snippets about his exciting doings. What he never mentioned, though, were his private sessions with Professor Waldman. Waldman had showed Victor one or two things, but still continued to keep his deepest mysteries a secret.

They were at dinner when Elizabeth brought out the letter she had received that day. Mrs. Moritz and Justine were helping to serve while Claude poured the wine into the goblets. They stopped eating and serving and pouring and listened with great interest while Elizabeth read out most (but not, of course, all) of what Victor had written.

"What's dissection?" asked Willie, sneaking a

glance at the letter which Elizabeth was folding up and putting away.

Elizabeth snatched the letter away with mock primness. "It's far too ghoulish for your young ears."

"That's where they slice people open and have a jolly good poke around their insides," Father told Willie with a wicked twinkle in his eye. He picked up his knife and pretended to stab Willie with it. The frightened little boy covered his face with his hands and started to wail.

"I didn't mean it," Dr. Frankenstein apologized contritely. Elizabeth and Justine immediately gathered little Willie up, cuddling and comforting him, murmuring, "It's all right, it's all right."

This would be an amusing tidbit to write to Victor in her next letter, thought Elizabeth.

Meanwhile, in Ingolstadt, tragedy struck the household of kindly Frau Brach. Her beloved Putzi, her companion and pet, was struck down by a carriage, and left bleeding and unconscious on the cobbles of the street. Hysterical with grief, Frau Brach had run to the only person she could think of, that nice young Dr. Frankenstein upstairs. He was a doctor, and he was fond of Putzi, maybe he could save her. He *had* to save her!

It took only one glance to tell Victor that the unconscious sheepdog was probably dying. Putzi's tongue protruded through her foaming lips. Her injuries were very severe. She had lost a lot of blood, and had already lapsed into a coma.

Two thoughts occurred to Victor simultaneously. The first was that he genuinely wanted to save Putzi's life, because he was fond of Frau Brach and he loved the sweet dog. The second was that here was the perfect opportunity to test the value of Professor Waldman's techniques.

Carrying Putzi in his arms, trailed by the sobbing landlady, Victor ran down winding cobbled streets until he reached Waldman's doorway. At his urgent knock, Waldman opened the door. Victor only managed to get a few words out, when the professor nodded agreement.

By now Frau Brach had reached the house, too, and although she was out of breath, she managed to cry hysterically as she sank into a chair. But she mustn't be allowed to stay. What Waldman and Victor would be doing must be shrouded in the deepest secrecy.

"Please, Frau Brach." Victor tried to calm her, lifting her up out of the chair and moving her gently but steadily toward the front door. "Come along, Frau Brach. We'll do what we can, Professor Waldman and I."

"The carriage didn't stop . . . she didn't see it in time," sobbed the old lady.

"I know, I know," said Victor soothingly, trying to maneuver her through the doorway. He was desperate to get her out of there so that he could join Waldman in the laboratory.

"Can I see her, please?"

"There's nothing you can do," he answered firmly. "You must go home, for your own sake, you must go home. We'll take the best possible care of Putzi. "We'll do everything we can. You'll feel better at home." He pushed her out of the door and closed it behind her, turning the key in the lock.

In Waldman's laboratory they worked frenziedly to save Putzi. The dog, partially bandaged, was hooked up to the electrical panel, wires and cables attached to every part of her. She lay twitching as streams of current coursed through her body. Waldman was looking through a surgical glass at her. "We're losing her," the professor said urgently.

"We'll have to risk another charge." Victor seemed in command here. He flicked another switch on.

Waldman pushed the instrument away from him. "Pulse?" asked Victor.

"Arrhythmic and decaying."

"Damn!" cried Victor, passionately, desperate. He gave her another jolt, and Putzi writhed uncontrollably as a violent burst of current surged through her body. He bent over the sheepdog, stroking her, soothing her, talking to her, looking into her eyes.

"There, girl. It's all right. Ssh. Be calm."

Waldman shook his head pessimistically. "We need an alternative power source," he said.

"Of course we do! And you know what it is!" Victor cried passionately.

Surprised by the young man's vehemence and shocked by the direction of his thoughts, Waldman answered slowly. "I know some things. I'm content to let God know the rest."

Victor raced around the laboratory, throwing switches, checking dials and gauges.

God. Always God. Whenever somebody didn't have the moral courage to go forward into the unknown, he blamed it on God. It infuriated Victor. "God gives us plague, God gives us war. God gives us death. God gave us a very imperfect world. But He also gave us the ability to improve it. Come on! What is it? Where is . . . the prime constituent . . . the link between matter and life?"

He was almost shouting in his desperation. Waldman shot Victor a concerned look. The lad seemed out of control. In her electrical harness, Putzi twitched and shuddered to a lifeless stop. It was over; her hard struggle to live and theirs to save her had come to an end.

The death of the dog struck Victor like a sharp blow in the chest. Tears formed in his eyes. She shouldn't have died. The alternative power source, whatever it might be, would have saved her life, would save many other lives.

"Now we have to find it!" Victor cried; he pushed past Waldman and stalked out of the room.

Waldman gazed after him, both shocked and impressed by Frankenstein's passion.

That evening, the three of them—Victor, Henry, and Professor Waldman—gathered in Waldman's parlor for a meal. They sat long over dinner, the two younger men helping themselves liberally to wine from the decanter on the table. Waldman sipped abstemiously at a single glass, maintaining a watchful silence. Almost in their cups, Victor and Henry were hammering at Victor's favorite topic—that death should not be a necessary evil in a modern world.

"I'm serious," Victor was saying. "Take vaccine for instance. Thirty years ago the entire concept of vaccine was unheard of. Now we save lives every day, but that isn't the whole answer."

"What do you mean?" asked Henry.

"That sooner or later the best way to cheat death will be to create life," Victor said simply but with great conviction.

"Oh, now you *have* gone too far," protested Henry in a shocked voice. "There's only one God, Victor."

God again. Victor scowled. "Leave God out of this. Listen, if you love someone and they have a sick heart wouldn't you give them a healthy one?" He leaned over the table, searching Henry Clerval's eyes for the answer.

"Why?"

Professor Waldman turned his deep-set eyes on Victor's face, and a long look passed between them. "Because they resulted in abomination."

He rose, took the book out of Victor's hands, and walked slowly into his laboratory.

"Good night, gentlemen."

8 The Work Begins

During the eighteenth century, that wonderful age of enlightenment and scientific advancement, great medical and technical strides were made against the cruelty of nature, but nature was by no means conquered. She struck back, hard. In less than a hundred years a devastating series of natural disasters had taken hundreds of thousands of lives. In 1737 the catastrophic Calcutta earthquake killed more than 300,000 men, women, and children. Other earthquakes occurred in Japan, northern Persia, and Guatemala, with enormous loss of life. In 1750, the city of Lisbon in Portugal suffered an offshore earthquake, a tidal wave, and a citywide fire that left more than 60,000 dead. Volcanos erupted in Iceland, in Japan's Mt. Fujiyama and Mt. Cotopaxi in South America, and more than tens of thousands were killed.

Epidemics—smallpox, typhus, yellow fever, and

especially the dreaded cholera—took heavy tolls in
the cities and villages. Overcrowded conditions combined with a lack of proper hygiene and a limited
understanding of how these diseases were contracted
caused contagious illnesses to become widespread
plagues, attacking entire populations. In 1730 the
Russian Czar Peter the First died of smallpox on his
wedding day. In 1740 a smallpox epidemic killed
many thousands in Berlin.

And now smallpox had come to Southern Germany, and people were beginning to die. Darmstadt,
not fifty miles away, was already riddled with the
pox, and it was highly probable that Ingolstadt would
be next.

But there was hope. An effective vaccine was
available, thanks to the ancient Turkish practice of
inoculating young children with small doses of smallpox to prevent more serious cases later on in life.
Some seventy-five years earlier, vaccination had been
brought to the attention of Lady Mary Wortley Mon-
tagu. Wife of thee English minister to Constantino-
ple, she witnessed at first hand the potency of smallpox injections. In 1718 she published *Inoculation
Against Smallpox*, and three years later, during the
London smallpox epidemic, she had her five-year-old
daughter inoculated; thanks mainly to her efforts,
King George I also had two of his grandchildren
inoculated as an example, and many other families
followed suit. The inoculated children survived the
epidemic, and the method of efficacious vaccination
spread throughout Europe.

Now, under potential attack by the plague, the
medical student and faculty of the University of Ingolstadt rallied to aid the citizens. By means of citywide inoculation, especially inoculation of the old,
the very young, and especially the poor, who lived

under the most appalling conditions and lack of sanitation, a handful of doctors could prevent the few cases of smallpox from spreading and becoming epidemic.

Inoculation centers were set up around the city, manned mostly by students performing community service, working feverishly to inoculate thousands of people a day with serum-filled needles.

In the city poorhouse, Victor, Henry, and Schiller formed one team, giving out vaccinations. They labored urgently and silently. Nearby, at his own bench, Professor Waldman proceeded efficiently and swiftly, doing two or three inoculations for every one a student managed to complete. All around, panicked citizens were getting eye-ear-nose-throat examinations and vaccinations.

A sharp-featured man mingled with the crowd, hobbling on his crutch. Blind in one eye, one-legged and drunk, the man bristled with an unpredictable and ferocious nervous energy. Though short in stature and lean, he had a torso of enviable strength. He was terrified about getting his vaccination, and he had to be dragged up to Waldman's bench.

"Yer not stickin' that in me!" he snarled, pushing the professor's hand away. "Got a pox in it, I hear tell!"

A nearby woman, thickset and with coarse features, pricked up her ears. "Pox? They givin' us pox?"

"That's right, pox." The sharp-featured man nodded angrily.

Impatiently, Waldman brandished his needle. "No, it's not pox, it's a vaccine that will prevent a plague in this city."

"What's that?" the rough woman demanded suspiciously.

"A tiny harmless quantity of anti-smallpox serum."

"You just said pox!" accused the sharp-featured man. His body was already riddled with a disease he'd had for years, the so-called "French pox," or syphilis, a disease that had already cost him the sight of one eye and the leg that had been amputated because of gangrene.

The man's stubborn ignorance made Waldman angry. "No, no, I said it's harmless. It's a necessary precaution without which this godforsaken city would be placed under immediate quarantine. Haven't you heard what's happening in Darmstadt? Don't you people have any idea what's at stake here?"

When they heard Professor Waldman's voice raised, Victor and Henry paused in their work, concerned. They moved closer, made uneasy by the frightened murmurs of "plague" and "pox" that could be heard running through the crowd. The sharp-featured man still struggling, was cornered and couldn't escape. Waldman picked up his needle.

"You doctors kill people," the one-legged man cried shrilly. "I don' care what you say, yer not stickin' that in me!"

"Yes, I am," said Waldman shortly. "It's the law. Sit him down, somebody. Come on."

A couple of students came forward to seize the struggling man, who kept crying out, "Yer not stickin' that thing in me!" But, finally overpowered, he was pushed down onto the bench as Waldman prepared to vaccinate.

Suddenly, unseen by Waldman or any of the others, the sharp-featured man pulled a knife from the handhold on his crutch and stabbed Waldman once, in the pit of his stomach. Then, with surprising swiftness for a man with only one leg, he hobbled off and disappeared.

Professor Waldman sank back on the bench, his hand pressed to his sternum, his lips tight, his face drained of color.

Henry took a step forward. "Professor?"

"Oh God," said Waldman softly. He looked down at his body, at the bright blood pumping through his fingers, spreading widely, dyeing his shirt scarlet. With a small moan, Waldman collapsed, and the poorhouse erupted into a frenzy.

The students rushed the dying man to the university operating theater and laid him on the table. Aided by Schiller, Victor and Henry Clerval worked desperately to save his life. But major arteries had been severed by the knife of the sharp-featured man, and Waldman had already lost masses of blood. Despite the young doctors' efforts to stanch the flow, the wound continued to pulsate, the operating table was covered in blood, and blood dripped from the side of the table to the floor, making the theater floor red and slippery. The three of them were also blood-spattered.

"Come on. Come on," muttered Victor through gritted teeth. He plunged his hands into the professor's body cavity and groped around. Finding a severed artery, he pulled it clear of the wound and stitched the ends together quickly with great skill. But Waldman lay still and silent, and very, very white.

"It's no use, Victor," said Henry in a low voice. "He's gone."

"No! No!" Victor shook his head frenziedly, pressing a sponge hard against the bleeding cavity.

"Let him go."

"No! No, Henry! It shouldn't happen, Henry. It shouldn't happen."

It was over. Victor drew back and looked at Waldman on the table, seeing him not as a beloved mentor but as a bloodless corpse. Blind with tears of grief and frustration, he swung wildly, pushing over the instrument table. It fell with a clang and a scattering of scalpels and needles.

"It needn't happen."

There was no question in Victor Frankenstein's mind about what he was intended to do. He was convinced that he had been chosen by events not only to carry on Jacob Heinrich Waldman's work, but to perfect it. The door to Waldman's laboratory was no barrier to his strength, determination, and a stout crowbar. As soon as the crowbar forced it open, taking it off its hinges, Victor entered and began to strip the laboratory of what he was going to need.

He ripped Leonardo da Vinci's anatomical drawing off the wall and took down the Chinese acupuncture chart, rolling both of them up together. Then he went after the prize, Waldman's notebook. For a long moment he held the precious journal in his hands, sensing how important this moment would be to him and to future generations of humankind. Then he opened it. Thank Heaven Waldman hadn't written his notes in code, as some scientists did to keep their experiments from prying eyes. Waldman's handwriting was bold, clear, and easy to read, and in German, which along with French was Victor's primary language.

He couldn't wait. Victor lit some candles, and sat down at the laboratory table to read. Once he'd begun, he couldn't stop. What he read left Victor breathless. In experiment after experiment, Professor

Waldman had documented results that no other scientist had ever achieved, had ever even approached.
It was all there, in the heavy journal.

"My God, you were so close. Of course. The
power. The materials were wrong . . . you needed
auxiliary sources." He picked up an anatomical drawing of a man, heavily annotated by symbols, mathe-
matical formulas, and electrical connections and
studied it carefully, then turned back to Waldman's
notes.

"Yes, 'Experiment a failure. Resulting reanimant
malformed and hideous to behold. This factor clearly
dependent on appropriate raw materials . . .' " Victor
closed the journal and rubbed at the bridge of his
nose, thinking hard.

". . . Raw materials . . ." Yes, of course. But where
to get them? How?

It wasn't difficult for the town constables to find
and arrest Waldman's murderer. How many men in
Ingolstadt were blind in one eye and had only one
leg? And how far could such a man get? They provided the culprit with nothing so elaborate as a trial:
a magistrate found him guilty in under five minutes
and sentenced him to be hanged. So why wait? By
the following day, a gray day, the sharp-featured
man was already standing on the scaffold in the town
square, ranting. A large crowd of spectators gathered
to pelt him with rotten vegetables and were shouting
abuse. But the man's hoarse harangue carried over
the crowd's voices.

"I don't want to die . . . Whatever you say,
whatever you call it, you doctors kill people . . .
you're murderers, you're killers . . . evil, you're evil
. . . you're the ones who deserve to die . . . God will

punish you . . . God will punish you . . . You'll all rot
in hell. . . ."

His ranting words became muffled and were
choked off as the black hood was drawn on over his
head and the noose pulled tight around his neck.
Without ceremony, without even a final word of
comfort or a prayer from a priest, the sharp-featured
man was pushed from the gallows by two town
officials. There was the thump of the body dropping,
followed by the sickening crack of a snapping neck.
The crowd burst into a cheer.

The body hung from the scaffold in the town
square all day, even as the gray skies fulfilled their
threat and poured down a heavy buffeting rain.
Whipped by the autumnal winds and lashed by the
rain, the small man twisted at the end of the rope,
lifeless yet somehow still imbued with a strange
menace. Because of the weather, the curiosity-seek-
ers had all gone home and the square was deserted.

The night was dark as the halls of Hades. A
booming crash of thunder split the silence and a flash
of lightning lit up the scaffold. Victor emerged from
the shadows, where he had been waiting for some
minutes. He gazed intently at the dead man, thinking
his own thoughts, then he took a knife out of his
greatcoat pocket, and cut through the rope. The body
dropped to the wet ground, and Victor raised it with
effort and hoisted it to his shoulder.

Then, staggering a little, Victor began the long
and difficult walk back to his garret, carrying the
murderer's stiff body. His pulses beat rapidly, his
mouth was dry with apprehension. He was grateful
that the night was so dark and the rain was so heavy
that his journey would be cloaked from curious eyes.
For what he was about to do, Victor Frankenstein
needed the utmost secrecy.

* * *

The smallpox epidemic continued to spread throughout Ingolstadt. Not enough people had been inoculated to stop the spread of the disease. The citizens were panic-stricken, most of them keeping to their homes, hoping that the plague would pass their front doors by, as it did Moses' people in Egypt, or so says the Old Testament. The streets were mostly deserted, except for the death carts that rattled by, carrying bodies. The grave diggers were kept working around the clock; they and the city's undertakers seemed to be the only ones profiting from the pox. Filth began to pile up in the alleyways; with nobody carting it off to burn it, the rotting offal was a breeding ground for every kid of deadly disease.

The next step in Victor's planned process was to get the stolen dead body ready for reanimation, but the task was overwhelming in its complexity, and he badly needed another person to help. His thoughts naturally turned to Henry Clerval, whom he was certain he could trust to keep his secrets, and who had been in his company through a number of those significant dinner conversations with Professor Waldman. So, the night after the sharp-featured man was hanged, when he and Henry were sitting in a tavern with a bottle of Rhenish on the table between them, Victor revealed his plan.

"Come on, Henry," he urged, "join with me. I could really use your help."

Henry shook his curly head and his eyes refused to meet his friend's. "No, Victor, I can't help you."

"You mean you won't. What are you frightened of?"

"Everything! What do you think? If the authorities were to find out—"

But Victor shook his head vigorously. "Listen. We

do this in secret. I've got the raw materials, I've got Waldman's journals. Between us we know more than Krempe's whole staff put together."

Henry's mouth opened in shock. "You stole Waldman's journals?"

Victor's lips set in a stubborn line. "We owe it to him to complete his work. He was one step away."

"He didn't want this," Henry said soberly.

Victor leaned forward over the table, his eye's probing Henry's. "He couldn't face it. There's a difference."

But Henry was far from convinced. "No, Victor. Waldman saw what you refuse to see. You can't cheat death."

"Henry, how are you going to look your children in the eye and tell them that you had the chance to save those whom you loved most, to recreate them, but you were too scared?"

"Even if it were possible—"

"I'm sure it is," interrupted Victor.

"Even if it were possible," Henry said firmly, "and even if you had the right, which you don't, to make this decision for us, do you imagine for one second that there wouldn't be a terrible price to pay? Waldman knew that to eradicate the border between life and death can only result in abomination." Henry's face was drawn, his eyes very serious and frightened.

Victor was equally serious. "I think for the chance to defeat death and disease, to let everyone on this earth have the chance of life, sustained healthy life, to allow people who love each other to be together forever . . . I think that's a risk worth taking. We won't know unless we try."

Henry shook his head. "That's the difference between you and me, Victor. I don't want to know."

Victor scowled at Henry's squeamishness. Didn't the man understand that no great advancement would ever be achieved through moral or physical cowardice? Only those who dared the infinite could achieve the infinite. He stood up from the table.

"Well, I have to try." Victor left the tavern, and went back out into the night.

It was better so. Victor was convinced of it as soon as he returned to the attic and saw the dead murderer lying covered in a sheet on the slab. Better for him to do this alone, better for Henry Clerval to retreat with repugnance, for who else could share the passion of his convictions? Waldman, perhaps, but Waldman was dead, and besides, Waldman had turned back from the very threshold of discovery, racked by pangs of conscience. What did conscience have to do with conferring the greatest boon upon the human race?

No, only Victor Frankenstein was the right man for the job. But how ironic, what a bitter jet, that the body of the very man who took Waldman's life should be used to prove Waldman's theories. If only it weren't so flawed a body. One eye, one leg, racked by disease. And yet, the greater the obstacles to success, the sweeter the eventual triumph over those obstacles.

Victor lifted the sheet at the bottom, to study the stump of the amputated leg. An entire new one would have to be found, the stump amputated, and the new leg attached to the trunk of the body. Now he picked the sheet up entirely, and peered closely at the corpse's face. Even in the eternal peace of death, the sharp-featured man still looked angry.

The face was scarred and pocked by syphilitic sores, and the blind eye was sunken in its socket. The left arm was also showing signs of disease. He would need a new one. A great deal of preparatory work had to be done here. With a stylus dipped in ink, Victor marked the truncated leg where it was to be taken off and then marked the incision points on the body's diseased face and around the blind eye and around the left shoulder.

Most important of all, what was the condition of the brain? He had to find out.

Taking up a pair of scissors, Victor began to cut the murderer's hair. It was coarse and thick and felt surprisingly alive under his fingers. When most of the hair was lying on the floor of the lab, he wiped the head with his hand, mixed shaving foam in a bowl, and brushed it on the corpse's head. With a surgically sharp straight razor, Victor shaved the head until it was completely bald. Now he could see the place of incision. He marked a circle around the skull, just as Waldman used to do at the university.

Victor oiled the bone saw, then he carefully sawed the skull open to reveal the brain. It was an amorphous, disease-riddled mass, completely useless. Removing it from the brain pan, he discarded the infected brain into a covered barrel of waste.

Now for the limbs. Victor moved around the table to the trunk of the right leg, and used the bone saw to remove the unwanted part. He then sawed vigorously at the left shoulder joint, until it gave way and he was able to remove and discard the diseased arm. When the arm was in the waste bin, he sagged against the table, exhausted. Yet he was also exhilarated. The first step was completed. What was left of the body was now disease-free and ready for new additions.

He still had to get the additions.

Victor had few options. There was really no other place than a graveyard where one could find a supply of human parts. Under the cover of darkness, with a pry bar in his hands, Victor managed to open the gates of a crypt that showed signs of a recent funeral. He was nervous, working up his courage as he opened the chains that kept the crypt secured. It was hard for him to accept that he, Victor Frankenstein of Geneva, a medical school graduate from a fine family, was now a grave-robber. "Raw materials," he mumbled to himself out loud. "That's all they are. Tissue to be reused."

Entering the crypt, he looked around. Yes, this was a new coffin; the body parts would no doubt be fresh enough. Taking a deep breath, he eased off the lid of the coffin and peered inside. Then he took a startled step back. The eyes were shut, and the jaw was bandaged up in line with common undertaker practices. But the face of the corpse was unmistakably Jacob Heinrich Waldman's.

For an instant Victor shut his eyes to blot out the sight. But he had come too far to turn back.

"The best raw materials," he said out loud. "That means the finest brain . . . forgive me, Professor . . ."

Two hours later, the body of Waldman was lying on Victor's table, its head shaved. Victor marked the skull and placed a scalpel on the tracing to start his incision. His hand did not falter. The top of the skull came off easily, and Waldman's brain was revealed in all its size and perfection. There seemed to Victor a real poetic justice in all of this, that Waldman's brain should be reanimated as part of his student Frankenstein's plan to benefit the world.

When the gray matter was removed intact, Victor packed it up, wrapping the new brain in cloth and placing it carefully in a trunk of ice. Soon it would live again; he was convinced of it.

His careful readings in Waldman's journals, and

the notations he was making in arcane books together with the notes he made on Waldman's text, kept Victor working into the small hours of the morning. What he was doing was very bold. Victor was assembling the plan for one master experiment, based on everything he himself had read and done, and everything that Waldman had done and recorded before him. Candle flame flickering low, Victor sat hunched over his specimens, referring back to Waldman's notes. At last he cut the pages of Waldman's books and with great care pasted them into his own journal. Then he began to reread his conclusions.

" 'So, the electrical charges must come from more than one source. Galvanic power alone is insufficient. The assembled organs must have the designated nutrients and heat, and, crucially, more direct power.' "

Victor closed his journal, thinking hard. Nutrients, heat, more direct power. Direct power, that is, charges of electricity flowing directly into the brain and muscles and limbs. Powerful surges into the tissue itself . . .

Yes, he had an idea! Bizarre, perhaps, and untried. But it could work! He knew now where to get direct power.

Victor grabbed up a slab of fresh meat, dripping with blood, and laid it on a butcher's block. Using the same meat cleaver he had used on Schiller's corpse, he sliced the slab in half. "More direct power," he said out loud, looking up at the waterproof sack that was hanging from a ceiling hook. He tossed the oozing carrion flesh up into it. The sack shuddered and spasmed as whatever was inside it flung itself on the fresh meat in a repulsive feeding frenzy. The noise was sickening.

"Power," whispered Victor. "Power."

* * *

In the very early morning, Victor sat hunched over his notebook, pale and unhealthy, scribbling notations next to a rendering of the human form. Although he had reluctantly allowed Henry, who had come knocking at the crack of dawn, to enter his garret, he had paid almost no attention to him since.

Henry Clerval just sat shaking his head and wondering. He barely recognized this fellow. What had become of the Victor Frankenstein he knew? When was the last time the man had shaved or bathed or changed his clothing? Victor, who was as neat and fastidious as a cat, was now unshaven, unkempt, dirty, and ragged. His linen, the stock around his neck and his shirtfront, once so white they dazzled the eye, were now gray with grime. His coat and trousers, once scrupulously clean and form-fitting, were now covered in stains and hanging on his skinny frame like a scarecrow's garment. What was he living on? Precious little, to judge by his gaunt appearance. Probably no more than bread and cheese, if that.

Henry let his eyes trail along the shelves of the garret, crammed now with formaldehyde jars of animals and organs. There was an unspeakable stench pervading the attic; it was a choking smell but Victor appeared to be oblivious to it. Other things—bags and bins—did not bear a close examination. And a wriggling sack suspended from the ceiling was so disgusting it made Henry's stomach churn. What on earth could be inside it? He didn't want to know.

"Look, Victor. This has got to stop. Nobody's seen you in weeks. You've been suspended from all your classes."

"I've been preoccupied," muttered Victor without interest.

His indifference made Henry angry. "Don't treat me like a fool," he snapped.

Victor looked up from his notes. "Henry, just go."

Stung, Clerval stood up and started to leave, then he turned back. "Look, there's something else."

"What?" Victor looked up, surprised at the edgy note in Henry's voice.

"Do you remember Schiller?"

"How could I forget?"

"He died last night," Henry said sadly. "They think it might be cholera."

Cholera? Here in Ingolstadt? Victor looked up from his work, but Henry was already out the door.

Victor remembered Schiller well. A big, muscular, strapping specimen of large muscles and small brain. What was it that Henry had called him? "Ornament of the playing field." Yes, he must have been, with his powerful arms and legs. Arms and legs . . .

The mortuary was crowded. Dead bodies were everywhere, and the female attendants were busy stealing from their pockets. They paid no attention to Frankenstein as he entered the room, his eyes darting everywhere. The stench in the room was overwhelming, but Victor barely noticed it.

Yes, there it was—a large, muscular body, lying in a corner. Victor went to it and lifted a massive left arm, scarred with cholera. The muscles of the corpse were intact. He checked the left leg. Perfect. He raised a glinting razor-sharp meat cleaver, and brought it down cleanly.

But, as he amputated its limbs, Victor didn't look at the face, only at Schiller's body.

Hundreds of miles away from Ingolstadt's plague and Victor's laboratory, there was a different kind of misery, a misery set against the magnificent backdrop of mountains and a cloudless blue sky. Justine Moritz ran after Elizabeth, trying to catch her before she tore up every one of Victor's precious letters. Elizabeth moved swiftly, her skirts and her hair streaming behind her in the wind, marching along beside the lake, the letters in her hands fast being reduced to shreds of useless paper caught up by the breezes.

"But I don't understand," Justine protested, uncomprehending. "all these letters—you read them to us yourself. Every week."

Elizabeth's lips trembled. "I wrote them. *I* wrote the letters. He hasn't written to me in months."

"Elizabeth!" cried Justine, shocked.

Now Elizabeth turned to her companion and Justine could see the suffering in those enormous dark eyes. Then she turned her face away again, staring off at the mountains that separated her from Victor. "Something horrific is happening to him. I can feel it. At first I wasn't sure, but I knew I had to hide it from Father. Now there are rumors of cholera . . ." She broke off as a well of tears choked her words.

"I can take care of Father and Willie. You go to Ingolstadt." Justine sounded sure of herself, firm and strong.

But Elizabeth was shaking her head. "No, that's not possible. He wouldn't want me there. He's probably found someone else there anyway. . . ."

Justine reached out suddenly, grabbed Elizabeth by the shoulders, and turned her around so that they were face to face. "If he were mine I would have left already. But he isn't mine, he's yours. And you must go to him."

For the first time, Elizabeth realized the depth of Justine's feelings for Victor. "Oh, Justine, I had no idea how much Victor meant to you," she cried.

Now it was Justine's time to turn her face away.

"You don't have to say a word, Elizabeth," she said with great dignity. "Just find him. Bring him home."

Elizabeth's face was suddenly alight with conviction. "I will find him. I must."

The two women hugged each other warmly and, without a further word passing between them, turned their steps toward home. Each knew what she had to do now.

9 Dawn of Creation

The compass of Victor's existence grew narrower and narrower until his life was now totally encapsulated, focusing only on the work in his laboratory. He forgot everything and everybody in the outside world. He had stopped writing home to Geneva, because he could not report any of his recent doings truthfully to Elizabeth or his family. Gradually, Geneva was becoming only a sweet, distant memory; like one of those pretty scenes enclosed in a sugary easter egg, Victor's childhood home receded in his recollection until it seemed very far away and a long time ago.

He stopped attending classes; he no longer gave thought to his enjoyable verbal duels with Professor Krempe, or to his friendship with Henry Clerval or any of his other university friends. His work and only his work took up every waking minute of his time.

It didn't even occur to Victor to wonder where his

landlady was, or why he hadn't seen or heard her moving around the house, when it used to be her frequent custom to come tapping at his door with the offer of a cup of tea or a nice plump bratwurst. In fact, devastated by the loss of Putzi, and afraid for her life in plague-ridden Ingolstadt, Frau Brach had taken herself off to the countryside. Her absence, unnoticed by Victor, allowed him to move larger and more elaborate pieces of equipment up to his attic without attracting her curious attention.

Eight years ago when his mother died, the adolescent Victor had fostered a secret wish of discovering immortality, a dream in which loved ones would live on forever. With the best of intentions, Victor Frankenstein daydreamed of making immortality his gift to the world. As he grew older, the wish/dream he fostered became a hope, the hope an ambition, the ambition a determination, until the determination had grown into an obsession that possessed him utterly. Now, the search for a method of reanimation had become an end in itself, and it drove him onward, in feverish disregard of any distractions that daily life might afford.

Perhaps if Henry Clerval had accepted his offer and agreed to work with him, Victor's obsession wouldn't have taken quite so firm a hold on his mind. But, all alone in his garret, with only his anatomical charts and his journals, his chemical, biological, and electrical equipment, his acupuncture needles, some severed limbs, his mentor's brain, and a murderer's corpse to keep him company, it's small wonder that Victor had unwittingly stepped over the border of reason into that dark realm where the rational mind loses control.

It is in the nature of the scientist to be dispassionate, questioning, observing, notating, experimenting, but all with an open mind. Scientists are not supposed to go out of control and cling to one idea and one only. But a dangerous fire had been lit in Victor, and it flamed in his brain, burning away his scientific objectivity. Was he mad? No. He was not mad as madness is defined, but he had lost his sense of rational direction and the ability to take a step backward to rethink. He was veering out of control.

Victor's high moral principles and single-mindedness, combined with the determination to recreate life, had somehow coalesced, as in a chemical experiment, and hardened into fanaticism. He was on the right track; he was certain of it. Soon he would abolish death. He didn't question the rights or wrongs of his endeavor. It didn't occur to him that death was perhaps only the last natural state, that the ending of life was in balance with the beginning of it, and that dying was a necessary adjunct to living, or—most important of all—that without death life would stagnate and never change, and that there would be little use for new generations to be born on an already-crowded planet.

He never doubted for a moment that what he was doing would benefit all people everywhere. He wasn't aware of it, but Victor Frankenstein's very goodness was about to betray him. He was aware of nothing but his burning need to create life. He didn't stop to think that he was taking into his own hands the prerogatives of the gods, and that the gods reserved their cruelest punishments for mortals who dared such arrogance.

Venturing out into the city only to commission and acquire the elaborate equipment he needed, Victor gave precise and explicit instructions on how to build it, what shape and size, what materials, instructions based on the careful notes in his journal.

In all his months in Ingolstadt of living thriftily and spending little, Victor had not yet drawn on the bank letter of credit his father had given him, but now he dispensed those funds lavishly, paying workmen well to follow his designs to the letter without asking questions.

In the smithy, the blacksmith and his assistant were close to completing their assigned task, beating a huge copper sheet into shape, when Victor came in. The workmen had no idea of what they were creating; if they had, they would refuse, and turn away in horror from such abominations. Not knowing, they greeted Victor with enthusiasm as a client with deep pockets who knew what he wanted. Running his hand over the surface of a finished piece, he nodded.

"Strong. That's good. But now make it even stronger."

Almost every day laborers struggled up the stairs to Victor's garret, delivering vast quantities of equipment to the laboratory. For every piece he acquired, Victor made a checkmark on his list. There were Voltaic piles, a primitive sort of battery which provided a steady flow of electric current. Copper disks—which produced a positive charge—were set at the bottom of the pile, covered by zinc discs—which produced a negative charge—and topped by cardboard disks wet with a saline solution. The pile consisted of many layers of the three materials. Wires protruded from the top and the bottom of the piles, and when those wires made contact and the circuit was closed, electrical current would be produced in an unbroken stream.

There were wheels for generating steam, glass beakers and retorts, a large quantity of newly forged metal chains, lengths of two-inch-wide rope and wires of all shapes and thicknesses. A huge metal grating, strong and heavy. A block and tackle and a pulley that was fastened to the wall, connected to tracks that ran across the roof the entire length of the garret. A large iron ring also hung from the ceiling. Used as a rack, it held a series of bottles and lines containing various liquids chemicals.

Victor also had created a special induction machine constructed for storing charges of static electricity, a hand-cranked wheel-and-pulley arrangement with wire brushes that struck sparks, and which built up charges of stray electricity, multiplied them many times and stored the enhanced charges in two attached Leyden jars.

It took four men, struggling mightily, to carry in the enormous bronze vat and, later the finished huge copper piece. Now the equipment was assembled, and the work couldn't wait much longer. Victor was keeping the corpse and Waldman's brain at icy temperatures to preserve them, but they wouldn't keep much longer. As for the separate arm and leg, Victor had them connected to batteries that stimulated them with surges of current, as Waldman had done with the chimpanzee's arm, but that was also a temporary expedient.

He had first to repair the body, make it whole, before he attempted reanimation. Victor had provided for power sources and heat. Warmth is a synonym for life, just as cold is for death. The murderer's body would be brought from freezing to a living temperature by the application of heat. Electrical power would stimulate the muscles and the nervous system. But one vital ingredient was still missing. Power, heat, nutrients. What nutrients? What vital substance could feed and nurture dead tissue back to life?

"What is it? What is it? What is it?" Victor muttered to himself. He tore at his hair and pounded his fist in frustration against his forehead. Nutrients. In all of Waldman's notes, in everything else he had read, there was no mention of the effective nutrients. "What constitutes the proper biogenic fluid?"

In science, there is something known as the "happy accident." A glass beaker filled with chemicals is left unattended overnight, and the wrong reaction takes place, but the mistake leads instead to a valuable new discovery. A mathematician sits under a tree and is hit on the head by a falling apple, and Newton's Laws of Gravity come into being.

Such a happy accident now befell Victor Frankenstein. Unable to think clearly due to his exhaustion, he went to a window and opened it a little for fresh air. Idly, he looked down into the street.

And then he saw it. A pregnant woman was moving slowly up the cobblestones, a hand pressed to her lumber region. With her was her husband, walking beside her, tender, concerned, helping his wife.

At once, Victor had a vision. His imagination penetrated the woman's swollen belly and he clearly saw the unborn child there, floating in a warm sea of nourishment, growing and developing and taking human shape in the uterine sac of amniotic fluid.

"That's it! That's the biogenic solution. Of course! It's amniotic fluid," he whispered.

And he knew where he could find it.

As late as it was tonight and even despite the spread of cholera, the charity hospital's maternity ward was still functioning. Childbirth knows no clock; no epidemic can prevent its happening.

In the ward, a woman was positioned in a birthing chair, screaming as she went into labor. With a great gush, her water broke, cascading into a steel bucket. One of the assistants snatched it up, and scurried around the corner. Victor stood waiting in the shadows. A sum of money changed hands, and the pail of birth-water was his.

At a run, Victor reached his house and rushed up the stairs to the attic. He had to process and test this precious amniotic fluid while it was still fresh. Boiling it off, he reduced the liquid to a thick, viscose mixture and examined it. When it had cooled down a little, he filled a metal scoop with the fluid and carried it over to where a dead but pulsating toad was lying in a glass petri dish, penetrated by needles connected to a source of electrical current. Pouring the fluid into a funnel, he pushed the liquid down the tube, which went into the toad's flesh. As he worked he muttered to himself, going over every step of the operation for his journal later.

"Amniotic fluid at optimum density and temperature . . . copper acupuncture needles piercing flesh at all key energy points . . . these carrying maximum voltage for the specified time. Yes, good. Now after removal of current, the subject should retain animation, but independently of external power sources."

He shut the flow of electricity off by removing the connector to the current. A spark, then nothing.

Victor bent over the petri dish, his eager eyes checking for any sign of life. "Now come on, come on."

Suddenly, the animal's back legs moved in a kick. An actual kick. A shout of triumphant laughter welled up out of Victor's throat. To his delight the toad had come back to life. It was living of its own accord, without further electrical stimulation. The biogenic fluid worked.

"Yes, that's it! That's the combination! The amniotic fluid. It works! That's it! That's what's missing! It works. . . . !"

He could barely contain his excitement. He felt like dancing around the garret, opening the attic window and shouting his news to the entire population of Ingolstadt. But he did neither. Instead, he turned his back on the toad to record his results in his journal. He was unaware that behind him the toad's back legs suddenly flexed in strong kick, powerful enough to crack the lid of the petri dish.

If he *had* noticed, would he have made the connection between the power of the reanimated toad's kick and the strength of the chimpanzee's arm that grasped Henry so tightly that evening at Waldman's? Would he have hypothesized that perhaps . . . just perhaps . . . reanimation somehow endowed its subject with enormous physical strength? Would he have asked, "and also endowed with what else?" But he did not see, did not make the connection, did not ask the question.

Time was running out. If it were to be done at all, it would have to be done now. He could be back from the maternity hospital with more biogenic fluid in less than an hour, and then his preparations would be complete.

Far into the night, Victor Frankenstein labored. The large copper vat that the blacksmith had fashioned so carefully was now filled with the processed amniotic fluid. He dipped his hand in, and examined the consistency and smell. Everything had to be exactly right. It was no mere coincidence that the vat was human in shape. It was a sarcophagus; it would hold the body as a uterus holds a fetus, surrounded by a field of the nutrient fluid. Copper, the best conductor of electricity then known, would help in producing the necessary power.

Now to put the pieces of his man together.

Schiller's severed arm was held by metal bands wired up to the Voltaic piles, and Victor busied himself testing reactions. As he turned on the switch, the arm began to move and writhe under the electric current. The hand clenched into a fist, and the heavy muscles in the forearm flexed. Suddenly, the metal bands broke. That same increased strength showed by the chimpanzee arm and the toad's legs seemed to be shared by Schiller's arm. The electrical power had been turned into muscular power.

Once again Victor didn't sense the significance of the increase of strength. As far as he saw, the arm was still biologically viable, still reactive. But for how much longer? Victor scraped off a small shred of tissue and dropped it into the test solution. With a sinking heart, he watched the tissue break apart. It didn't look good. The flesh was already beginning to decay. The tissues were degrading very rapidly; soon the arm would be useless. He glanced feverishly at his enemy the clock, and made a rapid decision. In his journal Victor scribbled, "Imperfect, but must use. No time to replace. Other organs can't wait."

Taking up a huge curved suturing needle threaded with thick catgut, Victor rapidly stitched the arm onto the torso of his corpse, yanking up hard to draw the catgut tight. The stitches were huge, and the flesh pucked angrily beneath them. But there was no time for esthetics, for tiny, neat stitches like embroidery. He was working fast, racing against time, and thereby rushing the stitches. There would be massive scarring.

Coming from the street below was the sound of increased bustle, a rising panic. But Victor did not hear it; he labored on relentlessly, sewing the leg to the torso, fitting the brain into the skull and stitching

the scalp back up with long lines of stitching around
the head and the eye socket, and across the face
down to the jawline. Once again, the stitches were
large and uneven.

At last, this part of the work was completed.
The body was now assembled, crudely perhaps, and
resembling a piece of rough patchwork, yet sewed
together into one piece. The arm and the leg Victor
had taken from Schiller's dead body were grotesquely
out of proportion to the rest of the sharp-featured
man's smaller, slender form, but they would function, and to Victor function was all that mattered.

The creature now lay on a pile of crates, draped
in rough sacking, like Christ in Michelangelo's *Pieta*.
On the laboratory table, chemical beakers filled with
battery fluid, saline solution, and other liquids, stood
bubbling and dripping. Victor checked the bottles of
fluids that dangled from the iron ring in the ceiling.
Intravenous lines led from the bottles to the needles
stuck all over the body, seeping and secreting. He
removed the clips that kept the liquids in the intravenous tubes, so that the fluids would enter the body
in small, steady streams. A chemical haze hung in
the air like a miasma.

Now it was only a matter of hours. The drips
would feed into the body slowly, imbuing the dead
tissues with the necessary chemicals. When the bottles were all empty, Victor could finish his work.
Until then, all he could do was wait. A sudden flash
of lightning ripped through the skylights. Overcome
by exhaustion, Victor Frankenstein's muscles gave
way and he collapsed into a profound sleep.

The intravenous drips were empty. Victor's creation had finished taking in the fluids that would
provide much-needed electrolytes and rehydration to

its tissues. Thin gray rays of late afternoon sunlight streamed through the windows, but Victor Franken-stein still lay sleeping like the dead, in the place by the Creature's feet where he had collapsed the night before. He had been sleeping for many hours.

In the street outside a great commotion was taking place—shouting, horses' hooves clattering on cobble-stone, an occasional scream or wail. But Victor didn't stir; he was dead to the world.

Suddenly, there was a great pounding of fists on the door. Somebody was out there, at the front door of the attic, knocking furiously. Victor roused himself groggily; for a moment he didn't remember where he was or how he got here, on the floor. Then he saw the patchwork of a man lying sprawled on the crates, and the events of the previous night came flooding back to him.

Lurching to his feet stiffly, Victor pulled the sack-ing over his inanimate creation to hide it from view. How long had he been sleeping? Now, for the first time he heard the street noises—carts rumbling, horses' hooves pounding, and the running of many feet on the cobblestones below. What was happening in Ingolstadt?

And who the devil was at his door, now of all inconvenient times?

At the top of the boardinghouse stairs Henry Clerval was pounding, trying to get Victor to answer. Below him, in the square, there was a growing panic in the city. Getting around was increasingly difficult, even dangerous. No time to lose. Damn it, man, answer the door!

Inside the garret, Victor ran to the inner open door. Thank heaven the outer door was still tightly locked and the bolt thrown across. He couldn't risk anybody coming in now. He heard Henry's voice yelling urgently.

"Victor. Open the door!"

From behind the locked and bolted door, Victor answered. "What do you want?"

Henry sounded genuinely panicked. "This cholera . . . it's an epidemic. Classes have been suspended. The city's been placed under martial law. We have three hours before they close the gates! Are you listening to me, Victor?"

"Yes? And?" Henry's frantic words meant little if anything to him.

Henry felt a stab of irritation. How could Victor be so damnably dense? Nothing he might be doing behind his locked doors was worth getting trapped in a city ravaged by cholera! "The militia's arriving to quarantine the city. Most of us are getting out while we still can. Look, Krempe knows you're here, for God's sake! What if he tells the authorities?"

Victor could not stand here bandying words with Henry Clerval. He had too much work to do. "Good-bye, Henry," he said through the door, dismissively.

"Victor," another voice said, a low, sweet woman's voice. "It's me. Elizabeth."

Elizabeth? Here in Ingolstadt? Victor staggered a little with the shock of it, his fatigued mind reeling with anguish and conflict.

"Can you hear me? Victor, I have to see you."

Ah, God. Elizabeth was here, no further away than the other side of this door. Part of him yearned to throw the door open wide and pull her into his arms. But he could not; he must send her away. Dimly, he remembered that Henry had just told him that cholera was sweeping through Ingolstadt. She mustn't stay here. It wasn't safe. But, oh, how he longed for just one look at her face! Laying his forehead against the door that stood between them, he braced himself for a self-inflicted wound.

"Please go away."

Elizabeth paled. How could he possibly ask this of her? After she had journeyed so far to see him? And why; what was he hiding?

"Please, Victor. I won't leave here until you see me."

There was no other way out. He had to face Elizabeth; he owed her at least that much consideration. But he couldn't allow Henry to come in with her, because, even without seeing the laboratory, Henry would probably sense what Victor was doing and how far he had progressed.

He left his lab and went out into his hallway. Closing the inner doors, he unbolted the main door. "Come through the side door," he instructed, going into the bedroom. Henry and Elizabeth entered.

"Alone," ordered Victor.

Henry remained behind, and Elizabeth followed Victor into the bedroom. Her face lost its color and her eyes opened wide in shock, appalled by the sight of him and the dreadful smell. Whatever she had feared for him back in Geneva, she had never expected to find him living like this, in a gloomy attic. Victor was ragged, and his face was drawn and thin; obviously he hadn't shaved or even bathed for a while, and his beard had grown in unevenly. His beautiful golden hair—that hair she so loved to caress—was now long and stringy and unwashed.

Worst of all was the expression on his face. It was distracted, as though he weren't seeing her at all.

In fact, Victor looked at Elizabeth almost without recognition. It was as if she had arrived from a distant unknown planet, so far away was her world from the one that was now his. In his deepest soul, Victor still loved her and desired her, but that desire had been replaced by another passion, a passion of creation.

"Oh, my God," Elizabeth cried, agonized, "what has happened to you? How can you live here like this? And that stench?" She took a few steps forward, in the direction of the laboratory door. Victor leaped to block her way, pushing her back.

"Don't go in there," he warned her.

"We have to leave," Elizabeth said. "This isn't safe."

"No! I have to stay."

She stared at him, astonished. "Even if it means you'll die?"

"Yes." He couldn't look at her.

Elizabeth was distraught. She hardly recognized this Victor; what had happened to the man she loved to change him so drastically? He was irrational, not making any sense; it was obvious to Elizabeth that Victor must be ill. How could she abandon him in this state, she who had sworn vows of a love that would last forever? She took a step toward him. "Well, let me help you."

Victor moved back, away from Elizabeth, and shook his head firmly. "No. That's impossible."

"We made a promise—"

"Don't," he pleaded, suddenly overcome, and he sat down on the edge of the bed and dropped his head in his hands.

Elizabeth's eyes filled with tears; she loved him so much, and now she pitied him. Victor was obviously going through some sort of private hell. But she couldn't allow him to shut her out, or he would be left all alone in hell. And that mustn't happen. "Victor, I beg you—"

He looked up at her, and when their eyes met, each of them perceived something of what the other was feeling. If only he could spare her more pain! But he couldn't tell her or anyone else why he was compelled to stay here, or what great work he was doing. It was a burden of his soul to carry alone. Slowly, and with difficulty, he spoke.

"I know this is hard for you to understand, but I cannot abandon this work now. It's too important, not just for me, but believe me, for everyone, and it must come first."

Elizabeth gasped, and her voice was filled with pain. "First? Before us?"

The suffering in her eyes only added to his own. But he saw their future life together, the peace and beauty of Geneva, their shared domestic harmony, the children they would have together, only as something remote and indistinct, as though he were viewing it through the wrong end of a telescope. The here, the now, were all that mattered, and Elizabeth had no place in Victor's here and now. Later, when all of this was behind him, when the human race was rejoicing in its immortality and acclaiming Victor Frankenstein as its genius savior, there would be plenty of time for them and their happiness. But not today, not today.

Victor moved closer to her, drawn by her irresistible magnetism, but with an effort he restrained himself from touching her. If he touched her smooth skin, he might be totally lost. "Elizabeth, I love you so much, but—"

Elizabeth gasped. There were worlds of meaning in that "but." Those three small letters stabbed Elizabeth to the heart, but she accepted the wound with dignity. "I love you, too, Victor," she said simply. "Goodbye."

Pushing past Henry, who was still waiting at the door, Elizabeth left. Henry threw Victor a look of reproach and followed her. For a long moment, Victor remained where he was, overcome by his feelings of anguish. He had lost her; he had lost his Elizabeth. He had sent her away. Then he pushed the door to the laboratory open to look at his creation. From under its wrapping of burlap sacking the body seemed to beckon to him, as irresistible as Elizabeth herself. Dismissing everything else from his mind, Victor Frankenstein entered the lab.

Outside, in the streets of Ingolstadt, pandemonium reigned, spreading from person to person as quickly as the cholera. With only hours to go before the city locked its gates, a mob of people in panic was rushing through the squares and streets. Loaded down by as many possessions as they could carry, men, women, children, and even cats and dogs were fleeing the city. They fled on horseback, in carts, on donkeys, on hay wagons, but many of them were running away on foot. Elizabeth and Henry found themselves caught up amongst the frightened citizens and swept along toward the city gates.

"You stay here. I'll get you out . . ." shouted Henry to Elizabeth. People were eddying around them, pushing at them from all sides, and he was afraid that in the crush they would be separated.

But Elizabeth had come to a decision. She was not going back to Geneva without Victor. Now that she'd seen him, there was no way that she could possibly leave him; Victor was in some kind of serious trouble and no power on earth—not plague, not fire or flood—could keep her from his side. She had to go back to his laboratory and find him. This time she wouldn't take no for an answer; she would stay with Victor until he agreed to come home with her, or else she would remain and share his hell with him.

Deliberately, she moved away from Henry Clerval, pushing against the mob, going who knows where, allowing the crowd to swallow her up. Suddenly, Henry lost sight of her. "Elizabeth! Elizabeth!!" he called anxiously.

But there was no reply. Elizabeth was nowhere to be seen.

10   Creation

After Elizabeth left with Henry, Victor worked on
without stopping for food or to rest. He cursed himself; he should never have slept so long; he might
have jeopardized his entire experiment. Now he put
all thoughts of Elizabeth firmly out of his mind; his
attention had to be focused only on the work before
him. This might be the once chance he would ever
have to prove his theories valid, and everything had
to be done exactly right, in the correct scientific order.

First, it was time to bring the body's temperature
up. Victor lit the boiler and turned it up to high. It
would take a long time for a large empty space like
the attic to warm up, but there was much to do while
the temperature was rising.

Outside in the street, the noises from the crowd
rushing to escape grew louder, as fighting broke out.
The ceiling of the garret flickered with the reflection

"Victor arrived early at the lecture hall, snagging a place
at the front of one of the upper galleries."

"Victor began to assemble the equipment for his laboratory
in the attic. . . ."

"The spirited dance came to an end
with a great flourish. . . ."

"Ever after, Victor would subconsciously associate
the tinkling of harpsichord music and the
rustle of silk with Elizabeth."

"It was the stranger's eyes that were most arresting. . . .
These were eyes that had looked upon horror."

"Beaten by the waves and winds, the *Nevsky* groaned and shuddered as she plowed through the swells."

" 'Captain, we're losing the topsail,' the first mate cried."

"A letter from Victor was always a great event
in the Frankenstein home."

"It was no mere coincidence that the copper vat
was human in shape."

"Victor labored on relentlessly. . . . Once again,
the stitches were large and uneven."

"It was time to bring the body's temperature up.
Victor lit the boiler and turned it up to high."

"The creature crept forward silently to listen,
drawn by the simple country tunes."

"The mob dragged Justine up some narrow steps
in a high wall."

"Did I request thee, Maker, from my clay
To mould me Man? Did I solicit thee
From Darkness to promote me?"
—John Milton, *Paradise Lost*

of the torches carried by the mob. In a way, this epidemic was a godsend to Victor. Who would pay attention now to what one man might be doing in a laboratory while an entire city was caught up in terror?

His foot pumped at the bellows, making the flames of the fire blaze high, casting shadows on the wall. The shadows played over the reproduction of the Da Vinci that Victor had taken from Waldman's workshop. Now he glanced up at *The Study of Man*, which he had daubed with red paint to show key acupuncture points. The perfectly proportioned figure looked as though it were bleeding. Victor dipped a swab in a bowl of iodine, and began to dab identical marks on the dead body before him. These would be the acupuncture points through which the primary current would flow into the creation. The shoulder, the top of the head, the knee, the neck, the foot—those parts of the body now bore dark red iodine stains not unlike the stigmata, the wounds of Christ.

The attic was getting noticeably warmer by the minute. The moment was close at hand. Victor sat down to scribble in his journal, "Time running out. Rioting in town. Decay of flesh accelerating. Must strike now . . ."

Everything was ready. Victor Frankenstein stood up from his writing table and marched through his laboratory like a modern-day Merlin. He switched on the induction machine and gave its wheel a powerful cranking that put it in motion. He set the steam engine wheels revolving as he passed. The boiler was putting out an enormous quantity of heat. It was getting unbearably hot. Victor stripped his shirt off and let it fall to the floor. Now, bare-chested, his face feverishly alight, all fatigue forgotten, he passed the point of no return.

"Now, let him live," he cried out, exultant. "Let the Creation begin!"

Power and heat were being produced in the laboratory, and, in the sarcophagus beyond, which was fitted out with glass portholes, the precious nutrients were reaching the optimum temperature, thanks to the bed of live coals on the track underneath it. Attached to the sarcophagus was a large spill tank, into which the runoff of the waste fluid would enter. Outside the skylights, there was a sudden great flash of lightning; a storm was coming. But to Victor the lightning was a significant and appropriate overture. The power and majesty of lightning were a symbol of life itself.

Frankenstein approached his creation, which was lying on its back on a large metal grating, covered in a shroudlike sheet. The grating was surrounded by a network of heavy chains; Victor had copied the idea from the cargo hoists he'd seen on great ships. He checked the chains, to make certain they were fastened tightly and would hold. Now he moved over to the wall where he unfastened a chain attached to the pulley. He tugged hard on the pulley chain, the other chains pulled taut, and the shrouded Creature on the grating-rig began to rise up slowly toward the roof. Its arms and legs were stretched out, reminiscent of Leonardo Da Vinci's anatomical drawing. Only its limbs showed from underneath its covering, its mismatched legs, one small, the other large, one puny arm, the other powerful.

When the grating reached the roof, Victor moved over to stand beneath it, looking up. Swinging slowly around in its network of chains, from below the body did indeed resemble the Da Vinci, although its proportions were far from the perfection represented in the drawing. Reaching up, Victor grasped the edge of the grating and gave it a mighty push. The grate took off along the track running along the roof of the garret, carrying the body toward the copper sarcophagus.

As it trundled along on the moving grating, Victor ran after the body, soon getting ahead of it, watching it as it passed down the length of the lab. When it reached the far wall, just above the sarcophagus, the track came to an end, hitting the wooden buffers in the wall, and the body stopped.

Victor clambered up to stand at the head end of the sarcophagus, looking down into the steaming liquid and then up to watch the body coming down from the roof. Hauling on the chain, he lowered the body on the grating down toward the murky liquid in the sarcophagus. Once it was in position, Victor tugged off the shroud that had covered the body all this time. Now it was naked.

Slowly, breathing heavily under its dead weight, Victor lowered the body the rest of the way, down into the murky liquid, the processed biogenic fluid. Then he pushed the sarcophagus along its rail toward the waiting bed of coals under the sarcophagus lid. Lining up the lid and the sarcophagus, Victor lowered the heavy lid into place. He slotted them together, tightened down the lid, and snapped the main lock shut on the lid. The bolts slid into place. Now the body was fully enclosed in its metal uterus, a fetus waiting to be born. Victor peered through the side porthole, seeing the body's arm floating in the liquid.

One by one, he took off the acupuncture needles hanging on a wooden rack, fitting them through the holes in the sarcophagus and into the Creature's iodine-marked skin. One in its neck, one into the top of its head, one in its shoulder, one in its knee. The last needle was fitted into the foot.

It was time for the power. Victor moved off to the power terminals. He clipped on the connectors so that electricity would race from the condensors through the Voltaic batteries and along the wires leading to the sarcophagus.

Turning up the heat in the coal firebed under the sarcophagus, Victor ran to the boiler, and read the needle on the gauge. It indicated hot, but it had to be hotter, much hotter. He raced over to the steam generator, and made adjustments to the flywheel. Steam hissed loudly; the wheel began to turn faster and faster, and the boiler needle began to move toward the uppermost setting.

Next, hurrying to the induction generator and giving several hard turns to its crank, Victor set the wheel with its moving wire brushes going. Sparks leaped across the gap between the conductor arms, then traveled crackling across the spiraling wires that led from the conductor to the collection of Voltaic piles, and sparked again from the battery piles to the overhead rigging.

Surges of power were being generated everywhere in the laboratory; all the electricity was controlled by the wires leading into a control panel, and out of the panel once again in wires that led directly to the sarcophagus, to the acupuncture needles that penetrated both the sarcophagus and the body's flesh. A throttle on the panel had the circuit presently open; voltage was leading in, but not out. Through the mists of hot steam and the haze of chemicals, Victor raced across the lab to the throttle, grabbed it with a pair of pliers, and threw it open. As the electrical circuit closed, there was a blinding flash, like a bolt of lightning. In fact, it *was* lightning, another herald of the approaching storm.

In the metal sarcophagus the body went into convulsions as massive jolts of electricity tore through it. The limbs quivered and thrashed, and the head beat hard against the porthole, jerking up and down. But it was only reflexive motion, like the jerks of the galvanized frog's dead severed legs. The Creature did not live. It did not live.

And Victor knew why; he was prepared for this result. One final step had to be taken. Auxiliary power; the alternative source of power that Waldman himself was never able to find.

Victor didn't stop to breathe; he ran to the sarcophagus and, with a thick rope, he guided a wide glass tube out of a huge bollock-shaped container bag hanging from the ceiling; the bag was thrashing madly. Whatever was in that container was very much alive. The glass tube had been made to fit tightly into a projection from the lid of the sarcophagus; Victor now fastened the two together and checked the fit. Perfect.

Once the wide glass tube was fitted exactly into the lid of the sarcophagus, making a tight seal, Victor pulled a chain; it released the cover of the large bollock-shaped container, and, in one mad rush, dozens of huge electric eels, angry and hungry, poured down the tube and into the sarcophagus. Their voracious mouths opened furiously, snapping, showing sharp teeth. Sparks came from them as they began to bite ravenously into the Creature's flesh and discharge their stored-up electricity directly into the dead body.

Electric eels—this was Victor's bizarre idea, dating back to when he had experimented with them as a boy. But these eels were a lot larger and more dangerous than the little ones he'd kept in a bucket in his old schoolroom. For days now he had been keeping them alive in a giant sack, feeding them raw, bloody carrion flesh that stank horrendously. The eels had feasted well, turning the raw meat into electricity within their own bodies. Now the eels would be Victor Frankenstein's auxiliary source of power.

Victor climbed to the top of the sarcophagus. He crawled forward on his stomach and peered through the porthole at the head end. He could see the eels thrashing around the Creature, moving swiftly from its feet to its head, biting crazily with their razor teeth, creating direct surges of power into the very flesh. He could see electricity pulsing through the amniotic fluid.

"Live," whispered Victor, then his voice rose. "Live, *Live*! LIVE!"

Suddenly, the Creature's head smashed against the porthole. On top of the sarcophagus, Victor sat back in surprise. Could this be life? So soon? He leapt to the floor and ran to the power supply, ripping off the clips. The power died down, and everything was suddenly quiet and still. No wheels turning, no sparks crackling, no humming of electrical wires, no hissing of steam. Inside the sarcophagus, the Creature went limp.

Victor walked slowly over to his creation and looked in through the head porthole. The body lay still; its arms and legs floating quietly in the biogenic fluid. Nothing was moving. No life.

Victor's shoulders slumped wearily. It was finished; he had done everything he knew how to do, and all of it in vain. He had cared for the body, he had found it the parts it needed to be whole. He had provided the three basics—heat, power, nutrients. And nothing had worked. All his theorizing, all his research, all his labor, had in the end come to nothing. So Victor Frankenstein was not a genius after all. He was nothing but a failure. Disappointment flooded through him, filling his mouth with the bitter taste of ashes.

Slowly he turned and walked away, unwilling to look again at the sarcophagus and its dead contents. He knew he would have to clean up the laboratory, dispose of the contents of the sarcophagus, but not now. He couldn't bear to think of it now. All he wanted now was to sleep.

Almost imperceptibly, the Creature's hand tapped on the glass of the porthole. Inside the sarcophagus the Creature's eyes, filled with panic, opened wide, and he banged on the glass again.

Hearing the sound, Victor turned. Could he be imagining it? No; it was true. The metal sarcophagus was beginning to convulse, to shake madly, as though something very powerful was trying to get out.

Victor's face lit up like a flame; his eyes shone like twin beacons. His exhaustion was forgotten in a surge of gleeful exaltation.

"It's alive! It's alive!"

With his heart pounding, Victor raced toward the sarcophagus, which was now quaking violently as the Creature's convulsing body and head beat at the porthole again and again. Swiftly, he pulled out and discarded the acupuncture needles one at a time. He unscrewed the lid, and reached to undo the main lock, but before he could get to them the lead bolts snapped, so great was the power exerted against them from inside the sarcophagus.

Suddenly, the lid burst off, sending Victor toppling backward into the spill tank as a wave of amniotic fluid surged out to drench him. The lid of the sarcophagus flew through the lab, knocking down shelves and crashing into equipment, breaking the glass retorts and beakers into hundreds of glistening shards. Finally ending up near the door, the lid knocked the shelf with Victor's greatcoat on it onto the ground.

Another loud clap of thunder sounded, and a jagged bolt of lightning suddenly illuminated the garret. Victor stared aghast at the sarcophagus. What power was this that could do so much damage? Slowly, he got to his feet and walked toward the now motionless vat, coming up to the side of it. He looked in, anticipating that his creation was alive, but everything inside was still; there was no sign of life.

Suddenly, with no warning, the Creature reared up in Victor's face, his slippery hands grabbing for his creator. As he did, the sarcophagus began to topple off its rail and tipped over onto its side. Victor and the Creature went flying across the spill tank, landing in the center of the sticky fluid and thrashing eels, the Creature on his belly, Victor on his back.

Victor scrambled to his feet, and turned to see the Creature crawling through the fluid. He started to go over to his creation, intending to lift him to his feet, but his leather shoes slipped in the slippery fluid, and he fell again. The Creature seemed to be as helpless as a newborn infant. And why not? What else could he be called but a newborn?

"Stand, please stand, come on. . . ." Raising himself to his knees, Victor spoke the words of encouragement as though to a child.

The Creature, his vision obscured by the viscous mask of amniotic fluid that hid his features and clouded his eyes, managed to get to his feet, but could not keep them. With Victor's help, half-standing, half-sliding, he managed to move. Victor was face to face with him, holding him upright under his arms, pushing him toward the wall. The Creature's body dangled heavily; it took real effort to move him.

When the Creature was standing, the smiling Victor took a step backward to admire his work. But as he gazed on his naked, slimy creation, the smile faded from his lips, and an expression of horror came over his face.

What he saw was grotesque, monstrous, a hideous parody of a human being, crisscrossed by long, irregular scars, its head, body, and face mutilated by scarred, stitched, puckered flesh. The eyes stared out of sunken sockets; the mismatched arms and legs mocked their creator by their ugliness. For the first time, Victor Frankenstein understood what he had done. His heart sank; with the best intentions in the world he had created an abomination. But the full horror of it had yet to sink in. Victor was to be spared nothing.

Slowly, he backed away from his creation, but the Creature, knowing no other person but Victor, came staggering after him, those horrible mismatched hands reaching for him. Victor felt the fallen sarcophagus behind him and took a step sideways to get out of the way, and the Creature stumbled and fell forward, against the sarcophagus. His great strength tipped the vessel back over, but the force of the push broke one of the hinges that kept it on track, and the sarcophagus rolled over to the opposite side of the track, into the ranks of the Voltaic piles. The batteries went flying, smashed to pieces.

The Creature hurtled forward onto the track, his body landing directly over the coal firebed that had heated the sarcophagus. The skin began to crackle and burn, and the Creature, with an incoherent shriek of pain, jumped to his feet and began to run. Frightened, Victor ducked out of his way.

With its arms flailing wildly and its mismatched legs hobbling its gait, the abomination shambled at an extraordinary speed to the grating that was held by chains controlling a pulley. The force of his headlong dash drove the Creature into the chains, which curled around his hands and arms, entangling him, holding him fast. Driven by the hoist chain, the pulley began to operate; little by little, the Creature began to rise up into the air, drawn up by the mechanism, the grating revolving slowly. He slumped in his prison of chains, and his hideous scarred head fell forward.

Now, in another flash of lightning, the abomination was revealed in all his dreadfulness, hanging there in midair, moaning and twitching in his deaththroes. Victor stood below, dripping slimy bigenic fluid, his chest heaving, staring up at the Creature. Another flash of lightning, and the full horror of what he had created hit him hard. It was monstrous; monstrous! The Creature gave one final twitch and went limp. His death-throes were over.

For a long moment, there was only silence in the garret. Then, out of the sickness of his soul, Victor asked softly, "What have I done?" But Heaven made no reply.

He sighed heavily, suddenly bone-weary. Picking up his journal, he walked away from the lifeless Creature hanging in the chains.

" 'Massive birth defects,' " he recorded. " 'Greatly enhanced physical strength but the resulting reanimant is malfunctional and vile, and dead. These experiments are at an end.' "

For a moment, the thought of Professor Waldman entered Victor's mind, and he realized that this was what Waldman was cautioning him about; this was why Waldman had turned away from his own experiments. If only he had listened!

" 'Tomorrow this journal and this evil will be destroyed . . . forever.' "

He stopped writing, closed the covers of the journal and went over to his greatcoat. Automatically, Victor placed his notes in the pocket of his coat where he always kept them. He picked his greatcoat up from the floor where it lay, and hung it back on its customary hook by the door, but it was another automatic act; he barely knew what he was doing. His heart was so heavy he thought his chest would burst.

Above his head, the Creature still hung limply in the chains, revolving slowly. But Victor didn't look up. He turned his back on it and left his laboratory.

Victor virtually dragged himself into his garret bedroom. Outside, a fierce thunderstorm was raging, and heavy raindrops beat at the roof and skylights of the attic. But he was unaware of rain, lightning, or anything else in the outside world. Black depression settled over him; he was disappointed, deeply humiliated and unutterably weary. All he ever intended was to do good; his theories were provable, but he hadn't taken consequences into consideration, and the consequences were catastrophic. Waldman had tried to warn him, but Victor had been so hotheaded, so sure of himself and his ideas that he wouldn't listen to any word of warning.

All his life Victor Frankenstein had worshipped science, thinking of pure science as something perfect, whole, attainable. Now he saw it with very different eyes. Its perfection was a snare, a delusion, a Siren song. Science was but a means to an end, and the end itself wasn't forseeable by mortal minds. So, was there a God in Heaven after all? No doubt there was, and He was laughing at Victor right now.

He caught sight of himself in the mirror and recoiled from the sight. He was filthy, haggard, drawn. Is this how he had appeared to Elizabeth? No wonder she had been appalled. It was a testimony to her goodness and purity that she'd wished to stay and help him. The thought of Elizabeth brought a choking lump into his throat. He had hoped to bring her honors and laurels, wealth and fame, and lay them at her feet. Instead, look at him, he was unworthy of her!

Turning away from the mirror, Victor staggered to the canopied bed, where he collapsed, exhausted and weeping. He drew the bed curtains, threw himself down on his pillows and fell instantly into the dark hole of sleep.

But Victor Frankenstein's sleep was far from untroubled. Through the legendary Gate of Horn bad dreams came in to haunt and torture him. In his sleep, he was searching for Elizabeth, begging for her forgiveness.

And then he found her, floating in an empty landscape. Elizabeth's face was drawn in a horrible grimace of pain, her beautiful dark, curly hair was damp and matted, and her expressive eyes were wide with fear. When she saw him, she screamed in terror.

"Victor! What have you done, why did you do it? I'll never forgive you." Her lovely hands reached out to him, and the terror in her eyes was painful for Victor to behold. "Please help me, he's coming after me! You shouldn't have done this!" She gave him one last long look of fear and reproach, and then she disappeared.

Elizabeth! Where are you? He had to find her again. There must be something he could say to allay her fears, some word of comfort for her anguish. After all, the Creature was dead. There was nothing to be afraid of. He had to go after her and tell her that the Creature was dead, that they were all safe, that their lives could go on as before.

Now he found himself running down an alley in Ingolstadt toward the university, calling to Elizabeth. But he saw that the heavy iron university gates were closed in front of him. On the other side of the gates Professor Krempe was standing, dressed in his academic gown, and his tone was exactly the same as when he was lecturing in the operating theater, pompous and impatient.

"You wouldn't be told, would you? You were determined to play God, and now you're scared."

"It's dead," Victor answered dully.

A sneering smile played around Krempe's bearded lips. "How do you know?" he taunted. "How do you know it isn't alive and breeding a whole tribe of demons?"

Victor's flesh crawled at the thought. "I saw it die."

The smile grew broader and more contemptuous. "But this 'thing' isn't subject to the normal laws of nature. You've proved that."

"But I never intended—" Victor started to protest.

"Your intentions are irrelevant," Krempe interrupted coldly. "You have shaken hands with the devil, Victor Frankenstein of Geneva, and your name will be forever linked with evil."

"But it's dead!" Victor cried.

Krempe shook his head with deep scorn. "You fool, Frankenstein. Evil does not die. How could you believe this 'thing' will thank you for its monstrous birth? Evil will have its revenge. God alone knows what kind of monster you have unleashed upon

yourself and your loved ones. God help your family."
But there was no pity in his voice, only contempt.

His loved ones! In danger! "No!" screamed Victor,
but there was nobody there to hear him. Krempe had
vanished. Ingolstadt had vanished.

Instead, he saw his home in Geneva, and lightning once again striking and burning the old oak tree
as it did on the night his mother died. The bare-
chested Victor was mounted on his horse, galloping
toward the Frankenstein mansion through the rain.
He pulled to a halt outside and dismounted. He felt
a panic-stricken urgency running through him.

From inside the house, he could hear Elizabeth
screaming his name out in fear. "Victor!!" It sounded
very far away. She was still afraid; he had to find her
and tell her there was nothing to fear.

His legs seemed to be made of lead, holding
him back. It took enormous effort for him to move.
Soaking wet and shirtless, Victor was now in a corridor leading from the mansion ballroom. He could
hear music playing, although he saw no musicians,
and suddenly he was engulfed by dancers, who
milled around him, caught up in the *valse* and apparently oblivious of Victor's presence. It was as though
they couldn't see him.

There she was! There was Elizabeth among the
dancers. Although her back was to him Victor recognized the masses of dark curls, her beautiful white
shoulders, and her gown. She had worn that gown
the night before he went off to Ingolstadt, the night
he asked Elizabeth to marry him. Now she was dancing with another man.

Victor ran to her, calling her name, and she
turned. But as she turned, he drew back in horror.
This was not his beautiful Elizabeth but a hideous
corpse! He realized suddenly that all the men were

dancing with beautifully dressed, bewigged corpses. Then he heard her voice, Elizabeth calling him again from somewhere in the house, and he ran from the corridor, taking the stairs two at a time.

He moved up the staircase following his beloved's voice, and into the attic. She was there, his Elizabeth, looking radiantly beautiful. Thank heaven!

"Elizabeth . . . I'm sorry . . . ," cried Victor. "Forgive me. Thank God you're safe." Victor reached out for her. Suddenly, a powerfully strong hand curled around his mouth, and the Creature, appearing from mowhere, launched himself on Victor and dragged him away from Elizabeth.

He woke up with a start, shivering in his bed behind the heavy curtains, his ears straining in the darkness. All he heard was rain on the roof and the slight creaking of the grating chains swinging slightly. The garret was empty, nothing was moving. Nothing had changed; the Creature was dead. With a deep sigh of relief, Victor fell back on his bed again and went back to wrestling with his troubled dreams.

11 The Creature

Victor slept as if dead for several more hours, but even in his deepest sleep he trembled with dread, tortured by guilty dreams. Suddenly, with a sharp cry, his eyes flew open and he was totally awake, staring up into the darkness surrounding his bed. But the feeling of nameless dread did not leave him as sleep dissolved. He drew in his breath, willing himself to move, but he still lay there, behind the curtains, paralyzed with fear. He felt a dark shadow on his skin, as though something or someone had touched him, and the hairs on the back of his neck rose and prickled. He couldn't act, couldn't scream. Unable to stand it any longer, he thrust out his arm and jerked the bed curtain aside.

The room was empty. There was nothing out there! Victor shook his head with relief, realizing that he was overworked, exhausted. He needed rest; he needed food; most of all he needed to have his peace of mind restored. Lying back down, he glanced to the other side of the bed.

The Creature was there, looming beside the bed like a spector of death. Naked. Beseeching. Victor gasped and recoiled in horror. How could this be? He had watched it die! And now it was alive, *alive!*

Body covered in bunched and twisted flesh, crudely sewn and held in place by large, irregular stitches, it looked as though the Creature was fastened together by barbed wire; with the mute pleading look in its eyes, it was a terrible sight, at once grotesque and pitiable.

The Creature reached its huge hand out toward Victor, to touch him.

"*No!*" shrieked Victor, lurching from his bed, knocking over his washstand as he tried to get away. The china pitcher and bowl smashed behind him, spilling water and broken crockery over the bedroom floor. Afraid for his life, Victor went careening out into the laboratory. Unsteady for a moment, the Creature followed after him with surprising speed. Victor raced through the lab with the Creature close behind him, almost catching up. In a frenzy of fear, Victor hurled a shelf full of glass jars in its path.

But nothing seemed to stop the Creature, not even the barrier of broken glass under his naked feet. Like Nemesis, inexorable and deadly, he kept coming on. He ran around the water tank, past the smashed shelves, after Victor, toward the door to the stairs.

But Victor reached the door first. He ripped it open, lunged through, and slammed it in the Creature's face. He didn't stop to take his greatcoat, and it fell to the floor with the force of the slam. As Victor Frankenstein ran down the stairs to the street, the

Creature was stopped by the door. He pressed his body against the unyielding wood, whimpering.

Abandoned and alone, he sank to the floor. He was shivering with the chill in the attic. The Creature was cold, very cold. He didn't understand the sensation, he had no words to describe it, but it was unpleasant, almost painful. Instinctively, he sought to protect his naked flesh from the cruel windy drafts. His eye fell on Victor's greatcoat lying where it fell, and he grabbed it and dragged it over to him, wrapping himself up inside it, shrouding himself with the greatcoat's capes.

But his naked feet were still freezing, so the Creature scavenged the laboratory for something to warm them. There were soiled rags and some rolls of bandage, and he gathered them up and bound his feet with them. Strange images flickered through his mind like pictures that move; were they thoughts? Impressions? Memories? Or only fears? The strongest image was that of Victor's face, contorted by fear.

His half-naked body streaming with rain, Victor Frankenstein searched frantically in the stables behind Frau Brach's house. His pulses were racing so fast he could barely get his thoughts together, but one thing was very clear. The abomination was not dead, but soon it would be. Victor himself would put an end to its hideous existence; he owed that to the world, to eradicate this terrible error he'd made. It was his responsibility; he and he alone was to blame. He felt shame at his cowardice; he had run away like a small boy, but now he cast that cowardice aside. From now on he would play the part of a man. But he would need a strong weapon, because the Creature was evidently possessed of incredible strength.

For the first time, Victor pieced together hints that he had been given and which he'd ignored. The chimpanzee's arm, so strong that Henry Clerval was brought to his knees in its grasp. The frog, breaking the petri dish cover with one kick. He should have known; he should have known. Fresh shame poured over him, like salt scalding his wounds. At every turn, Victor was being forced to acknowledge how wrong, how foolish, how headstrong he had been. His feelings of disgrace made him all the more determined to end the Creature's life without delay. Even if it cost him his own. He couldn't allow his beastly creation to be unleashed on an unsuspecting world.

Yes, there it was, hanging from a rope next to one of the mangers. A pickaxe. Sharp and heavy, it would be the perfect weapon. Victor grabbed it up, running back through the rainstorm to the boardinghouse. The streets were deserted; all was silent. The city gates had been locked hours ago; all those who were able to had escaped, by carriage or by wheelbarrow or by shank's mare. The remaining people of Ingolstadt were locked away in their homes, terrified of the plague. Now that the city was under quarantine, no more of them would be fleeing tomorrow, because when the gates opened again it would be to let out the dead, not the living.

Victor raced up the stairs to the garret, the pickaxe in his hand, ready to do battle, to die if necessary. But Armageddon would have to be postponed. He discovered the door literally torn off its hinges by superhuman strength. He entered, stunned. He looked around, then rushed through the laboratory and the bedroom, searching. But the Creature was gone.

Oh, my God! I must find him! He's very dangerous! With his heart in his mouth, Victor ran back out into the storm. There was no sign of the Creature. He didn't know which direction to follow or where to begin his search; all he knew was that he couldn't, he mustn't give up. If anything happened to the citizens of Ingolstadt, their blood would be on his hands. Slogging grimly on through the windswept rain, Victor ran down through streets and up through alleys, peering on all sides, looking into the doorways of buildings, finding nobody.

At last he could search no more. Victor's head was pounding with pain, and a fever had begun to run through his bloodstream, making him weak and ill. He felt lightheaded and his legs were trembling. Something was happening to him. He would try to make it back to his garret; maybe the Creature would return there. Once again, he vowed to himself that he would put an end to the abomination he had brought into being. What an irony! Victor Frankenstein had wanted to make a gift of immortality to the world and now his gift would be the destruction of the very being he made immortal.

"Listen to me, you demon from hell! I will find you! And I will kill you! Do you hear me? I will kill you!" Victor shouted his vow out loud to the empty streets. He stood there, arms outstretched, the rain pelting his face. Was there anybody to hear him? And, if he was listening, would the Creature understand?

The day dawned gray and drizzly. The cobblestones were slick and wet from the heavy rains of the night before. The alley was piled with stinking garbage, and a crew of rats was already busy tearing at it with their strong rodent teeth. Suddenly, a shifting, heaving motion scattered the rats, as the waking Creature opened his eyes and peered out from beneath the greatcoat. Lost and confused, he felt something new and painful, a gnawing hunger tearing at his gut. Without standing up, he scrabbled through the garbage for something to eat. Finding an old piece of meat, mostly gristle and bone with a little fat, he chewed at it ravenously.

The Creature lifted his head, hearing the sound of barking. Two feral dogs appeared suddenly from around a corner. They loped into the alley, emaciated and starving, looking for anything they could find to eat. Their keen noses brought them the rancid scent of the old meat in the Creature's hands. Breaking into a run, the dogs launched themselves on him, snarling and snapping. The Creature scrambled to his feet, but the dogs frightened him, and the food was torn from his hands. Fighting between themselves over the miserable bone, the dogs ran away.

He didn't understand that what he was feeling was mostly fear, but the Creature's instinct hurried him off in the opposite direction. As before, his instinct was for self-protection above everything else. As he lurched swiftly along he hugged the greatcoat to him, pulling the hood back over his head. The once-elegant coat was always large on Victor, but it was small for the Creature, a grotesque misfit. But to him it meant warmth, shelter from the elements. And the greatcoat was the only familiar thing the Creature had. It was his first and only possession.

A distant clanging took the Creature by surprise. A death cart, carrying out the cholera victims, clattered past the mouth of the alley, with the driver ringing his bell. The Creature watched, uncomprehending, until it had passed by, then pressed on. He had, of course, no idea at all of where he was going. He had no destination in mind, or any thoughts. Everything was strange and new; nothing was a memory.

But he kept going until he emerged into the city

square. It was still the center of activity for Ingolstadt, although not quite as bustling as before the epidemic. Yet the square held much more activity than the Creature had seen in his short hours of existence. The sight of so many men and women, all crying out their wares, made him uneasy.

People were still living in the city, although not as many as yesterday. But the mercantile life of the market square went on pretty much as before. Vendors were calling out, selling food to the men and women streaming past. The Creature moved warily through the square, hooded, his features and shape obscured by the greatcoat. He went unnoticed. People went trudging past him without a second look.

But now the Creature paused, sniffing the air. His mouth filled with water. An aroma, delicious and powerful, was drawing him to a vendor's stand. He saw a high pile of fresh loaves of bread. Of course he had no idea what they were, only that they smelled delicious and made his mouth water. He sniffed one, picked it up, and bit off a chunk. A sensation of enormous pleasure came over him as he chewed. He took another bite.

"Here! What do you think you're doing?" The rough voice took him by surprise, and the Creature glanced up. His eyes met those of an angry, red-faced woman. Although most of his head was hidden in the greatcoat's hood, the little she saw of his hideous face was enough for the vendor's wife. She was too stunned to scream.

More afraid of the angry woman than she was of him, the Creature dropped the loaf and backed away from her, straight into the arms of a rough man who pulled him up by his coat, dragging off the hood.

"Stupid bastard!" growled the man furiously.

The Creature whipped around, horrified, staring

from one person to the next. His shaved head was bare, and the angry scars that crisscrossed his head showed plainly. He saw terrified faces on all sides, and heard gasps of fear and disgust. He didn't know what anger was, but the looks on their faces increased his uneasiness.

The vendor's wife advanced toward him, her knife in her hand, her face a cloud of rage. "He's the cholera!" she shrieked. "He's the one been spreadin' the plague!"

At once, the crowd became an angry mob. They began to shout and wave their fists at the Creature; some of the men brandished makeshift weapons. He didn't understand any of it, not their words or their angry shouts, but he comprehended enough to be afraid. These people reminded him of the snarling dogs who'd stolen his meat. His strong instincts told him to get away from there.

He turned and ran away from them, but the crowd had already turned into a mob, and they started to follow, some of them picking up sticks and stones to use as weapons.

"Get him! Get him!" yelled the vendor's wife, encouraging the mob. They followed the Creature, who was running down a covered way that housed a row of shops. He heard them all shouting behind him, and their angry voices hurt his ears. He turned to look over his shoulder, but a tall shelf loaded with tin kitchen ladles was in front of him and he smashed straight into it.

As it fell over, the Creature fell over with it, and as soon as he was down the mob tumbled over themselves in an effort to get at him. His very ugliness was an affront to them, and it was plain to see that he bore the signs of some horrible contagious disease. They had to stamp him out, to teach this

Satan's spawn a lesson; how dared he come amongst decent folk with a face like that?

With hard wooden sticks pummeling him on his back and shoulders, the Creature managed to clamber out of the fallen shelves and run on. He hastened his steps, lurching through the middle of the market, the mob in pursuit, hitting him with their sticks and pelting him with their stones. He kept running until he could go no further. At the end of the street the market square was railed off. The Creature ran into the railings, but they didn't yield. He was trapped. A moan of fear escaped his lips, and he clung to the railings as though for support.

The mob moved in, surrounding him on three sides. The railings had this whatever-it-was stopped in its tracks. The Creature, like a trapped animal, turned and faced his tormentors. He was very afraid, and he whimpered imploringly, but the mob paid his cries no attention. They were bent on revenging themselves upon his ugliness.

Near him was a huge farm cart laden with barrels. The Creature had no way of knowing that a cart of this size and weight was something that even a big dray horse could only pull slowly and with difficulty. He grabbed at the handles and upended it with ease, sending out a flood of vegetables and heavy wooden barrels into the crowd.

For a moment, that stopped them, and the Creature tried to make good his escape, moving sideways along the railings. But one man ran from the mob and began hitting him with a stick, pummeling him without mercy. The Creature cowered, and tried to protect his head with his misshapen hands, but the man wouldn't stop his pounding. Desperate, the Creature pushed him away. The strength of that push propelled the man with unbelievable force backward

through the air, sending him crashing into the
square's drinking fountain. The fountain was actually
a deep well, with a wooden cover, and a common
ladle attached by a cord to a spigot.

As the citizen slammed into the fountain, his
body knocked the cover off. Screaming horribly, he
hurtled down into the deep water below, to an instant death. The mob gasped as if with one voice,
and shrank back. What kind of creature was this? No
human being had that kind of strength.

But the dead man's brother, mad with grief and
rage, ran pell-mell toward the Creature. With a frightened roar, the Creature picked up the man as though
he weighed less than a cat, and hurled him into the
crowd of people. Like ninepins, several men were
knocked down at once.

The diversion allowed the Creature to make good
his escape, but the mob took new courage at the
sight of him running away, and streamed after him.
Still, out of prudence, they kept their distance, content to hurl rocks and sticks, some of which found
their fleeing target.

The breadmaker and his wife watched him impassively, letting him go. "Leave it. Come and help these
people." Muttering, the mob subsided. It was the
cholera, it must be. Everyone knew that the cholera
would drive you mad, and a madman has the
strength of ten sane men. Better to leave him the hell
alone; the disease would kill him soon enough,
anyway.

The Creature turned a corner, and collapsed
against a wall to catch his breath. He could hear them
coming after him, shouting, and he knew that he had
to get away. He saw a flight of stone steps leading
up to a higher section of the city, and he headed
for them.

Suddenly his climbing feet touched something solid blocking his path. He gave a startled cry, stumbled and nearly fell. He looked down and cried out again, frightened by a pile of corpses that had recently been abandoned on the steps at his feet, awaiting the daily visit of the death cart. Dead of the plague, the bodies lay stiffly stacked, one on top of another, their arms and legs sticking out of the pile, their mouths open. Many of them had staring eyes and most were stripped naked and their contaminated clothing discarded.

The Creature bent down and picked up a bundle of clothes and ran a few steps further up. He could hear the creaking of wheels on the cobblestones. The death cart, already heaped with bodies, was approaching. He crouched down to conceal himself from the driver of the cart and, as soon as the fresh corpses were loaded and the driver had climbed on his seat ready to resume his doleful journey, the Creature hurled himself down onto the cart, and burrowed down among the bodies to hide himself among the corpses.

Something greater and more human than just instinct was beginning to work in the Creature's brain. Animal instinct caused him to run blindly, fleeing from his tormentors, but it was the dawning of human intelligence that suggested a way of concealing himself.

As the Creature moved among the bodies, the driver turned as if he'd heard something, then shrugged. The bodies were settling, that's all. This was a damned spooky job, but it paid well. He drove on, joining the other death carts at the town gates, at the point where they opened to let the dead leave the city. There was only one way out of the gates of

Ingolstadt in the quarantine. You either had to be in the cart or on it.

By a near-miracle, Henry Clerval had caught up with Elizabeth after all, and with much persuasion, convinced her to postpone her return to Victor's garret to the morning of the following day. Henry had some idea of what Victor must be up to behind those locked doors, and he knew that it was nothing that Elizabeth could be allowed to see.

But she was at his door before the rooster crowed in the morning, demanding that they go at once to Victor. All thought of leaving Ingolstadt without him deserted Henry as he saw the pleading look on that beautiful face. It would be the three of them or none of them.

They were astonished by what they saw as they came up the stairs of Victor's lodgings. The door stood off its hinges—what could possibly have done that?—and the debris inside was incredible. Broken glass and damaged equipment was everywhere. It looked as though an earthquake had struck the attic, so entensive was the devastation. For a moment the two of them stood in the doorway, stunned. Then Elizabeth dashed forward, crying out, "Oh, my God!"

Victor was lying sprawled unconscious on the floor, his sweaty face a deathly gray. He was barely alive.

The death cart rattled along the road outside Ingolstadt. Nearly smothered, the Creature crawled out from under the rotting pile of corpses, tumbling off the back of the cart onto the muddy road. As the cart trundled away, he picked himself up, carrying his little bundle of clothes, and headed off down the road.

After a few minutes of walking, the Creature stumbled off the road and into a small tract of woods. The trees were silent except for the singing of the birds in their branches, and the cooler air felt good on his wretched face. He shambled on for a while, and in less than an hour he had arrived at a river. Thirst was a new sensation to him. Scrambling to the water's edge, he bent down to drink, lapping the water into his mouth like an animal.

There was something moving in the water. The Creature paused in his drinking and watched it. It was his own broken reflection. As he sat still without moving, the reflection ceased to shimmer and became whole. With a cry, he started upright, terrified at his own image. Without being able to form words or even entire concepts, he knew that the face was . . . not right. Not like the other faces he had seen on the people of Ingolstadt.

He stirred the water to break the terrible image up, then his hands sought his face, touching it, feeling the massive jagged scars and the swellings. A sick "not right" feeling overwhelmed him, and he knew disgust and horror at himself. He sat up. With a moan of grief, he touched his face again.

Suddenly, the Creature heard the sound of dogs barking not very far away. He pushed to his feet. His experience had already taught him that barking dogs were not a pleasant thing. He began to run, faster and faster through the trees. He was gasping for breath as he went crashing through branches. The barking sounded closer now. The Creature hurled himself into a thicket, covering himself with dead leaves. A mingling of sensations coursed through him, overwhelming him in panic, exhaustion, mortal terror.

Lying not far from him he saw a dead doe, newly killed, two arrows sticking out of the wounds in her side. At that moment, a tiny fawn, only a few days old, stumbled into view, looking for his mother, panting with fear and exhaustion.

The Creature uttered a moan at the sight of the baby deer. The fawn turned and met his gaze. For a long moment, the two of them stared at each other and a rush of empathy passed between them. Both were hunted beasts, prey for the kill. Both were alone in the world.

The barking sounded louder as the dogs drew closer. To their excited yips was added the noise of hunters shouting. The Creature stood up and picked the fawn up in his hands and began to run. With a chorus of deep barks, the dogs gave chase. The Creature ran swiftly along the riverbank, looking for a place to ford. Amazingly, it seemed he could out-run hunting dogs.

Seeing a stream, he rushed across it, hugging the fawn to his chest. The dogs arrived at the other side, yapping furiously. They waited on the bank for a moment, but they had lost the scent in the stream, and they had no wish to cross running water, so they returned hungrily to the doe.

The Creature lowered the fawn away from his chest, joyous at their escape, only to realize that the small animal was limp and lifeless in his hands. He moaned unhappily. He was aware that, in trying to save it, he had crushed it to death. And the feeling that came over him was the same bad feeling he had when he recognized his reflection in the water. Not right.

In his brain inchoate thought were beginning to

form, but hardly thoughts to which he could give expression. Rather, the Creature had a series of mental impressions and physical sensations on which he based simple conclusions. Food and warmth were "right"; angry faces, raised voices, sticks and stones, barking dogs, dead fawns, were "not right." He had somehow grasped that he was stronger than other people, and that the others feared him because of his strength and also because of the hideous way he looked. He made no connection between himself and others—except for one man, the man he had seen when he first opened his eyes. To him the Creature felt a strong connection he didn't begin to understand.

He walked on for several hours. The sunlight that filtered through the leafy canopy of the trees thinned, and the sky began to darken. He heard and saw nobody. He was only a solitary figure in a greatcoat trudging through the woods, cold, hungry, wet, tired. He was still carrying his bundle of clothes. The wind began to rise. Soon it would be night.

Faint music came to his ears suddenly, carried on the breeze. The Creature paused, hearing the sound of a recorder, a wooden instrument not unlike a flute. He turned around, looking to see where the music was coming from. Then he set off again, in the direction of the sweet sounds. The music gave him a sensation of "right."

A small wooden house stood in a clearing, and the recorder music was coming from inside. The Creature approached cautiously, not eager to see men again. He eased up to a window, caught a glimpse inside, and drew back, listening. The music calmed him; it was a good feeling, a pleasant feeling. The tune came to an end. He heard the murmur of voices and then footsteps clumping across the floor.

The Creature recoiled in fear, and ran quickly around the side of the house as the door opened.

A poor, painfully undernourished young farmer came out of the house, heading in the same direction as the Creature. He walked around the corner of the house just as the Creature scrambled away, reaching a small door to a pigsty. The pigsty was attached to the cabin by a common wall between them.

"Felix," called a woman's voice from inside the house. "Remember those scraps in the bucket by the door. They're for the pigs."

"Oh yes," the young man called back. "I'd forgotten about them."

"Well, feed those pigs. And hurry up! Supper's almost ready."

"I won't be a minute."

The Creature managed to get the door open and go inside the sty as Felix rounded the corner, about to follow him inside. He found himself in the company of pigs. Seeing the Creature, the animals grunted and squealed in alarm.

"Stop that noise, I'm coming to feed you," called Felix from outside the pigsty. The Creature scurried further back into the shadows as the man came in carrying an overflowing bucket. The pigs, scenting dinner, began to grunt noisily. Felix upended the pail and slop poured into the trough. Felix left, and the pigs scurried to eat.

The Creature leaned forward intently. Food? He, too, smelled a combination of intoxicating aromas, and it drew him forward like a magnet. He crawled to the trough and squeezed in among the pigs. The pigs jostled him, but the Creature, driven nearly mad by hunger, jostled right back. Greedily, he lapped up the slop, shoving it into his mouth with his fingers. As the pigs grunted with pleasure, so did he.

Suddenly he stopped; a different sound had caught his attention. Someone inside the house was singing. The woman's song flooded him with pleasure, a pleasure so sweet it was almost unbearable. Drawn by the music, the Creature crawled back into the darkest recesses where the pigsty adjoined the wall of the house. He placed his eye to a chink between the logs, wiping his mouth. Through the chink in the common wall, the Creature could see inside the house.

What he saw was family's evening ritual. Grandfather was stirring a pot of soup. The Creature shifted his bulk for another view of the room, and saw the children, Maggie and Thomas, ages 6 and 8, setting the table for dinner. Felix's wife, Marie, was helping her husband clean his work-torn hands. Felix held his hands out. "Bleeding again," he sighed.

"How are the pigs?" she asked him.

Felix winced at the sting of the carbolic. "They're fine. I've fed them."

The sight of these simple domestic moments made the Creature moan with pleasure. They were so gentle, so natural, these people, so unlike the angry-faced men and women who had chased him with their sticks and hurtful sharp stones. It was a pleasure almost equal to eating the warm sticky food in the trough.

The moan was so soft that nobody in the cottage heard it except Grandfather. Totally blind, the old man possessed an enhanced sense of hearing equal to the barn owl's, who can hear a mouse's tiniest rustle in the grain sacks. Grandfather paused to gaze blindly toward the wall that separated the little house from the pigsty. But the moan was not repeated. Probably nothing, he decided. "Soup's ready," he announced.

"Come and sit down, Grandpa," Thomas said. The old man let the children lead him toward the table. Marie brought the pot from the stove. The little family sat down to bless their bread and eat their frugal meal.

The Creature eased back from the chink in the wall, and sat down with his back to it. He was no longer hungry; full at last, he was somehow satisfied in mind as he was in body. Feeling something in his pocket, he took out the journal and leafed through it, but not understanding what was written inside, he put it down. A great weariness came over him; this, the first full day of his life, had been long and eventful. Pulling the greatcoat over himself for warmth, the Creature laid himself down and went to sleep almost immediately.

12 The Journal

For several days, Victor Frankenstein lay hovering between life and death. Elizabeth never left his side; even when Henry persuaded her to get some rest, she would fall asleep reluctantly, overcome by fatigue, in a chair by Victor's bed. Henry ministered to his friend, using all his newly learned medical skill, but there were many moments when he despaired of Victor's survival. In his delirium, Victor kept crying out threats of murder and mysterious phrases that Elizabeth didn't understand—"biogenic fluid," "auxiliary power," "enhanced strength," "abomination."

But Henry comprehended at least a part of what had taken place in this laboratory, and although he couldn't possibly have foreseen the outcome of his friend's experiment, he was glad that it was over. He always thought it was a dangerous business, Victor's chasing after Waldman's bizarre experiments. It was breaking the laws of God and man.

Henry Clerval would never forget the strength in that severed ape's arm as it closed relentlessly around his hand. It seemed to Henry that Victor must have crossed over that line between experimenting and playing God, with catastrophic results. Victor's secret must surely be a terrible one to burden his soul so grievously even during his unconscious hours.

But one morning Victor's eyes opened as a cup of warm broth was being put to his lips, opened and focused on Henry's anxious face. He cried out weakly, "What?" and tried to move.

Clerval pushed him gently back onto his pillows. "There now, rest easy."

"Henry, you're here," said Victor weakly, in a wondering tone.

Henry Clerval chuckled. "Of course I'm here. Where else would I be? It was touch and go with you, though. Take just a bit more soup. You've been very ill, Victor. I feared cholera. Turned out to be pneumonia."

Could this be the old Clerval, who hated the thought of sick people? Victor looked at him in surprise.

"Yes, I've become something of a doctor." Henry laughed. "Even Krempe is pleased with me. At this rate I might even pass anatomy."

Victor struggled to sit up, pushing the soup away. Memories came flooding back to him. "The epidemic? What about the epidemic?"

Henry's grin faded and his face grew troubled. "It's dreadful. There is nothing we can do for them. Anyone vulnerable, anyone without food or shelter—the newborn especially—will die."

The newborn will die! Victor's heart gave a leap in his chest. He pictured the Creature, powerful but newborn, unable to speak or think, with no food, no shelter, with cholera raging, unable to survive. He imagined him dying of exposure or the plague, that scarred and maimed body falling still at last, becoming harmless in death. It was a wonderful thought, greatly comforting, if he could believe it. "Are you sure?" he asked Henry seriously.

"I'm certain of it."

"Thank God," whispered Victor.

"What do you mean?" cried Henry, perplexed. "Victor, what is it?" He wanted to know and yet at the same time he didn't. The puzzling equipment in the shattered laboratory had given him more than enough clues, especially that big copper vat shaped like an oversized coffin.

For a fraction of a second, Victor hesitated. He longed to tell Henry everything, to share this burden that weighed so heavily on his heart. But he knew it would be wrong. For the first time, he understood Waldman's evasions and his secrecy. Some things are best kept hidden forever. "Nothing," he said finally.

"Well, that's my shift finished," Henry said cheerfully. "I'll see you later." Taking the soup bowl, he left the bedroom; Victor was alone.

Victor fell back on his pillows with a sigh of relief. He felt weak and a little dizzy, but surprisingly well, considering that he'd nearly perished of pneumonia. He was close to euphoric. The certainty of the Creature's death had worked a greater medical miracle on him than all of Henry's nostrums and potions and broth put together.

Suddenly he was aware that he was hearing piano music, a soft air, gentle and soothing. Was he delirious again? Then the conviction. *No, it's real.* It was the song Elizabeth had sung at his farewell ball, "So, we'll go no more a-roving." Unsteadily, Victor got out of bed and went searching for the music's source. The bedroom door to the laboratory was open, and he saw that his scientific equipment had all been packed up into trunks, the broken glass cleared away. How innocuous the long room now looked, which had so recently been the stage on which loathsome acts had been played! It had become an attic again, nothing more.

The music seemed to swell as he searched for it; it drew him onward like magnetism. And then he saw her, Elizabeth, seated at the piano at the far end of the garret. His Elizabeth, no delirious dream, but real, flesh and blood and beauty. Victor felt such an onrush of joy that it nearly overcame him. He had to put his hand out and hold onto the wall to keep from falling down.

"Elizabeth! ELIZABETH!" he cried ecstatically. She turned from the keyboard and saw him—alive, standing, calling her name. Elizabeth rose from the piano and started to run to him, her skirts billowing. Her face was glowing with happiness and love.

Victor sped to her as fast as his unsteady legs would carry him. When they met at last he all but collapsed into her arms. They fell together, bodies pressing tightly, kissing, touching, holding. All rational thought was suspended, and only their great passion flowed between them like a torrent. They were young animals, children, unable to stop, unable to get enough of each other, unwilling ever to let each other go. They had come so close to losing each other; now they were reunited, and nothing must part them ever.

"Elizabeth," cried Victor passionately. "I thought I'd never see you again." Tears of gladness spilled from his eyes, mingled with a deep remorse, and he was not ashamed to weep before her.

"Sshhh. It's all right, it's all right . . ." Elizabeth comforted him with great tenderness, stroking his bent shoulders, kissing his hair.

"Please forgive me, please," he begged.

"Of course I do."

"I'm so sorry," Victor wept. He kissed Elizabeth with his entire soul, a kiss she returned with the same fervor. As they sunk onto their knees on the floor they didn't let go of each other. Elizabeth cradled Victor's head in her hands, and looked deeply into his face. How frail he seemed! Through her tears, she whispered urgently, "Victor, I don't know what you were working on . . . I don't want to know . . . but you must understand that it nearly killed you."

Victor nodded. "It's finished. It's over. It should never have been started. But it's over now. It's dead." He scanned her lovely features, so dear to him, so sweetly familiar. He must have been mad to forget Elizabeth, Geneva, his home. "I love you," he whispered.

Elizabeth smiled tremulously. "I love you, too."

They kissed again, passionately, tenderly, deeply. Weeping and laughing all the while. How lucky they were, they both thought. How incredibly lucky!

Inside the pigsty, the Creature and the pigs were asleep. They were curled up together in one heap, as though the Creature was just another littermate. Having slept like this for hours, warm and comforted, he opened his eyes gladly and roused himself, scattering the pigs. Then he crawled to the slats of the sty to look out. Through the slats in the front he could see the outside of the house and even the bit of yard in front of the door. It was very late afternoon, to judge from the thin sun's slanted rays.

While the Creature was studying his new little world, Felix returned from the fields with a basket on his back. Although he was very tired he stopped for a moment to pluck one of the small alpine flowers that always emerges from the ground when the weather turns cold in autumn.

When he heard footsteps outside, the Creature moved to his eyehole in the pigsty wall. The pleasures of his life were pretty much limited to being warm and feeling full, but watching Felix and his family through his peephole was what he enjoyed most of all. In the short time he had lived hidden away in the sty, the little family had become endlessly fascinating to the Creature, and every day he learned more and more from them. They were a textbook crammed with information.

For example, although he didn't know how to form words yet, he had already grasped that words were how these beings communicated with each other most of the time. One made sounds that the other seemed to understand and answer with different sounds of his or her own. And these people didn't use angry noises or raise their fists toward one another. Sometimes the old blind one would play the recorder, and sometimes the pretty one would sing, and that gave the Creature the greatest "right" feeling of all.

Sometimes they touched one another with gentle, loving hands, and the Creature had come to understand that these caresses, too, must be a form of silent speaking, because they were comprehended by both giver and receiver. He had even learned to tell the differences between the touching the parents gave their children, and the touching the man and woman reserved for each other.

Now he watched as Felix entered the house and dumped the basket out for Marie. The basket was nearly empty; only a few potatoes and turnips rolled out onto the kitchen table. The oncoming winter had brought with it very cold nights, and the earth had turned to ice, making it almost impossible for Felix's hoe to break through to dig their vegetables.

"We'll never get through the winter with this yield. The ground's frozen hard."

"We'll have to sell another pig at market," replied Marie with a sad little sigh.

"We can't," answered Felix, sitting down with a tired groan. "Not until they lift the quarantine. These days, nobody gets in or out of Ingolstadt. Even then it's one less pig for us. And there's last month's rent. He'll be back for that soon. . . ." His voice sounded bitter.

Marie sat down beside her husband. "Come on, we'll do this together," she said softly, taking his hand.

"You're right." Felix nodded wearily. "We've got to before the snow comes." The couple fell silent as they shared a tender moment. He handed her the flower that he picked earlier. "For you."

Through the chink in the wall, the Creature watched Marie and Felix, deeply moved by the tenderness they displayed. The softness in their voices when they spoke to each other was sweet to his ears, and their caresses seemed so very gentle. Also, the gift of the little flower moved him strangely. It seemed to be a symbol of their affection for each other. Suddenly, the Creature felt very alone. He desperately yearned to be a part of this little family, and this yearning raised his threshold of self-education to yet a higher level.

In the womb, the human fetus undergoes the same evolution that the human species once did, many millions of years before. At the moment of conception a one-celled organism divides and becomes a many-celled organism. Then it grows a tail and resembles a fish; losing the tail, it goes through stages resembling the amphibian and finally the mammal, exactly as the ancestors of the human race did when they came out of the sea eons ago. Scientists have a term for this: "Ontogony Recapitulates Philogony," which means that the individual goes through the same evolutionary development as its species. And all in only nine months in the womb.

So it was with the development of the Creature. When he was born, only days earlier, he had the mind of an infant, knowing no more than hunger and satiety, fear, and comfort. But with surprising speed his brain power was expanding, his intelligence growing almost by the hour. He was making quantum leaps forward in comprehension. He had yet to learn to speak, but he was beginning to understand simple words.

With these people as his notebook, and from the vantage point only of a pigsty, the Creature had already grasped the sophisticated concepts of "home" and "family." He knew that these people had names for themselves and one another—Felix, Marie, Thomas, Maggie, Grandfather. But the Creature had no name for himself. He knew that the family were not alone in the world, and that he himself was. And all this comprehension was his within a matter of a few days. The power of the Creature's body was being almost overmatched by the lightning power of his brain.

"Come on, then." Marie tried to sound cheerful. If they were going to dig their food from icy ground, they might as well do it right now, before night fell. They stood up; Felix took the hoe and shovel and Marie the baskets, and they left the house.

The Creature reached through the slats and picked up a potato, bringing it inside the sty. Wondering, he turned it over and over in his hands, puzzling over what it might be, and why they thought it was so important.

Out in the fields Felix was hacking furiously at the earth while Marie struggled with a shovel. The ground was covered in a hard frost. Their tools rang almost uselessly against the icy soil.

"The earth's frozen solid," Felix said bitterly. "We haven't the strength to do this. We'd need twenty men to work this field. It's useless." He hurled down his hoe, and his face looked desperate.

Marie straightened up and put a hand to her lower back, which was aching painfully. "We should stop now," she agreed wearily. "It's getting late."

They looked at each other. "We don't have enough to eat," Felix said with anguish in his voice. He hated this, seeing his little family going hungry. It made him feel unmanned and helpless.

"We'll manage," Marie reassured him softly. "Let's go, Felix." They picked up their nearly empty baskets and started wearily on the walk home, their arms around each other. Between them was the dreaded question remained unvoiced—without a crop how were they to survive the winter?

Unseen by them, the Creature was watching everything. Watching and learning.

Later, through the eyehole, the Creature observed the family eating their meager dinner of potatoes and turnips. A glimmer of understanding—this was their food, just as the pig slop was his. He looked at the raw potato he had taken from the cabin, and suddenly it held meaning for him.

He saw Felix and Marie each give up food so that blind Grandfather and the children would have enough. He saw the parents wait until the children had their eyes screwed shut as their grandfather said grace, then they silently slipped extra vegetables from their own plates onto the others'.

"Dear Lord, thank You, for the food You have given us. Thank You for our family. Amen." The old man finished his blessing, and the family ate slowly and silently, aware that this was all the food they would be getting.

Later that night, in the darkness, the Creature hacked away at the soil, using Marie's shovel. Many hours passed, but he did not feel fatigue, only a certain inner happiness. What he was doing felt to him "right."

By morning, all the baskets from the tool shed were stacked to overflowing in front of the little house's door. A bumper crop of root vegetables. Felix and Marie came out and gazed around in joyous wonder. Who could have given them this marvelous gift? Through the slat of the sty, the Creature peered out. Their happiness gave him a feeling of lightness, of joy. He was beginning to feel that he was one of them.

That evening, the meal was much more generous than last night's meal. The family feasted on their bounty of vegetables, and the talk around the table was of nothing but the strange surprise and how it might have come about.

"They must be gifts from the Good Spirit of the Forest," Grandfather said confidently.

But Felix shook his head and looked doubtful.

"Father, nothing in this life comes free of cost. I would like to know who and why."

"Was it, Grandpa, was it?" begged little Maggie. "Was it the Good Spirit?"

The blind man nodded. "I believe it was."

"Will you please stop filling their heads with nonsense," Felix grumbled testily.

"Is it, Mama? Did the Good Spirit give us all this food?" Thomas wanted to know.

Felix and Marie exchanged a look. He was not as amused as she was, but he let it go. How else could they explain it to the children, when they couldn't even explain it to each other? She smiled at the children. "Of course it is. Now eat up before it gets cold."

From his eyehole at the chink in the common wall, the Creature smiled to himself. He knew he had made life easier for these good people.

The next day, in the late afternoon, Grandfather took his cane and his recorder and walked to the pond, where he sat down on a log to enjoy the last rays of the October sun on his face and shoulders, and play his instrument. From the bushes behind him, the Creature crept forward silently to listen, drawn by the simple country tunes. The blind man's acute senses caught his presence, and he turned. But the Creature, not knowing "blind," ran away as swift as a deer. He hid himself back in the bushes again.

"Who's there? Felix? Children?" called Grandfather. But there was no response. The old man felt unsettled; this was not the first time in recent days he had sensed the presence of a stranger. Why would the person not reveal himself? What did he have to hide? Now too nervous to stay, Grandfather got up off his log, pocketed his recorder and walked away. Feeling sad and somehow bereft, the Creature crouched in the bushes and watched him go. He felt a longing to reach out to the old man, but he did not dare.

In the kitchen of the house, Marie was giving her daughter a lesson in reading. There weren't many good daylight hours in November, and it was a shame to waste any of them. At the peephole in the pigsty, the Creature watched with great interest. He saw a slate chalkboard, the word "Friend," unintelligible to him, written on it in chalk. Marie put the board on the table, next to Maggie.

"What's this one?" she quizzed her little girl, pointing to the word.

Maggie's young brows knotted as she sounded the word out. "Ff . . . reh . . . nn . . . nd. Friend?"

Marie grinned, hugging her daughter. "Friend! Well done. Let's do another one, shall we?"

Inside the pigsty, at his chink, the Creature echoed the reading lesson. "Freh . . . nnn . . . nd. Freehhnnnd." He spoke his first human word.

The days began to pass more quickly as the daylight hours grew shorter. The nights all brought frost, and the days were getting much colder, so the children went to the woods with their father to fetch back precious firewood. After several hours Felix's hands were bleeding from chopping lengths of wood from fallen trees, his axe already dulled by the task. At last he could cut no more.

"Children, pile these up. Quickly now, and we'll go home." Thomas and Maggie stacked the cut wood on a litter as their father put on his jacket, exhausted by his effort. With the litter of wood hitched to their cow, Felix and the children walked home slowly.

From inside the sty the Creature looked out to see

Felix stacking the last pile of wood under the eaves. Marie came from behind the house, and took his hands in hers.

"Felix, no more," she said anxiously. "Your hands are bleeding again. I'll bathe them. Come on inside the house."

Felix shook his head bitterly. "This wood is wet. It's useless, it won't burn." It seemed to him that he was getting to be less and less capable of providing for his family's basic needs.

"It doesn't matter," Marie said soothingly. But both of them knew that it mattered a great deal. The small wooden house would not withstand the winter unless it had a plentiful supply of firewood to burn. The house had been cold since October, and in November they had burned the last of their seasoned firewood. Now, in early December, all they could find that would burn was a few dry sticks.

They went inside. The door closed. It didn't occur to the Creature to wonder how he happened to understand almost every word they spoke. But he did. He understood so many things, now. And he could even speak a few words, words he'd seen written in Maggie's lessons, or common words the family spoke to one another. "Friend . . . brread . . . motherrr." He could say these words, and others, too. "Treeeeee." He said "tree" often that night in the forest, as he swung Felix's axe.

The following morning, Felix looked around his front dooryard, amazed. "Marie!" he called in excitement. "Marie! Come here, quickly."

Out of the kitchen, wiping her hands on her apron, Marie came to join her husband at the door. "What is it?"

"Just look." Felix waved his hand around at the yard.

Marie looked. "Jesus, Mary, and Joseph!" she exclaimed piously, crossing herself. The yard was piled high with cords of firewood, neatly cut and stacked. A supply large enough to last the winter.

"What's happening?" gasped Felix.

But it wasn't the time for unanswerable questions; it was the time for rejoicing at their good fortune. First the food, and now this! Wordlessly, they threw their arms around each other and hugged hard. Then they began to collect armfuls of wood to take into the house.

"Come on," laughed Felix, "let's have a fire," and his wife responded happily, "Yes, let's. It will be good to be warm again."

Warm again, thought the Creature, sharing in their joy through the slat in the pigsty wall. *Warm again.*

In the garret in Frau Brach's house Victor Frankenstein was packing, checking to make certain that the cases containing his equipment were secure, giving orders to a waiting servant. Victor was fully recovered now. The last three months had slipped by quickly as he regained his strength and his health. The beard that had grown during his illness was now neatly clipped; it suited him, he thought, and he'd decided to keep it. It made him look older and more like a doctor, gave him an air of mature responsibility, at least in his opinion.

Now he was intent on his instructions. The cases were marked FRANKENSTEIN GENEVA in large, bold letters painted on their sides.

"Now this is very important," he told the servant. "You must travel with them the entire journey. This equipment must not be left unattended."

"Yes, sir."

"My father will personally take delivery of them at Geneva, do you understand?

"I do, sir."

"Good. Thank you." He pressed a gold coin into the servant's palm.

"Going somewhere?" Henry Clerval was just coming in as the servant went out.

"Yes," answered Victor.

Elizabeth, all smiles, rushed across the long room to greet Henry. "Henry, look at the locket Victor gave me, isn't it lovely?"

Henry picked up the locket that was resting on Elizabeth's bosom and examined it. In a gold frame he saw a delicate portrait of Victor, painted on ivory. "Yes, it's lovely. Is this really you?"

"Bad likeness." Victor smiled, moving to him and looking at the locket over Henry's shoulder. "But for now it'll serve instead of a ring."

Aha, an engagement present! Henry Clerval threw his arms around his friend, embracing him. "Congratulations on the entirely expected. When, may I ask?"

Elizabeth joined in, embracing them both. "As soon as we get home. I can't believe we'll be there for New Year's Eve. Victor is going to take over Father's practice."

"And expand it," added Victor.

"I'm going ahead now that the quarantine's been lifted," said Elizabeth. "There's so much to do for the wedding." She was positively radiant with joy and there was a lightness in her step that had been missing during the long days of Victor's illness.

"By the way, the practice needs a partner," Victor said to Henry, grinning widely. "There's not much money. But there's food, board, and lots of good company. It's a perfect position for anyone who's finally passed anatomy. And we were wondering if there was anyone you could recommend."

Elizabeth laid one white hand on Clerval's sleeve. "Please, Henry," she added, and her dark eyes glowed at him.

"Victor, I . . . I . . . don't know what to say. . . ." stammered Henry, deeply moved.

"What you could say is yes."

"Yes." And he added, as Victor's grin widened, "And you write *that* down in your journal."

Remembering, Victor turned pale. "Oh, my God, the journal!" he whispered to himself. That incriminating document. What if someone found it and read it? No, that was impossible. The journal had perished months ago, together with the Creature.

But of course the journal had not perished, and neither had the Creature. Even now the journal was lying in the pigsty straw at his feet as he watched Thomas's reading lesson through his peephole. Young Thomas was struggling with the word "Geneva."

"Gen . . ." the little boy sounded out.

"Come on, you know it," encouraged Felix.

In the sty, the Creature sounded the word out, too. "Gen . . ." And then, amazingly, the Creature finished the word before the children did. ". . . Eva. Geneva."

Geneva. He had seen that word before. The Creature reached down into the straw and picked up the journal. He opened the covers and turned the pages until he reached a page with the words "Family" and "Geneva" written. He ran his index finger across the words as he read out loud, very slowly. "Family . . . Geneva . . ."

Then he made another of his quantum leaps.

Turning to the flyleaf of the journal, he read without hesitation. " 'This is the journal of Victor Frankenstein of Geneva.' " And he remembered the face of the man, which was the first face he had seen. And this greatcoat, which he kept wrapped around himself for warmth; it bore his scent now, but once it had smelled of that man. Victor Frankenstein of Geneva.

And he continued to read, as long as light from the kitchen came through the chink and fell on the pages in the journal.

" 'The first stages of the experiments were thus successfully completed. I was filled with elation. Waldman's vision was not fanatical. The way ahead was clear. His ideas possessed me and I had the skill and determination to pursue them to their ultimate, thrilling execution.' "

He paused, to let the words sink in. Some of them were incomprehensible to him, yet the Creature found that, as he read, certain ideas began to form in his brain from the words on the pages. And, the more he read, the clearer they became.

" 'But, even in this moment of triumph my heart returns often and always to my family and to my own dear Elizabeth, happy and safe in Geneva. I began the final phase of preparation . . .' "

He would go back and read the pages again. And again, until the Creature had them virtually memorized. And, each time he read them, each time the pages unfolded to him, Victor Frankenstein's journal became more and more understandable.

13   Geneva

"Why is it so quiet outside?" Maggie asked suddenly. The others stopped talking to listen. It was true. The world outside the little house had suddenly gone hushed; even the few remaining birds, the starlings and the jays and cardinals, the chickadees who spend every winter in the north, had ceased to chirp. All was silent.

"I know!" cried Thomas, his face alight. The children leaped to their feet in excitement and ran out of the house, banging the front door open. The adults followed as far as the door to watch them.

From the pigsty, the Creature, too, looked out at the dooryard. He drew in his breath in surprise. White flakes were drifting magically down from the heavens. Soft, silent, beautiful. The ground already wore a carpet of white; the Creature had never seen anything so lovely. He smiled as the flakes came down thicker and thicker. Soon the entire world would be white. He poked a few fingers out between the slats and caught a snowflake. But it melted before he could examine it, and all that was left on the Creature's hand was a small patch of moistness.

"Hurray!" yelled Thomas.

"It's snowing!" crowed Maggie. "There will be snow for Christmas!"

"Maggie! Thomas! You'll catch your death!" called Marie anxiously from the doorway.

Grandfather smiled. "Let them play. They'll soon get warm again. There's no shortage of wood for the fire."

Felix shot Marie a look. "You're right about that." She grinned sardonically. "We must thank that Good Spirit of yours." Before she could react, he grabbed Marie around the waist and dragged her shrieking out into the snow. They began to express their jubilation at the coming of the holiday. A snowball fight, wild but at the same time harmless. Together as a family they built a snowman, lumpy and lovable. Felix and Marie danced together in the snow while the children played amid screams of laughter. Christmas would be here in only a few days, and they had a good supply of food and fuel for the winter. Let it snow!

From his pigsty the Creature watched his beloved family cavorting in the whiteness. His face lit up with their shared joy and he said softly to himself, "It's snnowwinng."

The following day, Felix set off with Marie and the children to cut a tree. Bright sunshine was sparkling off the fresh ground cover of snow. Their spirits were high. Felix carried his axe on his right shoulder, with a coil of rope slung over his left. Marie was carrying a basket for winter berries and greens.

"Come on, Papa, hurry up." Thomas tugged impatiently at his father's winter tunic as he danced around under Felix's feet.

"Can I help pick the berries?" pleaded Maggie.

"We can all pick them." Marie smiled.

"And the holly," Thomas put in.

"And the Christmas tree," Maggie added.

"And the mistletoe," said Felix with a twinkle in his eye.

"What's mistletoe?" demanded Maggie.

"Ask your father," Marie said primly, looking a bit embarrassed, yet pleased nonetheless. She loved her husband very much, and welcomed his kisses always, mistletoe or no mistletoe.

"What is it?" Thomas asked his father.

"Ask your Mother," Felix replied maddeningly. "Now come on, no more questions. I'll race you . . ." And they ran happily into the forest.

That evening, the Creature gazed through the chink in the wall, and his scarred face lit up with wonder. Inside the house stood an evergreen tree, a dazzling vision of ornaments and light. His first Christmas tree. The house resounded with joy and song. Grandfather was playing his recorder by a roaring fire. The family was singing "Silent Night." The Creature had never seen them so happy. They seem to him transformed into magical beings by their joyousness. Just as the small balsam tree had been transformed into an object of reverence.

"Most beautiful . . . tree . . ." he whispered, and he, too, felt happy in his soul.

Suddenly, he saw the children go dashing across the room. The Creature moved from his eyehole to the pigsty slats as the door opened, throwing a spill of warm light out onto the snow.

The mother and father looked out of the door.

"Come back quickly," Marie called after them, "before you catch cold."

The children set something out in the snow. They called out into the darkness, "Merry Christmas!"

"Come on, time for bed," Felix told them, and Thomas and Maggie ran back inside the house. The door closed. The Creature crept from his sty and scurried closer to investigate. He found a covered plate sitting on the snow, with the children's slate beside it. On the slate was chalked a child's rendering of a glowing angel and a message. The Creature held the slate up to where light from the house could fall on it, and read the message out.

" 'For the . . . Goood Spirr-rit . . . of the . . . Forr-rest.' "

Picking up the plate, he took off the red cloth cover. On it was a red silk flower and a wonderful array of Christmas cookies. The Creature sniffed at the flower and the cookies and then hurried back with his precious burden toward his sty. He had not been forgotten. For the first time he thought he might even be a part of this family.

The following morning, Felix, Marie, and Thomas went to the woods, Felix to set traps for some small game, and the others to gather more Christmas berries and evergreens. Maggie was left alone with Grandfather. As soon as they were gone, she scampered into the dooryard to see if the Good Spirit had come for his cookies in the night.

Yes! He had, he had! The only thing left behind was the red cloth that had covered the plate. She picked the cloth up from the snow and stood gawping at it in wonder. Then it was true what Grandfather said; the Good Spirit *was* real.

A huge shadow suddenly fell across her, and Maggie squinted up. The sun was so dazzling on the fresh snow that she could only make out the shadowy outline of somebody large standing beside the snowman. She couldn't see his features.

"Are you the Good Spirit of the Forest?" she asked in wonder.

The landlord, Herr Koretz, smiled sardonically. "Not exactly. Where's your father?"

When the child didn't reply, the landlord bent down and grabbed her face, squeezing her round cheeks cruelly. Maggie squealed in pain.

"I said, where's your father?" He squeezed harder.

Roused by Maggie's cry. Grandfather appeared at the door. Seeing him, the landlord let go of Maggie, who darted off into the woods calling for her mother.

"Who's there?" called Grandfather blindly. "Maggie?"

"No! Not Maggie."

Grandfather stood listening intently as the landlord trudged up to him. Now the old man knew the identity of his visitor. He'd heard that step often enough. There was cruelty and arrogance even in the way Herr Koretz walked.

"Oh, it's you," the old man said defiantly. "Herr Koretz. What have you done to Maggie!"

The landlord tried to peer past Grandfather into the cottage doorway. He was looking for Felix. "Is he in there?" he demanded. "Hiding behind a blind old man?"

"My son is in the fields," said Grandfather stiffly. "They all are. When he returns, he'll pay you."

"I don't like to be kept waiting. Let's see what you've got lying around in there." The landlord tried to brush past Grandfather and get into the cottage. But Grandfather stood his ground, wildly brandishing his cane.

"Get away!" the blind man yelled. "Get away from here!"

Stepping behind Grandfather, the landlord tripped him up and grabbed his cane. The old man plunged face forward into the snow. Jabbing the cane into his back, the landlord snarled, "Don't blame me. Blame your son for not paying his rent on time!"

The landlord raised the cane and took a mean swipe at the head of the snowman. Then he turned to enter the house, but he stopped dead in his tracks with a cry of astonishment mingled with abject terror.

The doorway was filled by the massive frame of the Creature. Herr Koretz gazed up at the hideous figure, paralyzed by fear. His mouth opened and closed, opened and closed, but no sound came out. The Creature lifted the landlord bodily into the air and jammed his head through the overhanging porch thatch. And then he flung him, like a rag doll, into the snow.

Screaming hysterically, Herr Koretz pelted away into the woods, running for his life. Grandfather started to get to his feet. Hesitating for a moment, the Creature bent to help him and handed him back his cane.

In the woods Felix was laying traps, while Marie and Thomas collected berries and placed them in their baskets.

"I bet I can pick more berries than you can," Marie teased her son.

A sudden scream echoed across the countryside. Felix looked up from his traps, startled. Marie dropped her basket and ran to her husband. Mutely, her eyes searched for his. They held the same fear as hers. Their little girl and her blind old Grandfather, left behind alone, helpless.

"My God! No!" cried Felix. He ran toward the

house at top speed, with Marie and Thomas behind him.

Still breathless after his ordeal, Grandfather was standing by the fire to warm his old bones. The Creature remained behind on the doorsill. He didn't dare come into the house.

"Thank you, my friend, thank you so much. Won't you come and sit by the fire? Please?" Grandfather turned his blind face to the doorway.

The blind man caught a whiff of pigsty, and he recognized his savior by the scent and the sound of him. He knew that this was the man who had been lurking for some time around the small cottage, but who had never done any of them any harm. In fact, he probably had done them a great deal of good, for Grandfather had an inkling of just who the Good Spirit of the Woods might really be.

He beckoned, and sat down before the fire himself, on one of the two facing settles. He patted the seat as an invitation, but the Creature didn't move.

"Come in, please. Don't be afraid," the old man urged. "Come and warm yourself. Please come in. There's only me here, you mustn't be shy."

Very slowly, hesitating with every step, the Creature came in and sat down facing him. The warmth of the fire felt good to him.

"That's better." Grandfather smiled. "I'm glad you finally came in. A man shouldn't have to hide in the shadows."

"Better that way . . . for me," answered the Creature.

"Why?" The old man turned his blind face toward the sound of the rough voice, as though he could learn what he wanted to know merely from the sound of the other's words.

"I'm . . . very . . . people are afraid. Except you."

Grandfather smiled sweetly. "It can't be as bad as that," he said in an encouraging tone.

"Worse . . . worse," the Creature said in a very low voice. He felt unutterably sad; nobody had ever spoken gently to him before, nobody had ever been kind to him, and the generosity of this blind old man had touched a deep well of emotion in the Creature, which took him completely by surprise, and which he found difficult to deal with.

As they neared the house, Marie and Felix saw Maggie running to them. When she reached them, she ran straight into Felix's arms and held her father tight.

"Papa! Papa! He hurt Grandpa!" the little girl wailed.

Felix turned pale. "Who hurt Grandpa!" he demanded.

"What was that noise?" asked Marie.

"Who hurt Grandpa?" Thomas chimed in.

"Tell me what that noise was!" Felix sounded angry.

"What happened?" shrieked Marie.

This was all too much for little Maggie. She wanted to say "Herr Koretz, the landlord," but everybody was yelling at her at once, asking questions from all sides, and the child was frightened and confused. Nervous tears stung her eyes and began to roll down her cheeks.

"Try to remember what happened!" urged Felix.

"Is Grandfather all right?" Marie asked again.

"Who hurt Grandpa?" persisted Thomas. But Maggie, crying now, was too upset to tell.

There was no time for any more questions. Grandfather was in danger. Felix and his family began running back to the house through the forest.

"Father! Father!" cried the young farmer.

"We're coming!" his wife called.

"I can see you with my hands," Grandfather said very gently. "If you'll trust me."

Instinctively, the Creature jerked his head back from the seeking hands, but changed his mind, deciding to trust. He eased forward so that the old man could reach him.

Grandfather ran his sensitive fingers over his features, feeling the network of jagged scars and the lumpy, puckered skin. At last, he took his hand away. The old man's voice was very gentle as he asked, "You poor man. Have you no friends?"

"There are some people," said the Creature slowly, thinking of the little family, "but they don't know me."

"Do they live close by?" asked Grandfather. He took the Creature's hand into his own.

"Yes. Very close."

"Why do you not go to them?"

How could he tell the old man? How could the Creature reveal that he had been hiding here, spying on them, for how long he didn't know, but surely months. Or was this his chance? Would it be now that he'd be welcomed into the family as the Good Spirit, just as he must have been when the silk flower and the delicious cookies had been left out for him? Emotions were swirling around his brain. Tell or not tell? Speak or remain silent?

"I have been . . . afraid," he began tentatively. "I am afraid . . . they will hate me . . . because I am so very ugly . . . and they are so very beautiful."

Grandfather took the other hand in his, and

masked his surprise at the difference in size between the Creature's two hands. It was as though they'd come from two different individuals. All he said was, "People can be kinder than you think."

But the Creature shook his head. "I am afraid," he said simply.

"Perhaps I can help," the old man said quietly.

Kindness, which the Creature had never before experienced, now took his breath away. He felt a strange constriction in his chest and a thickening in his throat. His eyes welled up with tears as he tried to get the words out.

"I ll-love them . . . so vv-very much," he said at last with an enormous effort. "I want . . . I want . . . them to be my ff-family. I ll-love them ss-so very mm-mm-mmuch. . . ."

Felix raced in through the door, his family trailing. He cried out as he saw a sight horrible enough to chill the blood. A hideous creature, scarred and misshapen, had burst into their home and was holding his blind old father tightly by the hands. Thank God Grandfather was still alive! Felix let out a roar of fury.

The Creature turned eagerly to them, but he shrank back when he saw Felix grab up an iron poker and rush at him. The young farmer began hitting him hard across the back. The Creature cried out in pain and tried to move away.

"Get out! You're a monster, get out!" Felix shouted, flailing away with the poker.

"No!" begged the Creature. He scuttled toward the corner of the room with Felix in pursuit.

The children and Marie rushed to their grandfather as Felix continued to beat the shrieking Creature around the room. The Creature crashed into the Christmas tree, knocking it down. Grandfather stood

up from his settle and raised his feeble old voice
to protest.

"Leave him alone! No, leave him—"

But in the bedlam nobody paid any attention to
the words of the old man. The Creature was screaming under the hard blows, writhing in agony; Felix
was hurling curses at the monster's head even as he
was making his attack on the monster's unprotected
body. The children, crying loudly, were hiding behind their grandfather. The old man was dazed and
shouting incoherently, while Marie stood tugging on
his arm.

It was a madhouse. The family's screams unnerved the Creature even more than the painful beating. Loud, angry, and fearful voices—how they terrified him! Here he'd thought he was safe from them,
but he'd been wrong. He had to get out of here.

At last the Creature managed to roll away across
the floor, out from under the brutal beating; he stood
up and ran out the door.

Felix watched him go, then he turned urgently to
his family. "We have to leave here! Now! Before that
inhuman thing returns!"

The family, panic-stricken, began to gather up
some belongings, only what they could carry. They
recognized the peril of their situation. A monster had
invaded their home, and had almost killed a helpless
blind man. God alone knew what he would do to the
rest of them when he returned!

Bleeding and sobbing, his greatcoat billowing behind him, the Creature ran blindly toward the
woods, to get away from the screams. He ran until
he could run no more, until the breath rasped in
his lungs.

He stopped at last, leaning against a tree, trying
to catch his breath. He sank to his knees, hands

clutched to his chest, and bowed his head in misery, weeping. That they should have beaten him and shouted at him, called him "monster!" His own family, his! Then he pulled the little red silk flower from the cuff of his coat. It lay glittering in his huge, misshapen palm. The flower, yes. The gift to the Good Spirit. If they saw it again, then they would know. They would understand where the firewood and the good food had come from. He must show them. With the decision, the Creature's heart felt lighter; he stood and ran back toward the clearing.

The sky was brewing; another snow storm was on the way and would be here before nightfall. The Creature ran across the dooryard toward the house, breathless, holding his palm out with the silk flower in it.

"It's me! It's mmmmeeeeee! Look!"

But there was nothing. Nothing. No sound, no movement, no people, no animals. The Creature's eyes went wide, first with surprise and then with fear. He dashed into the house and stood in the doorway. The room was empty. The family's possessions were scattered and most of them had been left behind. Books, clothes, even the old man's recorder. On the floor, the beautiful tree was smashed and the ornaments broken.

"No! No . . . noo," cried the Creature, devastated. Alone. He was alone again. The beautiful family was gone, driven away by his ugliness. They feared and hated his ugliness, just as everybody did. His ugliness . . .

He raced into the sty. The pigs were gone, but the Creature didn't even notice. He grabbed up the journal he kept hidden there. With mounting apprehension he turned the pages until he found what he was looking for: it was Victor's sketch of his "patchwork man." The Creature gazed at the drawing for a long time, his eyes going wider. Revelation was slowly dawning until at last, the Creature understood everything. He dropped the journal, clawing at his coat in a surge of panic, wrenching it open to reveal his chest. He saw the massive suture scars down his torso in an exact match of the drawing.

This was he, and he was this, not a human being but an experiment. Something created out of bits and pieces of human flesh, something created to be despised, reviled, driven away by everyone, something without a friend, something without a right to live, without a soul. The man whose face he remembered was his creator, who had brought him into being and then fled away in horror, leaving him helpless.

From the very depths of himself came an unearthly moan, deep and chilling, then the Creature threw his head back and howled, an animalistic primal scream.

He knew what he had to do, and where he had to go.

The Creature hurried back to the house, and frantically stuffed various objects such as books, the recorder, and a couple of animal skins, into a battered satchel. He worked quickly, intently, scowling. When he had finished, when he had taken everything he wanted and needed, he started on the rest of the work.

He broke up furniture until it was little more than sticks, and piled it up into a bonfire inside the house. He took a pan of oil from a trivet standing in the fireplace which was still glowing hot and poured it over the pile, throwing the pan down as well. Then he lit a torch and set fire to the pile of smashed wood and family possessions. As the fire caught and the flames leaped up, the Creature stood back, his eyes on the colorful dancing fire.

When the fire began to spread to the rest of the house the Creature left the cottage and stood outside, watching the house burn. The flames rose higher, reaching the thatch of the roof, which was quickly engulfed. The family's cottage, through the wall of which the Creature had witnessed so many acts of love and kindness, where he had learned to speak and read, was soon completely consumed by the fire. At last it was nothing more than a pile of smoldering ashes.

This part was over, but his work was only beginning. The Creature turned his face up to look toward the dark night sky and, raising his arms above his head, gave a name to his rage.

"FRANKENSTEIN!"

He kept away from cities and farms. He avoided habitations and people, and, especially, dogs who could scent him. Walking mostly through forests and down shallow streams that would cover his tracks and footsteps, he headed southwest. In his memory only one face burned, and only one destination sent him onward. Frankenstein. Geneva.

He moved very swiftly, more swiftly than a man on horseback who would have to stop for rest and a night's sleep. The Creature didn't stop to rest. He was hungry, but he discovered that he could do without food for very long stretches of time if he had to. Sometimes he came upon small animals, rabbits and squirrels, and he caught them and ate them raw without stopping. For water, there were always the streams. If he wasn't near water, he'd eat handfuls of snow to quench his thirst. There was plenty of snow, for the winter had come in hard. But what was snow or hunger or thirst or fatigue compared with the burning in his brain?

At last he reached the Alps. Oddly enough, he felt at home here, traversing the glacier with a walking staff, his greatcoat streaking out behind him in the wind. These endless wastes of snow, the silent majesty of these mountains were somehow soothing to the Creature. Up here, anybody would be lonely; up here one would not have to be hideously scarred and patched together to be solitary. He even welcomed the cold air and the strong winds, because they kept other people away from the Alps. Cold was his element, not theirs.

From the Mont Blanc glacier he looked down toward where a large city lay nestled in the mountains' shadow, built around a glittering lake. The sight of the city made the Creature scowl in anger.

"Geneva," he growled in his throat savagely. "Geneva."

It was late in the day when Elizabeth arrived home from Ingolstadt, but everyone ran down the front steps to meet her. They had been listening for her carriage wheels for hours.

How glad she was to be home at last, how happy to see all those beloved faces! And how happy to see their reactions to the wonderful news she had written them—that Victor was entirely well, that he would be following very soon, that they were engaged and were planning to be married within a short time.

"She's here! She's here!" Willie cried, as he was the first one down the steps, the first to see Elizabeth being handed down from the carriage by the footman. "We got your letter! We got your letter! It's the first one I was allowed to read."

Laughing, Elizabeth picked him up and hugged him.

"It's wonderful news, my dear," Dr. Frankenstein said, kissing her on both cheeks.

Justine approached her somewhat shyly. "Congratulations, Elizabeth. I'm happy for you."

Elizabeth understood how much pain the words must have cost Justine, yet she knew the girl was sincere. "Thank you, Justine," she said simply.

"Is that the locket?" Justine examined Victor's portrait, which was hanging around Elizabeth's neck on a fine gold chain. Drawing the chain over her bonnet, Elizabeth handed the locket to Justine.

"Congratulations," added Mrs. Moritz.

"Thank you, Mrs. Moritz."

Justine showed the portrait to Willie. "He looks so handsome."

The boy took the locket into his own hands. "Elizabeth? Can I take this to show my friend Peter?"

"Willie, it's not a toy," Elizabeth reproved him gently. But William was already tearing off down the lawn with the locket in his fist.

"Oh, let him go," Dr. Frankenstein said indulgently. He shouted after his son. "William, don't dawdle. It will be dark soon!" Then he turned to Elizabeth. "Let me look at you. Today I am the happiest father in the world." Elizabeth gave him a warm hug and they moved off together into the house.

Willie raced down the gravel drive away from the house as the carriage pulled away toward the stables. He was heading into the miles of wooded acreage behind the house. It was his favorite shortcut to Peter's house.

As soon as Elizabeth's trunks were unpacked, revealing the riot of white silks and laces she had purchased in Ingolstadt, the ballroom was requisitioned for the fitting of the wedding dress, because, between the high windows and the huge chandeliers, it always had the most light available. With the marriage celebration so close at hand, the construction of the dress commanded top priority. In no time, the vast room was bustling with activity.

The bride-to-be stood on a table in front of a huge mirror as her wedding dress was fitted. Justine and Mrs. Moritz were kneeling on the table sewing a part of the train, working urgently, but laughing and conversing. Justine wielded needle and thread while her mother held the fabric steady. Justine looked up at Elizabeth, which caused her a momentary loss of concentration. By accident, she drove her needle into Mrs. Moritz's thumb.

"Justine, you idiot!" the housekeeper shouted brutally. The girl's clumsiness was a sore point with her mother, who felt little more than contempt for Justine. "Pay attention! Anyone would think that you're the one who's getting married!"

"Yes, Mother," Justine answered tightly.

Elizabeth sensed that the girl was upset. "What's wrong?" she asked, genuinely concerned.

"Nothing," Justine said with her eyes averted. Then she saw that Elizabeth was really worried, and she softened. "Really," she added. "Really nothing."

"Just leave it," snapped her mother. "You've ruined it now." But, under her breath to Justine, she hissed, "How I loathe you. I absolutely loathe you." How could she have given birth to a dolt like Justine? Why couldn't she have a daughter as beautiful and clever as Elizabeth?

Despite his father's caution not to dawdle, William Frankenstein did dawdle along as children do, the precious locket clutched in his hands where he could admire it. He could hardly wait to show his big brother's portrait off to his friend Peter. Even so, he didn't hurry. Instead, he stopped to cut a thin switch from a tree with the little silver pocket knife of which he was so proud, and continued walking, using the switch to slice at the branches in his way.

Faint tones of music came to him suddenly, carried on the breeze, eerie and flutelike. A recorder. Willie paused, his ears pricked, listening. He began to follow the sounds farther into the woods.

Inside the grand ballroom of the mansion Elizabeth was now trying on her basted-together wedding dress, while Mrs. Moritz bustled around her with pins, making the last adjustments to the fitting. No longer needed, Justine was standing apart and alone, as usual. Her heart was in her eyes, which looked with envy on Elizabeth's charm, vivacity, and beauty, and most of all, she envied Victor's love for her. At that moment, Dr. Frankenstein came into the ballroom with Claude. Both men looked worried.

"Elizabeth, have you seen Willie?" asked her father, his face grave.

"Isn't he back yet?" Instinctively, Elizabeth glanced at the gilded baroque clock on the mantel. It was later than she'd supposed. Time had flown by with the alterations to her wedding dress taking up all her attention.

"No, Claude rode over there to Peter's to see if he'd lost track of time. They say he never arrived."

Never arrived, and soon it would be dark. "It's far too late for him to still be out," Elizabeth said anxiously. She followed Dr. Frankenstein out of the ballroom, Justine trailing after them. What were they to do? They had to look for Willie, of course. The servants and the tenant farmers would help, but

Elizabeth insisted on going along and Justine would not be left behind. Elizabeth slipped out of her wedding gown, and Mrs. Moritz gathered it up. She stood in her silk underwear, but she had not time to dress. She would just throw on her cloak.

"You don't look well, Father," Elizabeth told the old man gently. "It might be better if you stayed here."

But Dr. Frankenstein wouldn't hear of remaining behind. Little Willie, who reminded him so much like his beloved lost Caroline, was his heart's darling, his joy in his old age. How could he not go out looking for him? His son might be in trouble!

Out in the countryside, a massive search was soon organized and in progress. People fanned out, scouring the fields on horse and on foot, shouting William's name.

"William! . . . Willie! . . . Everybody spread out . . . some of you go and check by the bridge . . ." Claude was the search leader.

"WILLIE!" shouted Elizabeth, who was in the van of the search party. She heard thunder in the distance. A storm was approaching. They had to find the little boy before it started to rain. He was only eight years old, and there was a good chance he would not survive a night out of doors in the wet bitter cold. Where could he have gone?

Dr. Frankenstein was forced to quit the search before it had gone very far. His face was gray with pain and his breathing had become labored. Mrs. Moritz, who was on the watch, saw him return unwell, and rushed forward to help him into the house. As they started up the front steps to the mansion, they heard the clattering of horses' hooves. Victor came riding up with Henry Clerval.

"Father," Victor cried out warmly. "I'm so pleased to see you." Dismounting, he ran to hug his father, but stopped dead as he saw Dr. Frankenstein taking off his wig. The old man's head was covered in sweat, and the look on his face told the story.

"What's wrong?" Victor gasped.

Willie heard the music long before he saw anything. Distant, sweet, delicate, the tune carried through the trees as though wood nymphs were playing on pipes. The little boy couldn't help but be drawn to it. It seemed to be coming from the pond, and he pushed branches out of his face and stepped over fallen logs until he came into view of the pond. A figure was sitting half concealed among the tall reeds, gazing off across the water and playing a simple country air on his wooden wind instrument with oddly pleasing dissonance. Willie drew closer, curious. He didn't want to intrude, he just wanted to listen to the pretty music. The figure in the reeds still hadn't noticed him.

And then, abruptly, the man's head whipped around. Although he was bundled in a large greatcoat, the man's face could be seen clearly. They stared at each other for a moment, child and Creature. Willie gasped in terror. He'd never seen anything like this hideous monster in his life! It was much worse than his worst nightmare. As the monster in the reeds lunged to its feet, the boy turned and ran.

It was standing up! It was taking steps! It was going to come after him! "No!" Willie screamed and ran as fast as he could. Branches whipped into his face and twigs poked him sharply, tearing at his clothing. But the boy didn't stop.

"Wait! Don't be afraid!" the Creature called after him. He would never harm a child. Why didn't anybody understand that? He didn't mean harm to anybody . . . except one man. Except the creator, who had done this to him, made him so ugly that little children ran away in fear.

But the boy kept running. He didn't dare look back over his shoulder. Soon he was out of sight. Sadly, the Creature came shambling up from the pond. He was sorry he had frightened the child; he meant no harm. Seeing something lying in the grass, he picked up the fallen object. As he got back up to his feet, he found himself staring at the locket that Willie had dropped in his flight. He opened it and examined the small painting if contained.

He knew that face. He'd seen it on the day he was created. It was the first face to show him that look of horror he had come to hate so much. Victor Frankenstein. The Creature raised his gaze after the fleeing boy.

"Frankenstein. . . ." he muttered, and he felt the rage rising within him. "Frankenstein!"

The Creature started after William, the locket clenched in his fist. His anger was going out of control. His teeth ground together as his fury built; his eyes were wild, rolling in his head. The Creature moved very quickly, and little Willie's childish legs were so short. They took such small steps. He would be easy to catch.

14 Mont Blanc

Justine had been lost in these woods for more than an hour. She was alone, angry, wandering first here and then there, anxious and upset. She had separated from the search party, knowing that William had a shortcut to Peter's somewhere around here. But she couldn't find the shortcut and she couldn't find the boy. Her mother's contemptuous words still burned in her ears; *why does she hate me so much?* Justine never understood the reason for Mrs. Moritz's sudden flashes of rage against her. Her mother was a total enigma. Sometimes, the woman was affectionate and kindly to her daughter, but at other times she turned into a virago, cursing at Justine and wishing her dead. Now she was lost, and it was beginning to rain hard. Suppose she never got back; would her mother even care?

"I hate her, I hate her!" Justine muttered to herself. "I want this to stop. Why does she do this?" She raised her voice again, letting it echo through the woods. "WILLIE! THIS ISN'T A GAME!" Justine desperately wanted to be the one to find Willie and bring him home safe; then her mother, who was devoted to the Frankenstein family, would have to acknowledge her value and give her some respect. "WILLIE!"

But it was raining too hard now for her to go on. It had become a real thunderstorm. Ahead of her, Justine could dimly see a large old barn, lashed by rain and lightning. She made for it, hoping it would be warm and dry; maybe even Willie was sheltering there.

Hours passed. The rain was coming down much harder now, and the trees offered little shelter. The Creature was wet through and through; water had even seeped through his greatcoat, and he was chilled and very uncomfortable. He went in search of an empty place he could hide in until the rain stopped.

A barn. The Creature smiled; he liked barns. He enjoyed the smell of the hay and the quiet movements of the animals. The cows didn't know he was hideous. Goats and sheep didn't flinch back from him in terror or disgust. He crept quietly inside and looked for a place to lie down.

But the barn wasn't empty. Justine was lying asleep in the haymow. Haggard, wet, exhausted, she, too, had found shelter here from the lightning and the rain.

The Creature turned to flee, but something held him back. He turned to look at her again; she was so pretty. She reminded him of Marie, and he remembered the sweet caresses Marie and Felix always exchanged. Those touches, which set the man and woman apart from the others and joined them in intimacy, always gave the Creature a special feeling, and he felt it again now when he saw the sleeping girl. He moved closer to her, very silently, afraid she might wake up, but Justine was sleeping very deeply, and she didn't stir.

The Creature loomed over her, gazing on her beauty, a monstrous shape of darkness occasionally lit up by flashes of lightning. His hand reached down, hovering reverently, feeling desires he had not felt before, strongly wishing to caress the swell of her young white breasts at the neckline of her bodice. But he didn't touch her. Instead he gave her a gift as gratitude for her beauty; he no longer needed the locket with Victor's picture, so he laid it gently on her arm.

Looking at Justine, a new idea entered the Creature's mind. Perhaps he had relieved his blood-lust and wanted no more killing. Perhaps he now saw the revelations in Victor's journal in a somewhat different light. There were new possibilities to explore. Thinking hard, he got to his feet and went back out into the storm.

A driving rain lashed the environs of Geneva, and heavy winds came down from the Alps bringing a sharp, bitter cold. The search had gone on for hours now, and nobody had yet found Willie. Victor and Henry completed a sweeping search of their assigned segment, finding nothing, and returned to the mansion to report, and to find out if anybody else had spotted the boy. Dr. Frankenstein and Mrs. Moritz were waiting at their post at the front door; nothing could persuade the old man to go upstairs to bed until he was certain his William was safe.

"I've checked the East Ridge. There's nothing

there," Victor shouted into the rain, which was carrying his words away.

Suddenly, through the gloom, they saw a figure moving toward them. It was Elizabeth, with only a cloak thrown over her silken undergarments, emerging from the woods. She came to a stop in the downpour at the far edge of the lawn, suddenly revealed drenched and weeping by the flashes of lightning. She was holding a dark bundle in her arms.

"Elizabeth? *Elizabeth!*" Victor started to run toward her across the lawn, with Henry, Claude, and Mrs. Moritz close behind him, and Dr. Frankenstein following more slowly. Elizabeth staggered on, her knees buckling under her burden. It was Willie in her arms, his bright new clothing all muddy, the boy's arms hanging limp, his head dangling back. His neck was obviously broken.

"I found him . . . I found him . . ." sobbed Elizabeth, distraught. Victor reached her first as the others crowded around, crushing and jostling as she collapsed into Victor's arms, cradling William to the muddy ground. The golden curls of the child's head were dark with rain, and his face was wet with raindrops and Elizabeth's tears.

And then Father was there, shoving his way through. Seeing his dead boy, he screamed and, clutching his chest, collapsed in the muck. Henry and Mrs. Moritz, Claude and the other servants rushed to surround him, lifting him and carrying the unconscious man home. This was by far the worst day in the annals of the Frankenstein family since the night Caroline died.

They brought Dr. Frankenstein home and put him to bed in the large bedroom he once shared with Caroline. For a long time he didn't regain consciousness. When he opened his eyes at last it was only to moan feebly at the recollection of his precious little son lying dead in the rain. Then his eyes shut again, and he muttered incoherently. He was gravely ill. In his silent room, with the only sound the soft ticking of the clock, Henry Clerval tenderly ministered to his patient.

"We did everything we could, sir. Rest now, just rest now. We did everything we could. . . ."

But Dr. Frankenstein was too ill to hear.

Downstairs, Elizabeth sat dazed, her face ashen. She was still in shock and was having a great deal of trouble holding herself together. Finding her baby brother dead was a nightmare from which she would never recover. Who could murder an innocent child like Willie? She couldn't imagine anything so brutal.

Victor stood beside her, lending as much support as he could while dealing with his own grief. On the long ride from Germany to Switzerland, all he could think of was his happiness, of his coming marriage to Elizabeth, of his practicing medicine with his father and his closest friend. It seemed to Victor that the future held nothing but joy. And then, the minute he arrived, to find this instead! His family in disarray, his home shattered, his brother dead, his father possibly dying! Where was happiness now?

All he could do was cling tightly to Elizabeth's hand, reassuring her of his presence.

Mrs. Moritz came into the parlor, her eyes swimming with tears. "Sir, oh, sir! I'm terrified for my girl. She's still out looking for William." Her words came out in a torrent. "You know how she adored him. We parted badly, you see, I was cruel to her. I didn't mean it. Sometimes I can't seem to stop myself. I think she finds it very hard now, with your wedding. She loves you dearly. I couldn't bear it if anything happened to her. Please help me—"

"We'll organize another search now that it's light enough," Victor replied gently. "We'll find her, Mrs. Moritz, I promise."

Henry came down from Dr. Frankenstein's room and drew Victor aside, conferring with him in whispers. Elizabeth turned to them.

"How is Father?" she asked in an anxious voice.

"His heart is breaking," Henry answered simply.

There was a loud, urgent knocking at the front door. Victor went to see who it was, and Henry moved over to take Elizabeth's hand in his friend's place. She was still trembling from her ordeal.

A footman opened the door. Victor saw a uniformed militiaman hovering outside, his face grim. "Mr. Frankenstein, we've apprehended the murderer. Not five miles from here, hiding in a barn." The militiaman reached into his jacket pocket and produced the locket. "We found this on her, it is yours, I believe? Sir, you must come immediately, the townspeople have gone mad—"

They left at once on horseback, Victor, Elizabeth who insisted on coming along, and the militiaman. Within minutes they were in the heart of Geneva, in the town square. A large crowd, buzzing with fury, rushed past them. They heard angry shouting from all directions.

"My God, what are they doing?" gasped Elizabeth.

The militiaman looked grave. "They must have broken into the jail."

"For God's sake, man, can't you stop this!" Victor cried.

"They've gone wild. This is a lynching mob." The militiaman shook his head. Suddenly a door flew open and a crowd of men surged through it, dragging out a screaming Justine. The girl looked as terrified as a young deer facing a hunter's bow.

"Justine!!" shouted Elizabeth and Victor, running toward her.

The Calvinist minister was with them, trying to stay close to Justine to protect her, shouting to make his voice heard over the angry mob.

"No! no! I beseech you! This is unlawful!" the minister pleaded, but the crowd of angry people paid him no attention, pushing him aside. As Victor and Elizabeth tried to get closer to Justine, the mob shoved them away viciously. Many hands picked the girl up and carried her above the crowd, passing her along. There were ear-shattering shouts of "child killer!" and "Hang her! Hang her!" As Justine was dragged along, others in the mob fought to get at her, to beat her with their fists and kick her. Elizabeth and Victor ran desperately on the outskirts of the crowd, trying to get closer to her.

"JUSTINE!" Victor belowed.

She heard his voice and her wild, frightened eyes searched for him in the mob, and found him. As soon as she saw him, Justine burst into hysterical pleading, sobbing "Victor! Help me! I was going to find him. I was looking for him everywhere. He must be there for the wedding. I went to the lake, but it was dark. He's such a baby. He's so tiny. I'm sorry. Forgive me—"

By now the mob had dragged her up some narrow steps in a high wall. In a minute she appeared at the top of the wall, pinned between two burly men. Screaming and struggling, she was pushed to her knees. The men put a noose around her neck.

"No!" cried Elizabeth. "Victor, don't let them! Do

something!" But Victor was helpless, trapped in the crowd, unable to get closer.

Mrs. Moritz and Claude ran into the square. When she saw her daughter, the woman screamed out her name. "Justine! Justine, my child!"

Now the men on top of the high wall pulled Justine back up to her feet and, without ceremony, without a last word from the condemned, without the comforting presence of a man of God, they threw her off.

"NO!" cried Victor. "Justine!" Elizabeth sobbed. She sank, half fainting, against Victor's shoulder.

As the girl hung there, dying, the mob cheered lustily. One of Justine's shoes flew off, and the yelling crowd started to throw stones at it and at Justine's body.

Mrs. Moritz ran to the swaying body, trying, unsuccessfully, to grab it. Her face was desperate, and there was a mad glint in her eyes. "Justine, come down now! Let's go home now. There's a good girl. Leave her alone! Come down now, we'll go home now."

The crowd, coarsely jeering and catcalling, was enjoying this madly grotesque display of bereavement. They continued to throw rocks at Mrs. Moritz and Justine's body. There was a real danger now that the woman might be seriously injured. Claude rushed to grab Mrs. Moritz and lead her away, just as the mob surrounded the body and made a grab for it.

"She's my baby," the woman sobbed to Claude. "She's my only little girl."

As Elizabeth wept on his shoulder, Victor Frankenstein just stood there staring. He couldn't understand why Justine would want to kill Willie, when she'd looked after him like a loving older sister for all the little boy's life. Was Mrs. Moritz right? Had she

been in love with him? Did she kill his baby brother
in a fit of jealous rage over his wedding to another?
Was he somehow responsible for Justine's homicidal
insanity? There would never be a solution to the
mystery, he thought. He sighed deeply, and took
Elizabeth's arm firmly, leading her away from the
ghastly scene.

Another storm was gathering. Lightning flashes
in the distance presaged long, low rumbles of thunder. Victor crossed the lawn, his heart heavy. Would
there ever be an end to the horrors that were stalking
his family? Claude was waiting for him.

"Claude," he acknowledged.

"We have cut her down, sir," Claude said sadly.
"We can bury her in the morning."

Poor Justine. At least her travail was over now.
"Thank you, Claude. Get to bed." He moved with
slow, dragging footsteps up to the house when,
suddenly, a heavy strong hand grabbed his shoulder.

"Frankenstein." His name was spoken close to
his ear. Victor whirled. There was a sudden flash of
lightning and the sky brightened for a second. Victor
found himself looking up into a hideously scarred
face, a face he never expected to see again, the face
of his creation. He stared in wordless horror. Alive?
Here? How was this possible?

The Creature raised his arm. "I will wait for you
there," he said quietly, pointing upward. Lightning
danced in the sky, illuminating Mont Blanc with a
crackling halo of electricity. Darkness fell again, and
the Creature vanished.

Victor fell gasping. His head was spinning with
questions, but, through the vortex of questions, some
answers emerged, terrible, inexorable. Willie. Justine.
He realized now what must have happened. Guilt

and shame flooded over him. Rising to his knees, he bowed his head. "Oh, God. My brother. Justine. Forgive me."

All, all of these dreadful events were his own fault. On his head was the sole responsibility for the death of two people, innocents, beloved to him. And, if his father died, that would make three deaths for which he, Victor Frankenstein, would bear the guilt. Three people who would have lived except for his own stubborn recklessness. How could he have assumed—without a shred of proof—that the Creature was dead? How could he have just walked away from his shattered laboratory without a backward look?

Never counting consequences, Victor Frankenstein had driven himself onward, with reanimation the only thing in his mind. All he wanted was to be first to conquer the unknown, the first to show the world what great heights science could reach. Now, the consequences were here, and they were dreadful indeed. How many more would have to die because of Victor Frankenstein's foolishness? No, he resolved. No more. *I will finish this business on Mont Blanc, as I should have done months ago in Ingolstadt.*

Early next morning, Victor armed himself with a pair of pistols. Each of the guns had four barrels; Victor primed all eight barrels with powder and shot, and slung a powder horn and ammunition bag over the pommel of his saddle. He told Elizabeth and Henry next to nothing of what he was about to do. All they knew was that Victor was going out to hunt down the man responsible for the deaths of Justine and Willie.

But that was hardly enough for them. They followed him out of the house as he headed across the lawn to his horse. "Who is this man? How do you know he's responsible?" demanded Elizabeth.

"I will tell you everything after I've destroyed him," Victor replied, distracted and impatient.

"If what you say is true, then surely this is a matter for the police," Henry said.

Victor shook his head firmly. "They wouldn't understand." He turned his back on them and checked the saddle girths on his gelding.

"Neither do I," cried Elizabeth, exasperated.

Victor mounted his horse. He turned to Elizabeth and his face was closed, stony. "Then just accept it."

Never had he spoken to her like that, so brusquely, so dismissively. Stung to the marrow, Elizabeth watched Victor ride off. Why had he shut her out? Why couldn't he confide in her? She was hurt and angry, but she was also deeply worried. She had never seen Victor this adamant, and he was riding off all alone into who knew what sort of danger.

Victor Frankenstein left his horse abandoned in the foothills of Mont Blanc, and, a rucksack on his back, trudged his way on foot up the crags of the icy mountain. It was a long climb, and he had time to think and to wonder. Was he hallucinating when he saw the Creature? Did he actually hear it speak his name? How was it that it could speak, and how did it come to find him here, in Geneva?

The air was very thin and cold. Victor paused for a moment to catch his breath, and climbed on up, his pickaxe in his hand. Farther up the glacier, he stopped and whispered to himself, "Where are you?"

He looked around. All he saw were a wall of ice ahead of him and his own footprints in the snow behind him. Of his adversary there was no sign. Victor knew he had to go forward; there was no turning back until the Creature—or he himself, or both—was dead. He climbed farther, making slow progress up the jagged wall of the glacier. It was difficult going, and took all the skill he had acquired over his years of Alpine climbing. He turned once more, his eyes scanning his surroundings, but he saw nothing but emptiness and ice.

"Where are you?" shouted Victor. His voice echoed around the icy mountains, but there was no reply. He didn't dare shout again, for fear of causing an avalanche. He resumed slowly climbing the steep face of the glacier. At last he reached the upper part of the crag, and found himself in a strange kind of ice world. Tall walls of ice surrounded him, like the parapets of a fortress. He had never been this high up Mont Blanc before. Victor climbed up onto a ridge and looked around.

At first he saw nothing, but then he perceived a movement out of the corner of his eye and he turned toward it. There! It was the figure of the Creature, ducking behind an ice wall. Victor moved down along the ice wall, trying to follow the figure, but it had disappeared.

All at once, Victor made a misstep; his feet flew out from under him, and he went tumbling down the ice face, slipping and sliding until he hit the soft snow at the bottom. As Victor struggled to stand up he thought he heard something, but when he looked around he saw nothing. His guns had fallen out of his rucksack, and he picked them up, leaving the pack behind, and moved on.

There was that sound again; this time Victor was sure he was hearing something. He listened hard. Yes, it was a voice. The Creature must have been watching him. Now he was calling to him, luring him on.

"Victor . . . over here . . . Frankenstein, this way. . . ."

He tried to follow the sound of the voice, but he couldn't. The very thinness of the mountain air was not a good conductor of sound, and every way Victor turned, he was faced by a sheer wall of ice. The walls appeared to be closing in on him. As the voice continued to call him, he became frantic. He *had* to find his creation.

Suddenly, he saw a figure duck behind a wall and disappear, only to appear again in another gap in the ice. Victor raised his heavy pistol and fired, but the Creature leaped out of the way. Like a hunting cat toying with a mouse, the figure appeared again, showing through another gap in the ice. Victor fired again, a second barrel, and again he missed. The Creature seemed to be everywhere at once. In front of Victor, behind him. Now Victor saw the Creature down below him. He ran toward it, sliding through the snow.

By the time he reached the place he last saw the Creature, it had gone, vanished. He looked madly around and then above him and behind him. Nothing. And then, suddenly, as if from nowhere, the Creature leaped toward him. Victor whirled to face him and, as the Creature landed, it pushed Victor away. Impelled by its phenomenal strength, Victor literally flew through the air backward, landing in the snow. He lost his footing and began to fall, tumbling down a steep slope, and on down another slope and another, continuing to fall. His head and body slamming into projecting crags, Victor disappeared into a crevice and down a natural tunnel to land in a misty pool of cold water in an ice cave. The fall knocked him unconscious.

The Creature studied him for a long moment, then he moved toward the unconscious Victor and dragged him out of the pool to safety. Some time later, Victor Frankenstein woke up and took a startled look around. He was surprised to find himself alive, and even more surprised to find himself in the company of the Creature, who sat watching him quietly on the far side of a small fire. The being was wearing a familiar garment, the very greatcoat Victor had lost in Ingolstadt, and this cave of ice seemed to be its home, to judge by a scattering of possessions, including—Victor saw with astonishment—a musical instrument and a small pile of books.

"Come and warm yourself by the fire," it said.

"You speak," marveled Victor.

The Creature looked impassively at him. "Yes, I speak. And read. And think, and know the ways of Man." He paused, and added, "I've been waiting for you."

Victor tried to get to his feet, but he was covered in bruises and his head was hurting so much that he sank back down again. "How did you find me?"

The Creature indicated the books beside him. "A geography book . . . and . . . yes! Your journal."

The journal! Victor remembered now; he had put it away in the pocket of his greatcoat, the very coat which, now ragged and filthy, the Creature was wearing. "Oh, my God!" he breathed. "Then you have everything! Waldman's notes, my diary—"

"Elizabeth sounds lovely," the Creature said softly.

Victor's mind was reeling with this series of revelations. He hardly knew what to think of first, but there was one thing he had to know, and he asked, "You mean to kill me?"

The terribly scarred brow wrinkled as the Creature looked at his creator. "Kill you? No."

"Then why am I here?" Victor demanded. "What did you want with me?"

"More to the point, why am *I* here? What did you want with *me*?" the Creature parried.

"You murdered my brother, didn't you?"

The Creature's hand moved in a dismissive gesture. "Do you think I am evil?"

"Yes," Victor said bitterly.

"Do you think the dying cries of your brother were music in my ears?"

"Yes," Victor said again, his voice breaking with grief.

The Creature raised his hand before Victor's eyes, his bony fingers curling as if to clutch an invisible neck. "I took him by the throat with one hand . . . lifted him off the ground . . . and slowly crushed his neck." A moan of horror escaped Victor's lips, but the Creature, caught up in a fierce emotion, did not hear, but continued to relate his story with tears shining in his monstrous eyes.

"And as I killed him I saw your face. Later, when they were searching, I followed the pretty lady who got lost in the woods. She was so lovely. I longed to touch her . . . but I simply returned the object that had triggered my crime, hoping in some small way to atone. . . ."

Listening to this recital of horrors, Victor could only stare at his creation, sick at heart. It was all clear to him now, all of it—the magnitude of what he had done so unthinkingly, the suffering he had caused with all good intentions. He had been vain; he had been proud; he had been heedless, and what a terrible price there was to pay!

Now the Creature turned his hideously marred face to Victor, and the corners of his mouth were trembling. "You gave me these emotions, but you didn't tell me how to use them," he said with deep reproach. "Now two people are dead. Because of us."

Us. He was right. Crushed by remorse, Victor dropped his head. He could not meet the Creature's accusing gaze. A sob escaped him.

"Why? Why? What were you thinking?" So plaintive was the Creature's voice it was almost a wail.

"I don't know," Victor confessed, weeping. "May God have mercy on my soul."

"What of *my* soul?" the Creature demanded bitterly. "Do I have one? Or was that something you left out?" He spread out his mismatched hands for Victor to see clearly. "Who were these people of which I am comprised? Good people? Bad people?"

"Materials. Nothing more," Victor said dully.

"You're wrong." The Creature picked up the recorder. "Do you know I knew how to play this?" He put the recorder down again. "In which part of me did this knowledge reside? In these hands? In this mind? In this heart? And reading and speaking. Not things learned . . . so much as things remembered."

The scientist in Victor automatically responded to the question. "Trace memories in the brain, perhaps." He hadn't thought of that. Could the genius of Professor Waldman and the brutal nature of his murderer be at conflict within this patchwork being?

Now the Creature looked sharply at Victor. "Did you ever consider the consequence of your actions? You gave me life, and then left me to die. Who am I?"

Ah, how could he answer that? For the first time, Victor looked at his creation and saw a "he" and not an "it," a he who was asking what he had an innate right to know, and for which there was no answer. "You . . . you . . . I don't know," stammered Victor.

"And you think *I* am evil." A bitter ironic smile crossed his dreadful face. ◄

There was undeniable justice in every word the Creature spoke. The realization of his guilt was crushing Victor's heart like a heavy boulder on his chest. Now he felt remorse not only for Willie and Justine, but for what he'd done to his own creation. Very slowly, he said, "What can I do?"

"There is something I want," the Creature replied. "A friend."

"Friend?" echoed Victor, uncomprehending.

"A companion," continued the Creature. "A female. Someone like me, so she won't hate me."

Hearing these words, Victor was aghast. "Like you? Oh, God! You don't know what you're asking!"

But the Creature would not be denied. "I do know that for the sympathy of one living being, I would make peace with all. I have love in me the likes of which you can scarcely imagine. And rage the likes of which you would not believe. If I cannot satisfy the one, I will indulge the other. That choice is yours."

Hearing this threat, Victor shook his head vigorously in denial. "You're the one who set this in motion, Frankenstein," the Creature pointed out accusingly.

Victor closed his eyes to blot out the Creature's face. The very thought of attempting another reanimation was abhorrent to him. Especially the reanimation of a female. There was something obscenely grotesque in a patchwork man wanting companionship and love from a patchwork woman. If it weren't so tragic, it might even be funny. Bitterly funny, like a Punch and Judy show from Hell.

But he knew that the Creature was deathly serious about carrying out his threats, and he recalled with a shudder the malevolent violence of which he had already shown himself capable. His strength and his brutality were incalculable. "And if I consent?" Victor asked quietly.

The Creature's face softened at the thought. "We'd travel north, my bride and I. To the farthest reaches of the Pole, where no man has ever set foot. There we would live out our lives. Together. No human eye would ever see us again."

He and Victor exchanged long, serious glances. "This I vow," said the Creature. "You must help me. Please."

Victor's shoulders slumped in defeat. What other choice did he have?

15   Materials

With a grim face and a teeming brain Victor Frankenstein rode down from Mont Blanc. The burden that
the Creature had laid upon him in the ice cave was
the heaviest a man was ever forced to bear, composed
of guilt and remorse mingled with doubt and a sense
of abhorrent purpose. Suppose he did commit the
morally unlawful act of reanimation once again—
could he trust the Creature to keep his word, take his
ghastly bride and disappear from the neighborhoods
of humans forever? Would that redeem Victor's sins,
or was he damned for eternity?

Or should he have lain in wait for the Creature,
snuffed out its life with his pistols, and then taken
his own? Damned was damned, and if Victor was
damned already, why shouldn't he rid the earth of
this scourge?

No; it was no longer as simple as that. Having

met his creation face to face, and having spoken with him and listened to him articulating intelligent thoughts, Victor felt a stab of pity for the poor Creature. None of this was his fault; he hadn't asked to be made, he didn't deserve to be so ugly, or so physically powerful, or to possess so deep a strain of violence in his nature.

Sitting face to face with his creation had left Victor with a series of unforgettable impressions. When he'd reanimated him, back in his Ingolstadt laboratory, Victor Frankenstein had not attempted to foresee a future that would include his patchwork being. Focused only on his creation coming back to life, he had given no thought to how he would turn out, how he would "grow up," or "the consequences," in the Creature's own words.

In that, he was not unlike a young married couple who want to have a baby, picturing only a dimpled, lisping totally dependent little darling, never considering that the infant would be with them for many years, and would have to be housed, fed, clothed, and educated, and that all too soon the baby would grow into an adolescent—sullen, rebellious, insulting, demanding its rights. In short, another person.

The Creature was just such another person, although endowed with extra-human abilities. Victor was impressed by his powers to speak and to reason, to read and play music, to feel the sting of injustice, and by his agility in movement. The Creature he had fled from at the beginning had been a shambling, helpless neonatal being. The Creature on Mont Blanc was surefooted and swift, clever and terribly strong. And all in three months' time! And who knows what powers he had that might still be only in the developmental stage! Victor had never considered the future education of his patchwork man, but his creation seemed to have done that by himself, and not so badly, either.

And there was something else eating away at his brain; Victor Frankenstein would not deserve the name of scientist if he didn't think about it with enormous curiosity. What if the Creature were right? What if the choice of "materials" determined the nature of the reanimant? Suppose that, instead of a murderer without an arm or leg Victor had been given the perfect, intact body of say, an artist who'd died young? And what if into that body had gone the brain of a mathematician or a philosopher? Or a saint? Would the resultant creation be a noble super-human? Would Victor have created the forerunner of a superior race of humans?

"Trace memories," Victor had said, but suppose it was much more than that? Suppose that he'd been able to operate immediately upon death, instead of allowing the "materials" to begin rotting over time. Would Waldman's brain, if it had been implanted within hours after his death, have infused the Creature with a high sense of morals and a horror of violence? Victor tried to put these thoughts out of his mind; he was through with all that. Seeing the consequences, he had turned his back on all that. Only this one last time would he go back into his laboratory, to reanimate a "friend," so that the Creature would be content to take his mate and go far, far away. But he couldn't help thinking . . .

What if it were possible to create a race of human beings who possessed only desirable attributes— great brains, sound bodies, benevolent natures, un-sullied souls? What if the very best brains, hearts, bodies of the century were recombined and reani-mated immediately after death, with enhanced pow-ers? A super-race, as it were, to cleanse the human race from evil, to attain new heights of discovery and art, of music and literature, chemistry and medicine, a boon for all mankind.

No; Victor forced the intriguing idea from his mind. Hadn't he learned his lesson? If he had been taught anything, it was that humans were not yet enough advanced to take on the prerogatives of God.

Another thought he blocked out of his mind, shrinking away from it and refusing to consider it, was the answer to the Creature's plaintive question, "Do I have a soul?" Because, if he did, then Victor's responsibility would be magnified a thousandfold.

As his horse picked its way with delicate hooves over the foothills down to Geneva, Victor sat listlessly in the saddle, his mind so crammed with conflicting ideas that it was almost numb. He would keep his promise to the Creature; he would make a female friend for him; he owed him that much. He owed him much more than that. It occurred to Victor suddenly that he had never given the Creature a name. Now it was too late.

He would have to reorganize his laboratory. The empty attic in the mansion would serve. It was a good thing he'd sent all his equipment back to Geneva; he'd been tempted to leave it behind, recoiling from the idea of ever practicing reanimation again, but his Swiss prudence and thrift rebelled against waste. Besides, much of the equipment had been expensively custom-built and could be used in other experiments; other bits of it might come in useful some day, in the practice of conventional medicine. Victor shook his head bitterly as he thought of its usefulness now.

He'd need new beakers, new retorts, and new Voltaic batteries, because the Creature had smashed the old ones in his destruction of the laboratory. But they wouldn't be hard to find in a city like Geneva, which was home to so many scientists. The essentials—the machines for generating electricity, the glass tube for the eels, and above all, the sarcophagus, these were mercifully intact.

The precious biogenic fluid could be obtained from the medical school, just as Victor had purchased it in Ingolstadt. As for the other "materials," well, he'd cross that bridge when he came to it. The Creature had undertaken to provide them.

As the gelding turned down the gravel drive leading to the Frankenstein mansion, Victor roused himself. It would not do to alarm Elizabeth or make Henry suspicious. They were already anxiously waiting outside the house for him, along with Claude. As soon as they saw Victor riding up, they all rushed across the lawn calling out his name. Victor dismounted as they approached, and handed the reins to the stable boy. Elizabeth flung herself into his arm and he embraced her tightly, kissing her brow and her hair.

"It's all right. It's all right I'm safe." Victor forced a smile.

"What happened?" asked Henry.

"Tell us . . . tell us, Victor," Elizabeth pleaded.

But Victor merely shook his head, walked on past her and away toward the house. She followed him, determined to get the story out of him at any cost. "Victor, you have to tell us what happened," she demanded fiercely.

Claude pulled the pistols from the saddlebags and caught a strong whiff of powder. "These have been fired. Many times." He and Henry Clerval exchanged significant looks.

Elizabeth followed Victor swiftly, catching him up, and they appeared to be in heated conversation as they made their way into the house. Elizabeth would not accept Victor's keeping from her secrets as important as this one; what kind of life together would they have if her position was not to be a full partner in everything pertaining to their lives? Look at what had happened in Ingolstadt. Victor had sent her away, and if she hadn't disobeyed him and come back on her own, he would have died of pneumonia, all alone.

Victor, on the other hand, was determined not to drag Elizabeth into any of this. Once he'd decided that it was best for everybody that he accede to the Creature's request, he knew that the sooner he did so, the sooner they would all be free of him and safe. He told her he was working on an experiment, and that he would be spending time in a laboratory he'd be setting up in the attic. It was an experiment begun in Ingolstadt and requiring completion. But he promised that all of this would not take long, and he pleaded for time.

"Look, a month at most, that's all I ask," he told her earnestly. "And then we can be married and forget this whole business. I promise."

Elizabeth stopped in her tracks and turned to face him. Her dark eyes flashed fire and her nostrils flared scornfully. "Promise! Promise! Don't dare use that word to me. You promised to tell me who that man was. You promised to abandon this work for good. . . . Your promises don't mean anything."

"Elizabeth—"

"I have to leave this house," she said decisively. Her lips were pressed tightly together, and her small hands clenched into fists.

"What are you saying? Where will you go?" cried Victor, stupefied by her sudden announcement.

Elizabeth shook her head. "I don't know. Somewhere where I can recover."

"This is ridiculous," Victor sputtered. "I haven't got time to argue."

His words and especially Victor's injured tone made Elizabeth explode. "Isn't it convenient? Doesn't it fit in with your plans?" she demanded indignantly. "Don't you ever think of anyone or anything but yourself?" Turning away from him with fury in her face, she ran up the stairs, leaving Victor baffled and uneasy.

With a feeling of despair, Victor went to sit at his father's bedside, holding tightly to Dr. Frankenstein's bony hands. The old man, a weak and frail shadow of his former self, attempted a faint smile. Victor squeezed his hand and whispered, "We're all safe now. I promise."

Father clung tightly to Victor's hand. "It is better to find peace than safety, my son. Marry her. Marry her now."

Oh, if only he could!

In the mansion's empty attic Victor started at once to set up his laboratory. Claude's first task was to carry up the heavy packing crates and set them down in a line. Victor went down the line, one crate at a time, opening the cases with a crowbar and checking off the contents on the manifest he had made before they left Germany.

When he came to one huge box he stopped. Just looking at the crate brought back a flood of terrifying memories.

"God forgive me," Victor whispered. He nodded to Claude, who lifted the cover from the case to reveal the gleaming copper of the sarcophagus. Victor hauled on the rope that brought it out of its box, and together, the two men lifted out the sarcophagus in pieces.

Little by little, with Claude's assistance, the laboratory in the attic began to take shape. The acupuncture needles were tested for sharpness; a load of Galvanic flux jars was lifted onto a trestle. The sarcophagus was bolted together and placed in its cradle. Claude and Victor threaded up the ropes that ran the electricity-generating machine. Roof tracks were installed for the body grid, the chains were attached to the grating, and the entire assembly checked and adjusted for smooth operation. Voltaic batteries were obtained and hooked up. Wiring was completed, with copper wire strung out across the ceiling beams. Behind thick protective goggles, Victor tested the electrical circuit and was rewarded by a giant shower of sparks.

The fishmonger delivered a huge barrel of live electric eels, and the butcher brought forty pounds of blood-dripping raw meat. The fire was lit under the sarcophagus. It was time for Claude to go, for Victor to continue alone, with strong locks on the laboratory door.

Meanwhile, two floors below, Elizabeth was packing, quickly and angrily, without the benefit of one of the maids to help her. She threw a handful of books into a trunk, dragged dresses out of the wardrobe without even looking to see which ones they were, and bundled them in on top of the books, and tossed sheets of piano music in a packing case. When she came to one particular song sheet, she hesitated, and her lips trembled. *So we'll go no more a-roving* was Victor's favorite.

Then, squaring her shoulders, she tossed the music in along with the others. It was only a song after all.

Mrs. Moritz sent one of the servants up to cover the furniture in sheets to protect the fragile satin upholstery from dust. While the footman was doing that, Elizabeth covered her cherished wedding dress in a black drape.

That was it, then, all of it. Taking a last look at her room, furniture shrouded in white sheets, Elizabeth left, closing the doors firmly behind her.

Inside the mansion attic preparations were just about complete. The laboratory now was looking very much like the one at Ingolstadt. Victor went back and forth around the now restored garret, giving his equipment a final check. As he started to hang up Leonardo's anatomical drawing, he heard Henry Clerval's voice behind him.

"I prayed to God never to see all this again."

Victor turned. Henry was standing at the top of the stairs, studying the laboratory with a look of great sorrow mingled with revulsion. He stared at the drawing, with its acupuncture points demarcated by bloody red.

"You don't understand. I have no choice," Victor answered bitterly.

"Of course you have a choice!" Henry snapped. His usually good-humored face was dark with anger. "You've always had a choice. The choice between good and evil."

Victor shook his head. "It isn't as simple as that," he said in a low voice.

"Then make it as simple as that." Henry's face softened a little, but his voice was still thick with urgency. "Think of what's happened to your family. Think of Elizabeth, and if there's any chance that she might still have you, then leave this place. Both of you leave, now."

But all Victor could do was to shake his head mutely. He couldn't leave until this dreadful business was finished.

Henry turned heavily and walked slowly down the stairs. Sadly, Victor watched him go. Henry Clerval was the best friend he had ever had. If only he would understand! But it wasn't Henry's fault that he had glimpsed only part of the truth; Victor could not confide all of it to him.

That night, in a cemetery on the outskirts of Geneva, an eerie figure might be seen among the tombstones, hunched in a grave, digging madly, dirt flying. There was a ringing sound as the iron shovel hit wood. Frantically, the Creature frantically tore the lid off the coffin, and peered inside. When he saw the corpse, he drew back, and a dreadful smile played over his mangled features.

With the body bundled in a sack, the Creature sped through the night, keeping to the back alleyways until the city gave way to the elegance of the large surrounding estates. Then he doubled low, running swiftly until the Frankenstein mansion came into view. The body slung over his shoulder, he scaled the house wall easily, hand over hand, until he reached the cupola at the top of the house, where Victor Frankenstein had left a window open, by prearrangement.

He dropped heavily to the floor of the laboratory, and disburdened himself; Victor was waiting. The sack was untied, the winding sheet and shroud removed, and Victor found himself looking into the mottled face of . . . the corpse of Justine Moritz.

"I want her," said the Creature.

Victor stared down in utter horror at Justine's cold, dead face. The grave-worms had not been slow in beginning their fell work. Her blue lips were already shrinking back from her teeth in the death-shrivel. Purple, sunken eyes stared back at him as though in reproach. *Victor, I loved you and now I'm dead. It's your fault. You did this to me.*

He could barely get the words out. "Why . . . her?"

"Her body pleases me."

A wave of nausea washed over Victor, and, retching, he turned away from that dead countenance. It was more than Victor could bear. It made him physically ill, the thought of what he was about to do, the thought of two reanimated corpses mating in a macabre love dance, the Creature and his "friend," who had once been the sweet, fresh-faced Justine.

The Creature looked sardonically at his creator. "Materials, remember? Nothing more. Your words."

Victor nodded. "My words," he answered softly. Pulling himself together, he turned back to Justine, forcing himself to examine the body, trying to think of the dead girl as no more than "materials." He cradled the head, probing the back of the neck with his fingers.

"The brain stem was destroyed in the hanging," he told the Creature. "We'll need another. The rest of the body looks as though it will do, but some of the extremities are too decayed. They'll have to be replaced. The fresher the better."

The Creature nodded wordlessly, and headed for the window. Climbing out, he disappeared into the night. Victor Frankenstein watched him go, and he was filled with revulsion imagining him running—with that incredible loping gait that ate up the miles—back to the graveyard to rummage around in newly dug graves in search of "fresher" materials.

But it was not to the cemetery that the Creature was going. He knew the ways of Man.

He watched from the shadows of the alley while the prostitute and her client finished their tawdry business against a wall in a sheltered doorway, her skirt up, his trousers unbuttoned. He saw the pitifully small sum of money change hands, and he saw the man button up and walk away, and heard the prostitute mutter "Bastard!" after him.

He saw the prostitute arrange her skirt and fluff her hair up with her fingers, and sashay up the alley under the pine-torch street lamps looking for new business. He took one step from the shadows, enough to be noticed, not enough to be seen. He saw the bright, mechanical smile come over the prostitute's face as she approached him.

"Want some yourself? Or do you just want to watch?" she asked him saucily. She came closer. "What do you say, lover?" she wheedled.

The Creature leaned into the light of the street lamp, so that she could see his face. He yearned to see the look of horror on it, watch her eyes go wide with fear, watch her mouth open to scream. He smiled as he clamped his powerful hand over her mouth, enjoying her struggles as he wrapped his other arm around the prostitute's neck and wrenched hard, snapping her spine.

Hoisting the body onto his shoulder, the Creature loped back to the Frankenstein mansion, scaled the wall to the roof cupola, and entered the laboratory through the open window.

"What is this?" gasped Victor, staring down at the dead woman. The blood at the corners of her mouth was still red and oozing, her eyes were fixed, wide open, and had not yet begun sinking into their sockets. She could not have been dead an hour, probably less.

"What is this?" echoed the Creature. "A brain. Extremities."

"This was not taken from a grave."

The Creature shrugged. "What does it matter? She'll live again. You'll make her."

Horror upon horror! Was there no end to these horrors? Victor's blood ran cold, and his entire body went numb with the realization that the Creature was driven by no moral imperative, and could not or would not distinguish right from wrong. It was one thing to kill at the height of passion, regretting it afterward, and quite another to kill deliberately, without remorse, saying only "What does it matter?" Evidently, the Creature was capable of doing both. He was not to be trusted with a mate. They might breed a race of murderous monsters.

"No!" exclaimed Victor. "I draw the line!" He turned his back and began to walk away, but the Creature, enraged, raced after him, seized him, and hurled him down on the table next to the corpse of Justine. His strong fingers tightened around Victor's throat.

"You will honor your promise to me!" he roared.

Revulsion washed over Victor Frankenstein. Even the thought of using the body of that poor dead woman for the benefit of her murderer was repugnant to him. Through gritted teeth, Victor defied him. "I will not! Kill me now!"

But Victor had no idea how deep ran the strain of malevolence in the bosom of the Creature. Nor had Victor in his innocence even begun to plumb the depth of the galling anger which possessed that maimed and scar-crossed body.

"Kill you?" the Creature laughed scornfully.

"That is mild compared to what will come. If you deny me *my* wedding night . . . I will be with you on *yours.*" He released his grip on Victor's throat, sprinted to the open window and disappeared, leaving Victor gasping for breath beside the putrefying body of the dead Justine.

Staggering off the table, Victor ran to the attic stairs, closing the laboratory door and locking it with a padlock. The only thought in his mind was Elizabeth . . . he must find Elizabeth. She was not safe. The Creature had made a threat against her. Henry was right. He *did* have a choice. He must find her and take her away, far away where the Creature would never locate them. They must run and they must hide.

Elizabeth wasn't in her room. The furniture was all shrouded with ghostly sheets; it looked like a gathering of phantoms. Good God, could he have missed her? As he sped down the stairs, Victor prayed to Heaven that he had not. He collared one of the servants, who told him that Mistress Elizabeth was just on her way out, but was planning to stop at the family chapel for one last prayer before going.

The chapel! Victor sped through the ballroom to the other end, where the family chapel was located. He could see Elizabeth, who was dressed in her traveling cloak and a feathered hat, just going in at one of the doors. Victor ran from one chapel entrance to another, trying the doors, but they were all locked. Finally, he managed to get in, near the altar. Elizabeth, having uttered brief prayers for the safe recovery of her father, and for Victor's health and happiness, was at the far end, just about to leave.

"Elizabeth! Wait! Don't go! Please, I have to talk to you."

She turned, and asked him coolly, "What do you want to say?"

"Don't go," Victor pleaded. "Please don't go. I'm frightened."

Frightened, Victor? Elizabeth had never heard him even use that word. She looked at him keenly, and he *did* appear frightened. Elizabeth had never seen him looking so distraught. "Of what?"

"I have done something so terrible . . . so evil . . . and I'm so frightened . . . if . . . I tell you the truth . . . that I will lose you."

"You'll lose me if you don't," she said simply.

Her words made him break down completely. He sank to his knees, weeping. "I don't know what to do," he sobbed, and bowed his head in misery.

The sight of him would have melted a stone, and Elizabeth's heart was not made of stone. Never had she stopped loving Victor for a moment, and never could she love another. All she had ever wanted was his complete trust, to be his wife, to share with him the bad times as well as the good. Her anger was only because he didn't seem to have faith in her.

But now he was begging to trust her, to confide in her. Victor needed Elizabeth, and she needed him to need her. He claimed to have done something monstrously evil. She couldn't begin to picture Victor doing evil, for evil was not in his nature. But, whatever crime he might have committed, whatever trouble he might be in, she would accept an equal share of it, she would stand with him and they'd face it side by side.

Elizabeth came up the chapel aisle, and sank to her knees face to face with Victor. He lifted his tear-streaked face and looked deeply into hers. The spark that so often jumped between them jumped between them once again. In this solemn place he felt a joining of their souls, and in that moment he half believed that everything would be all right.

"Will you marry me, Victor?" Elizabeth asked quietly. "Marry me today, and tomorrow tell me everything." She held him with her serious gaze. "But you must tell me the truth. Then together we can face anything. Whatever you've done, whatever has happened, I love you. So don't be frightened."

Her words lifted a great weight from his heart. He'd been so afraid of losing Elizabeth, but he hadn't lost her. She was still here, and still his. She loved him and was willing to become his wife. How could he have doubted her even for an instant? Victor managed a teary smile. "I won't if you won't," he joked, recalling the first time they had met as children. It was a dear and familiar jest between them. "I love you, Elizabeth."

And so it was agreed between them. Tomorrow he would tell her everything. Today they would marry. And later, they would have tonight.

Elizabeth changed into her wedding dress without delay, and a fresh floral wreath was bound around her brow. She wore no jewels except her own youth, beauty, and radiance. This was not the wedding the young woman had dreamed of for many years, a splendid affair with many guests in their brightest clothes dancing in the ballroom, feasting from long tables laden with pheasant, venison, roasted boar, delicate cakes, and rare fruits, drinking Madeira and champagne, toasting bride and groom. There would be no guests, no music or dancing, no feasting or toasting. But it was Victor she was marrying and that was all that really mattered to Elizabeth.

In his own room, Victor washed himself, put on clean linen and his gold-buttoned blue tailcoat, and groomed his dark gold hair and beard, but even as he wound his stock around his neck and tied it in a bow, his mind was distracted by anxieties. They would have to leave immediately after the wedding, and ride far and fast all afternoon. No time for a cumbersome carriage; they would go on horseback.

Victor knew that the Creature was both dangerous and unpredictable, and he knew, too, that the monster would try to make good his threats. They had to leave this place before the Creature returned.

A quick and simple wedding ceremony was arranged, to take place beside Dr. Frankenstein's bedside, with only two others present—Henry as best man and Claude as witness. The old man's frail body trembled with happiness as he saw Victor and Elizabeth exchange their vows. Now his son and his daughter were united as man and wife, just as everyone had always hoped they would be. If only Caroline were alive! thought Victor's father, his joy colored for one moment by a tinge of sorrow.

The minister joined the hands of the bride and groom, and began the recital of the sacred vows. ". . . To share the truth and the whole truth . . . for good or ill . . . to stand by each other in sickness and in health . . . and in joy, from this day forward till death do you part. . . ."

Till death do you part. Looking deeply into each other's eyes, trading pieces of their souls one with another, Victor and Elizabeth took that vow and sealed their love forever. It would be the last happy moment that either of them would know.

16 The Wedding Night

The brief ceremony over, immediate preparations were made for departure. Because Victor urged haste, Elizabeth kept her wedding dress on, putting over it a long red cloak, and wound a scarf around her hair. Meanwhile, Victor selected which guards would be accompanying them, three of them recruited from the best men—young, strong, and level-headed—among his own servants, and gave orders for their arming.

Claude was put in charge of the detail, and armed with a rifle. The other servants were given rifles, also multiple-shot pistols from the mansion's excellent armory.

"Who is this man, sir?" asked a stable hand. "How shall we know him?"

Victor hesitated. How could he even begin to

describe the Creature without terrifying his guards? "Believe me, you'll know him."

"He killed Master William and Justine Moritz died for it," said Claude. "No hesitation, lads! Shoot on sight!" There were cheers and cries of agreement.

The horses were brought around, saddled and bridled, their saddlebags packed. Victor's chestnut gelding carried a rifle and two Collier pistols, each with four barrels. Elizabeth was already waiting with Henry, and Victor now joined them. His strong sense of urgency made him impatient to leave, and yet he was reluctant to say goodbye to his family home, his father, and his best friend.

"Henry—" began Victor, then stopped. What could he say in gratitude? No man ever had a braver or truer friend than Victor Frankenstein had in Henry Clerval. He was staying behind to be in charge of a situation he didn't even understand, but he had asked no questions; Henry was ready to accept danger and act on Victor's word alone.

"Don't worry about a thing." Henry smiled. "You look after each other. I'll look after your father." He embraced Elizabeth, kissing her on both cheeks, and he and Victor stepped toward each other and hugged hard.

Then, without another word, Victor and Elizabeth swung into their saddles and rode away.

Up in his bed, Dr. Frankenstein slept fitfully, his remaining strength waning. He heard a noise somewhere in the room, and cried out, "Who's there? Henry?"

At the window, where he was watching Victor and Elizabeth ride away accompanied by guards, and noting the direction they had taken, the Creature turned. Slowly, he came toward the bed. The old man's eyes focused on the approaching figure until he could see the face. He shrank back against the pillows, his heart filled with dread. That face! Never had Dr. Frankenstein seen anything so hideous, a death mask of scarred tissue and malevolence. What demon from Hell was stalking toward him to snatch away his soul?

The old man opened his mouth to scream, but before any sound could emerge, the Creature's hand whipped out and closed over Dr. Frankenstein's mouth. For only a moment, the old man kicked and fought, but his strength was not equal to the struggle and, with no air in his lungs, his heart gave out. Very soon he lay still.

For a long moment the Creature stood looking down on the dead face of his enemy's father. His feelings were mixed—rage, of course, and satisfaction, but also he felt a sort of kinship with the corpse, as though they were related, which in a sense they were. But he couldn't tarry here; he had more important work to do.

There was a sound behind him, and the Creature whirled. A man dressed all in black had just entered the room, carrying a cup of tea for a bedside visit with Dr. Frankenstein; it was the minister. When he saw the Creature's face, the minister gasped and backed away, and the teacup went shattering to the floor, its contents forming a brown pool on the carpet.

"You're the Devil himself!" The minister put up one hand in a feeble gesture to protect himself; he was breathless with horror.

The Creature grinned evilly. "Yes, and I've come to snatch your soul . . ." He swooped across the room, pressing the terrified minister against the wall, bringing his mangled face very close to the other's

pale cheeks. ". . . Unless you tell me where they've
gone."

Victor and Elizabeth Frankenstein galloped along
the road, keeping just ahead of Claude and their
three guards. They'd been on horseback for hours
without, at Victor's insistence, stopping for food or
to rest. The afternoon wore away as they rode west
and north, around the shoreline of Lake Geneva.
Their intention was to cross the lake by boat, and
from there to ride north all the way into Germany,
where Victor's family had some distant cousins.

Behind them in the west, a magnificent sunset
was bathing the mountains in gold and purple, while
storm clouds came rolling in from the east. They
pounded onward, hooves beating a rhythmic tatto on
the stony road, approaching the ferry that would
carry them across the wide lake. Soon it would be
dark. Bending lower over their pommels, they rode
harder, determined to make the ferry before it pulled
away over Lake Geneva. But, as they road up to the
slip, they could see that the ferry had already left, its
wake making a line of white-capped ripples in the
lake's surface.

They dismounted with worried faces, and Claude
went to find out the time of the next boat. "I'm sorry,
sir," he told Victor on his return, "the last ferry's
gone. There's nothing now until morning."

"Damn!" Victor exclaimed softly. His flesh prickled with apprehension; every minute lost waiting
here increased the danger. They must hold onto their
lead at any cost! It was their sole protection from the
Creature, who was able to travel like the wind. Victor
had no idea how far behind them his enemy might
be. But they certainly couldn't wait here, at the ferry
slip, all night long. To judge from the lowering sky,

another heavy storm was on its way, and by now Elizabeth must be hungry, cold, and tired. They would have to seek shelter; Victor grudgingly agreed, although every nerve in his body cried out for them to keep moving.

"I'll ride on ahead and secure you lodging for the night."

"Thank you, Claude."

By the time they reached the fishing lodge, the storm was raging. Rain pelted them, and strong winds whipped branches into their faces as they rode. The chalet was a welcome sight—large, warm, and inviting, nestled in a copse of woods by the lake. Before he went upstairs with his wife, Victor positioned his men at the entrances. "Make sure you keep your pistols dry," he instructed.

"They're dry enough," replied one of the guards. "And if they fail, we have others. And if those fail, well, we can always get the bastard." He punched at the empty air to prove his courage. *If they only knew what they were up against*, thought Victor, but he said nothing.

"Get to your post," Claude ordered. "Don't worry, sir, you'll be well guarded. Now, why don't you go upstairs to your wife? It's not often a man has his wedding night."

Victor smiled. "Thank you, Claude," he said gratefully. Claude was a good man, strong and brave and noble-hearted. They were in good hands with Claude.

His wedding night. The night when Victor and his Elizabeth would unite their bodies as man and wife; as for their souls, well, those had already been united for many years. At last he would be free to embrace her totally, to touch her magnificent breasts with his lips and caress the softness of her skin with his eager hands. In his mind he had pictured the consummation of their love a thousand times. Tonight it would finally happen.

In the large room upstairs that would serve as their bridal chamber, Elizabeth sang to herself as she took her wedding dress off and carefully hung it away in the armoire. Over her naked body she slipped a peignoir of pure white silk, with lacings up the bodice to the neckline and ribbons at the elbows. The silken fabric stroked and caressed her skin as Victor would soon do with his hands. Her cheeks reddened and her breasts tingled at the thought of it. How many times she had imagined them making love, his strong, lithe body joined to her soft, yielding one! Tonight it would finally happen.

She took her dark hair out of the pins that bound it up, and let it fall tumbling down her back, a dark cascade of perfumed curls. Victor loved to kiss her hair. She brushed it out dreamily, waiting for her lover, longing for his kisses, only half hearing the rain pounding at the windows. When her hair was brushed, Elizabeth donned again her wedding chaplet of fresh flowers entwined with leaves, pressing it down onto her brows. With the wreath and her flowing silk robe, she resembled one of the nymphs of classical antiquity, perhaps a dryad, a young goddess of the woods.

Now she moved like drifting water from place to place around the large room, lighting candles, dozens of candles, until the entire room was aglow and the large canopied bed, its posts embellished by magnificent wood carvings, was bathed in soft light. When Victor came in, taking off his rain-soaked jacket and toweling his hair dry, he was met by candlelight and by the vision of beauty that was his bride. In her white silk gown and chaplet of flowers,

Elizabeth was ethereal, somehow otherworldly, like a bride from the kingdom of faerie.

Victor touched Elizabeth's soft neck, and she laid one hand on his shoulder, then drew it back. "You're soaking," she said with concern.

"I know." He smiled. "It doesn't matter." Drawing her into his arms, he kissed her deeply. Elizabeth wound her arms around his neck and returned the kiss with all the stored-up passion of her virgin heart.

"Brother and sister no more," she said softly, as they finally drew apart.

"Now, husband and wife," Victor replied huskily. He couldn't take his eyes off her face, for she was glowing brighter than the candles, more beautiful than he had ever seen her. And she was his, he thought, all of her was his, to love, to protect, to caress and kiss . . . and possess. . . .

Elizabeth pressed up against him, her red lips seeking his, her husband's. Their hands reached for each other's bodies—touching, finding, loving. Victor stripped his wet shirt off and flung it away. He reached for the laces of Elizabeth's bodice and, slowly, slowly, began to untie them, revealing the soft prominence of her white breasts.

Burning with passion, he turned her around, so that Elizabeth's back was to him, and he could kiss the back of her neck and bury his face in the perfume of her long hair. He reached around to cup her breasts in his hand, and she moaned softly, pressing her back tightly against him so that she could feel his lean body against hers. His hands dipped lower, reaching between her legs, and Elizabeth moaned again and shuddered.

Now they were on the bed together, their lips joined in a long kiss, tongues twining. Elizabeth lay back, trembling with desire as Victor moved down her body, caressing her thighs and the secret place between them, pushing the white silk upward. He knelt on the bed, removing her robe, while her fingers trembled on the buttons of his breeches. In the glow of the candles, her soft, voluptuous body shone like a star. His Elizabeth, his bride, his wife.

Suddenly, a not-distant strain of plaintive music reached Victor's ears. He knew that music; it was the sound of a recorder. Hearing it, Victor froze. *"Dear God, no!"* Outside, he could hear his men shouting to one another; the guards must have seen something. It was true; the Creature was here, very close by.

Victor leaped up from the bed, grabbing up his shirt and his guns, yelling to Elizabeth, "Lock the door!" and running down the stairs and outside.

The men who were standing guard had converged in front of the chalet, shouting confusedly to one another over the howling of the rain.

"I saw him in a flash of lightning!" cried one of the three guards. "He vanished toward the lake!"

"You two, stay here!" Claude ordered. "Johann, you wait outside Mistress Elizabeth's . . . Mrs. Frankenstein's . . . window, on the balcony. And keep your eyes open, everybody!" He and Victor raced off toward the lakeshore in pursuit of the Creature, leaving Elizabeth behind alone.

But the Creature was not at the lake. He was perched in a tree overhanging the roof of the chalet, clinging to the branches with hands and feet, like some malevolent spider. As he watched Victor disappear into the trees, his lips parted in a dreadful smile.

In the bridal chamber, Elizabeth sat up in bed and began to lace up her bodice. She wasn't sure whether to be puzzled or angry. Or frightened. For Victor to leap up and dash out at a moment like this, when they were just about to consummate their marriage!

And yet, she had seen that look of fear on his face only a few times, and every time there had been good reason for it. Something made her shudder, and she laughed out loud a little nervously. *Goose ran over my grave*, she told herself, a bit of country lore from her childhood.

She had forgotten to lock the door, but now she thought she heard a noise in the corridor outside.

"Victor, is that you?" she called, rising and going out in the hall. There was no Victor, and yet Elizabeth suddenly became uneasy. Something wasn't quite the way it should be.

On the balcony outside the bridal chamber, the Creature let the guard slip from his fingers and fall dead on the ground, his neck snapped like a twig.

Elizabeth left the corridor and went back into her room. This time she remembered to lock the door behind her. Slowly, tensely, she lay back on the bed. She had no idea why she was disturbed, but all her senses were tingling with apprehension. Somehow she felt things were going very wrong. There was danger here. For the first time, she was glad that guards had been posted.

She glanced upward, to the canopy over her bed, and recoiled with a gasp. The dark outline of a large figure was silhouetted against the cloth, on top of the canopy. But before she could utter a sound, a huge, powerful hand ripped through the heavy cloth as if it were tissue paper, and covered her mouth.

"Don't bother to scream," said the Creature.

At the very instant that the Creature plunged through the canopy, Victor Frankenstein stopped in his tracks. Suddenly, he knew with absolute certainty that the creature was not anywhere near the lake. He had cleverly deceived the guards; he had never left the chalet. The mystical union between Victor's soul and Elizabeth's told Victor now that his wife was in the gravest danger; he could actually feel her fear.

"Back!" he urged Claude. "We must go back at once! Hurry! There's not a second to lose."

As they neared the lodge, they could see one of the guards coming toward them, out of breath. "We lost him," the man admitted.

Victor's eyes went immediately to the window of the bridal chamber, and the breath caught in his throat. There was no guard visible on the balcony and . . . and . . . the French windows leading to the room were wide open. The curtains were billowing in the rain and wind. Oh, Heaven! He looked again, and this time he saw the balcony guard, hanging over the rail, obviously dead. The last remaining guard was slumped in the doorway, his dead hand still clutching his pistol. Even with guards posted at the door and the windows, the Creature had managed to break in.

I should have known it was a trick to get me away. I should never have left her, thought Victor.

"Elizabeth!" His blood pumping fiercely with dread, he sped toward the chalet with Claude at his heels. Both men drew their pistols and cocked them.

Elizabeth's eyes were fixed on the Creature kneeling over her. She was a gentle, loving creature who had lived a sheltered and protected life. How could she ever have imagined that she would find herself in the presence of such monstrous evil, or feel so much fear and not die of it? In that brief moment since he had clamped his massive hand over her mouth, she had come to understand something of what Victor was running from, trying to protect her from. But how? Why? Even in her terror, she needed to know, to comprehend what was happening to her.

Slowly the Creature took his hand from her

mouth. "Please, please don't hurt me," Elizabeth begged.

But the being did not even hear her. His eyes were fixed upon her features, studying her beauty, his face so close to hers that their lips were almost touching. He looked at her with something close to awe, mingled with an overpowering desire. "You're more lovely than I ever could have imagined," he breathed.

Despite her fear and revulsion, Elizabeth peered closely at the lumpy skin and jagged scarring of the Creature's face. "Who are you?" she asked in a whisper. She needed to know.

But before he could answer, the sound of footsteps came pounding up the stairs, and the crash of men slamming their shoulders against the locked door of the corridor.

"Elizabeth!" cried Victor as he broke through into the corridor outside the room. The interior door was also locked; Elizabeth had carried out his instructions only too well.

At the sound of Victor's voice, the Creature uttered a low, animal growl of hate. All other emotions fled—awe, desire, even pity—and he was left only with this gnawing rage and loathing. He cocked his arm back and, with the force of a heavy machine, plunged his clenched fist into Elizabeth Frankenstein's chest. His heavy fist broke through her flesh, breaking the ribs in its path, destroying muscle, tendon, bone, ripping through veins and arteries.

Elizabeth's body arched up in agony, and fell back on the bed, dead. Before she died, she uttered one long scream, but it was choked off, as the Creature pulled the living heart right out of her body. It lay pulsing in his hand.

The men outside rushed frantically at the door

once again, breaking it open at last, and Victor rushed through it, his eyes wild. The sight they saw was enough to strike them blind.

Elizabeth lay on her back on the bed, staring upward. Upon her head the virgin's bridal chaplet was still fresh, but the front of her white silk gown was stained the deep scarlet of heart's blood. And, there, at her breast, where Elizabeth's heart should have still been beating, there was only a red gaping wound and a dreadful emptiness.

The Creature held the heart in his hand, offering it to Victor as one would a gift. On his face was a vicious, crooked, jagged smile. "I keep my promises," he said.

For an instant, Victor stood paralyzed, unable to comprehend the magnitude of the horror that was burning holes in his retinas. Then, as full realization came crashing down on him, he uttered one long cry of grief and despair, calling her name, "Eliza . . . beth!"

As he heard the cry, the Creature swept Elizabeth's dead body off the bed onto the table holding the candles she had lighted with such joyful anticipation not an hour earlier. Her face smashed against the wood and the glass, and blood burst from her head. Candles tipped over onto her, setting her long, dark hair on fire.

The Creature raced across the room to the window. At once, the men opened fire, the fusillade of their heavy pistol shot shredding the wall to pieces near his head. But the Creature was too fast for them. He hit the leaded window head-on with the force of a hammer striking an anvil, and went sailing out into empty space in a cataract of splintered glass. Crashing into a low-hanging branch, he dropped forty feet to the grass below, and vanished like the wind.

Victor rushed to the bed and, with a long, anguished howl of misery, frantically put out the flames in Elizabeth's hair with his bare hands. Then he cradled the limp form of his murdered bride to his breast, his screams trailing off into wracking, agonized moans and sobs of sorrow and despair. "Oh, God, he took her heart . . . he took her heart from me . . . he's taken her heart. . . ."

If the Creature had pulled the heart out of Victor Frankenstein's own chest, it could not have hurt any more than seeing Elizabeth's naked heart in that loathsome hand. In one instant it made a savage mockery of Victor Frankenstein and his entire life—his dreams, his aspirations, his skills, and even his precious science—all, all, were mocked and reviled, and Victor was stripped bare forever of the last vestige of hope and joy. No mortal, no, not even an immortal demigod like Prometheus had ever been punished so cruelly for setting his foot on forbidden ground.

All that was left to him was the gift of the apple given to Adam in the Garden—knowledge of the difference between good and evil—and the terrible realization that good intentions are worth nothing when weighed in the scales of eternal justice. And his rage, oh, yes, he still had that. A rage and a hatred that cut so deeply into his soul that they scarred it as horribly as the Creature's face was scarred.

Victor didn't know it, but he was now quite mad. How could he not be mad, who had witnessed such abominations and suffered such great loss? What sane man could hold on to his sanity in circumstances like these? He wrapped his dead wife in her red traveling cloak and carried her in his arms down the steps and into the night, unaware of the downpour. He propped her body up on his saddle in front of him as he had done so many times while she lived. And he raced through the storm, faster and faster, whipping the horse into a frenzy, all his thoughts on the work ahead of him.

The storm increased its intensity; great, jagged forks of lightning split the sky and thunder crackled in his ears, but Victor Frankenstein paid it no attention. Ahead of him was his destination . . . home . . . and his laboratory. Reaching the mansion, he leaped from his horse, gathered up Elizabeth's body and ran up the steps, slamming the door behind him.

Henry pursued him through the ballroom to the stairs, appalled at the sight of his best friend, streaming with rain, carrying the dead body of the precious Elizabeth. "What happened? Tell me what happened—" he begged frantically.

"There's no point," Victor said tersely. "I know what I have to do."

Henry Clerval realized immediately what his friend had in mind, and the mere thought of it sent him into panic. "No, Victor!" he protested. "You can't do this!" He placed himself directly in Victor's path, and put out a hand to stop him, but Victor looked at him and Henry saw stern resolution in his face, combined with a glint of something that made him shrink away in fear.

"You'll have to kill me first," said Victor. Then his face crumpled, and the anguish showed through. "Henry, I have no choice. She's gone. I love her. What would you do?"

"Leave her in peace," Henry said quietly.

"Peace," repeated Victor bitterly, his voice breaking. "You call this peace? You think my father wouldn't have done this for my mother?"

"Your father's dead."

Victor's eyes shut for one moment, as he bade his father a silent farewell, then he looked again at Henry. "Well, then, I have nothing left to lose."

"Nothing except your soul," Henry Clerval said seriously.

Victor shook his head ruefully. "I lost that a long time ago, Henry."

He pushed past his friend, and Henry Clerval did nothing more to stop him. There was no further word he could say; Victor was adamant and nothing would dissuade him. He watched in sorrow, pitying tears streaming from his eyes, as Victor carried Elizabeth up the stairs to the attic. Her long, blood-red cloak streamed behind her, and her dark hair tumbled over her husband's arm, curly and lustrous. Henry could see one small, delicate arched foot peeping out from beneath her cloak, and the sight nearly broke his heart.

This was their wedding night. Victor and Elizabeth should have been going up together to their marriage bed, thought Henry. A stranger seeing them thus, the wife carried lovingly in her husband's strong arms, might imagine it so. Instead, Victor was taking Elizabeth to a bed so monstrous that Henry's brain recoiled from naming it. And Henry Clerval knew with certainty that Victor had been driven quite, quite mad.

17 Reanimation

Bolts of lightning crackled and flashed through the high cupola windows as Victor carried Elizabeth's body along the corridor leading to the locked attic. With fumbling hands he unfastened the padlock and carried her into the dark laboratory. With one hand he swept his books off a table, and slid his wife's body onto it. Now, with maniacal speed and single-ness of purpose, he began the forbidden process of reanimation.

The lab and all its equipment were standing ready, thank . . . what? Thank Heaven? Thank God? Rather, thank the Creature, who had demanded a friend. It was because Victor Frankenstein had been willing to break God's laws a second time that every-thing was now ready for the work to begin; even the amniotic fluid had been procured and was already in the sarcophagus. And with the corpse of Justine, he had the "materials." Only the journal was missing; the Creature still had that in his possession, but Victor didn't need his notes. The procedure for reanimation was burned into his brain like a living image.

He took the covers off the two dead bodies, and ran to switch on the generators, turn the wheels that stored the generated electricity in the Leyden jars, and connect up the Voltaic piles. Under the copper sarcophagus, Victor lit the coals and worked the bellows with his foot, building up the heat until the coals glowed a dull red.

Now he had to check his "materials." He turned Elizabeth over and examined her body, fighting down his nausea and guilt, fighting to hold onto a shred of scientific objectivity. He had to work quickly; he didn't have time to think of this body as his beloved wife, only as something to be reanimated while the brain was still viable.

He would have to use Justine's body and heart. The body of the prostitute was fresher than Justine's, but Victor couldn't bear to think of his virgin bride, so pure and so radiant, sharing a body with a whore's sullied flesh. He would use Justine's, but he'd have to replace one of the hands, because it was already putrefying. The other hand was still usable.

Elizabeth's hand. Elizabeth's head. The cleaver and the bone saw did their gruesome work, and Victor Frankenstein, a man possessed, worked feverishly, a lone runner in a race against time.

He sewed the body parts together, creating one woman out of two. He cut away the charred remains of her hair, clipping and shaving away around the horrible burns. A sob escaped him; he could not hold it back. Elizabeth's hair, so beautiful, had always fascinated and attracted Victor. He had loved it so, as it escaped its pins, curling in riotous tendrils over her brow and flowed down her slender back. How often had he caught it up in his hands and pressed the perfumed mass of it to his nose and lips! But he was determined that he would do so again.

When the body was complete and lying shrouded on the chain-enclosed grating, he hauled on the pulley rope. Arms and legs extended like the Leonardo drawing, the body lifted slowly to the ceiling to the waiting rail. The buffer slammed it, sending the grating across the ceiling track, sparking, to come to a swinging halt above the sarcophagus.

Victor pulled on the chain to lower it into its copper uterus, pulling the shroud off the body's nakedness just before it was submerged in the amniotic fluid. He pumped the bellows again, and the fire rose high, then higher. Victor positioned the sarcophagus over the firebed.

The needles now, and quickly. He rammed the first acupuncture needle home, and then more needles, through the side of the sarcophagus and into the body. Victor worked automatically, one step after another, almost without thinking, his hands working feverishly. He was conscious of nothing but the minutes passing, the urgency to finish in time.

The eel sack positioned above the sarcophagus, Victor locked down the lid and pulled the glass tube down into its position. Frenziedly, he grabbed the connectors at the main power point and clipped them onto the terminals. When they touched, sparks flew, but Victor was indifferent to them. All they meant was that the circuit was working. Power surged through the cylinders and along the copper wires. The wheels turned madly, the machines generated the voltage, the current flew around the attic, along the wires and into the batteries, and from the batteries through the needles into the sarcophagus.

Victor Frankenstein leaped to the top of the sarcophagus and released the electric eels. They came writhing and thrashing down the glass tube and into the amniotic fluid, where they sank their teeth into the female flesh. Current flowed through the fluid, powerful, constant.

The body in the sarcophagus arched and convulsed, its head slamming against the porthole.

"Live!!!" screamed Victor.

Outside the laboratory, Henry sat on the steps to the attic, his head buried in his hands. The death of Elizabeth, coming so soon after the death of Victor's father, the enormity of Victor's actions, the extent of his madness, had infected him as well. He was trembling, sweating, weeping, and close to a breakdown. Henry had a pretty good idea of what Victor was doing there, in the locked laboratory, and it was monstrous, monstrous! When he heard Victor scream out, Henry couldn't stop himself from screaming, too. "NO!"

It was finished. Victor Frankenstein turned off the power, taking the main connector off the switches. He went to the sarcophagus and opened it, lifting the lid off the tank and peering inside. Then he reached down into the steaming fluid, and gently, as though he were in truth handling a newborn baby from its mother's uterus, he pulled out his creation.

Cradling her head and neck, he whispered, "Live."

Her mouth was gaping to draw air, but there was fluid in her lungs, and she couldn't breathe. Victor clutched her tightly, pounding her back to start her breathing, as her lungs heaved violently to dispel the fluid. Massive sutures bisected her neck and collarbone where pieces were joined. She was a hideous amalgam of Elizabeth's head and face, and Justine Moritz's body.

But Victor didn't see her as hideous; in his dementia he saw her only as beautiful, and his only love. Stroking her on the head and still hitting her on her back, he started to lift her out of the sarcophagus.

As she shivered and coughed, Victor wiped the slimy muck from her face, gently, tenderly, with infinite love. He dressed her in her wedding dress, and forced the wedding ring onto her finger, Justine's finger. Now he led her to a box and sat her down. This thing that was Elizabeth, yet not Elizabeth, sat slumped, her head drooping. Victor stood in front of her, trembling with anticipation.

"Say my name," he begged. "Say my name."

She was dazed, stunned. In her blank eyes there was not a flicker of recognition. Victor knelt at her feet. "Say my name. Please, you must remember. Elizabeth! Elizabeth!"

She lifted her head to look at him. Was there some flicker in her eyes? Was it that hearing Victor calling "Elizabeth" triggered some memory? Did that brain, so recently dead, contain the trace memories of their life together? Of their undying love?

Victor saw the flicker, and his heart leaped up with joy. "That's it, you remember," he cried joyfully. "It's all right. It's all right. I'll help you remember. Don't be frightened. I won't if you won't." *We will never die. We promised each other long ago that we would never die.*

Slowly she reached out to touch his face. Victor began to help her to her feet, begging her all the while to "Remember, please remember."

He could see the trace memories beginning to come back to her. "You remember, you remember . . ." he murmured lovingly.

A mad strain of music came flowing into Victor's brain; it was the waltz that he and Elizabeth had danced to so often in the ballroom over the years. What was it Mrs. Moritz used to say? Something about partners in the dance being partners in life. Why, it was true after all!

"Stand, my darling. Stand. Yes, yes, come on, come on," he coaxed her, smiling encouragingly into her face. Slowly, Victor helped Elizabeth to her feet. And slowly, ever so slowly, she raised her bony white hand before her eyes. She stared at it, trying to puzzle it out—its meaning, perhaps the vaguest shred of recognition—and the hand continued to rise, creeping slowly toward his shoulder and coming to rest there. The kerosene lantern shone its light on the wedding ring on her finger.

At first her movements were imperceptible, just the slightest motion, nothing more than a swaying, but then she took a step, and another step, and another. Tears glistened in Victor's eyes as Elizabeth began to move . . . lurching, faltering, unsure.

Victor smiled. Sweeping his Elizabeth into his arms, he began to waltz with her around the laboratory, dancing to imaginary music that only he could hear.

Yes! Oh, yes, it was Elizabeth, his Elizabeth returned to him from the grave! In his derangement, Victor Frankenstein believed that they were in their blue ballroom, with all the candles burning, and the musicians playing for their sole delight. He refused to perceive the horror of it all—the scars, the burn scars, the empty eyes, the jerky movements like those of an automaton, the laboratory surroundings, and . . . the very worst thing of all.

There, on the shelf, was a large formaldehyde jar from which Justine's severed head was watching them through the glass with dead, sightless eyes. Watching them dance. Still a wallflower? No. She was finally finishing her dance with Victor . . . at least her body was waltzing, if not her head or her hand.

The dancers dipped and turned, and the waltz went on, madder and madder, sweeping in glorious circles, a macabre parody of all the waltzes they had danced in all the years they'd been partners. Elizabeth dropped her head back and they danced on, Elizabeth laughing. Victor picked her up and swept her around the room, joining in with her laughter.

This was their wedding dance, the waltz they should have had earlier, but didn't. In Victor's head the insane music was swelling louder and louder, climbing higher and higher, reaching toward its crescendo, and, when the music had passed its fever pitch, he would make her his true wife. . . .

There! Silhouetted in a sudden flash of lightning, the Creature was standing by the sarcophagus, watching them dance. In Victor's brain, the music echoed away abruptly into silence. He could hear nothing now but the beating of the rain and the low rumble of distant thunder.

"She's beautiful," the Creature said in a low, guttural tone. He didn't take his eyes off Elizabeth.

Victor's eyes flashed defiance. "She's not for you."

The Creature smiled. "I'm sure the lady knows her own mind." He raised one hand in a beckoning gesture. Elizabeth took a faltering step in his direction, somehow drawn to him.

Victor felt a panic rising in his breast. This must not be! He could not, would not lose her twice! *She is mine!* "Say my name . . . Elizabeth . . . say my name . . ." he pleaded.

Elizabeth stopped in the middle of the room and turned to look back at Victor. She was not sure which way to go.

"Elizabeth, you're beautiful . . . you're beautiful . . ." murmured the Creature hypnotically. "I've waited all this time, Come to me . . . come to me."

"You don't belong to him, you're mine," Victor urged desperately. "Say my name . . . you remember. Trust me, Elizabeth, trust me."

Elizabeth stood frozen to the spot, looking from one to the other, her face reflecting horror and shame. She knew that she was supposed to remember something, but she couldn't remember what remembering meant.

Both of them were beckoning to her, each trying to draw her toward him. Cajoling. Begging. She was caught between them, pulled like a piece of rope in a tug of war. "Please . . . come with me," insisted one. "Please . . . remember," was the other's litany. Finally, she moved off toward the Creature.

"No!" shouted Victor. "He's a murderer, Elizabeth, he's a murderer!"

But Elizabeth walked over slowly to the Creature. It was as though he had some mesmeric power over her. She gazed into his eyes, studying his face. Her fingertips traced his massively scarred flesh. She frowned, puzzled. Did she remember that her last words spoken alive were spoken to him? "Who are you?" she had asked. Was she asking it silently again, with the tips of her fingers? The Creature's appearance seemed to baffle Elizabeth. This wasn't right. People don't look like this. They're not stitched together out of pieces of flesh like a patchwork.

She looked down at her own hands. One of them was her own, the other dead and white, suture scars marring the wrist. Her eyes traveled down her own body. This body wasn't hers. How was this possible? Elizabeth tried to think, to remember. Realization came creeping into her eyes, realization and horror. She turned mutely to Victor, her eyes asking for answers.

Why do I look like this? What's happened to me? Oh God, what's happened to me? "Vic—tor?"

"I'm sorry, Elizabeth . . . it'll be all right . . . Yes . . . I'm Victor . . . you remember. . . ." His face was alive with a manic sort of joy.

"No!" snarled the Creature. "You're mine . . . you're mine." He reached out to grab her, turning her to face him, and began to dance with her, whirling her 'round and 'round, as he'd seen Victor do, in a ghastly parody of the parody that was Victor's lovers' waltz.

"No," Victor cried out, "don't touch her!" He could stand it no longer. Lunging forward, he tried to snatch her away from the Creature's arms. They tussled for her, Victor trying desperately to loosen the Creature's arm from around Elizabeth's waist.

"*Get away from her! She's mine!*" roared the angry Creature.

"*She'll never be yours! She said my name! She remembers!*" Victor roared back.

And, suddenly, Elizabeth did remember. Not much, but enough, enough to fill her with horror and loathing. She knew that she had been dead, and now she was somehow . . . not dead. The revelation was more than she could bear. Uttering a piercing shriek, she struggled to get free of them. Finally, she broke away and ran.

Shrieking "No!" she sailed across the room, pulling the cloth off an covered instrument chest, staring down at the huge, curved suture needles. She looked around her frantically, taking in the laboratory and all of Victor's bizarre equipment—the sarcophagus, the Voltaic batteries, the large electricity-generating wheel. She saw Justine's severed head in the formaldehyde jar. Suddenly, she understood everything, everything. She was not Elizabeth, but some mangled, made-up, stitched-together creature, part herself and part Justine, reanimated by electricity. She was not alive; neither was she totally dead. She was one of Victor Frankenstein's horrid experiments, the kind she'd made fun of as a girl. And, most loathsome of all, fighting over her body were her husband and some vile reanimated Creature, who dared to claim her as his right.

This must not be! Elizabeth turned to Victor one last time, running her hands over her scarred hand and face. Then, before they could stop her, she headed straight for the kerosene lamp, snatching it up.

"NO!" Victor cried out.

Elizabeth spun around to face them, holding them breathlessly at bay with the threat of the lamp, twitching from one to the other. But it was not only the lamp that held the Creature and Victor paralyzed, it was the look of sheer loathing in her eyes. Loathing for them for what they'd done to her, loathing for herself for what she had become.

She was finished; she wanted no part of this or of them. With her bare hands, she crushed the lamp, drenching herself in a cascade of burning kerosene. Instantly, the delicate fabric of the gown went up in a ball of flame. Elizabeth shrieked in agony as the flames ate at her flesh, and went running across the corridor and down the attic stairs to the main house. Victor flew after her, followed by the Creature.

In the upper hallway of the mansion, Elizabeth,

now burning like a torch, ran screaming, still trying to claw the dead flesh away, pulling off giant flaming pieces of herself as she careened out the door to the attic and down the broad staircase, sailing down the hallway, setting fire to everything she passed.

Victor raced after her, but the Creature only followed as far as the attic stairs, where he waited, watching everything.

Elizabeth's agony was unendurable. She spun around, screaming for the final torment to end. Coming to the banister rail that looked down on the grand entrance below, she hurled herself over the edge, plummeting to the floor far below. A pillar of flame leaped up on her impact, and then she lay very still.

As she was falling, Henry and Claude rushed in, in time to look on in horror as she landed. "Elizabeth," whispered Henry, disbelieving his eyes. He rushed toward the bottom of the stairs; Claude turned and dashed the length of the ballroom to fetch help.

"Water! Fetch water! . . . FIRE!" he shouted.

In the upper hallway Victor and the Creature confronted each other at either end of the flaming corridor.

"You killed her! You killed her!" Tears of grief and despair streamed down Victor's face.

"*We* killed her," the Creature retorted coldly. And then, lifting his arms, he flourished the journal, and vanished through the smoke and flames back up the attic steps.

"I will find you," Victor promised, from the depths of his broken heart. Elizabeth was dead, and he was alone. As alone as the Creature he'd made out of spare materials and a desire to save the world. Poor Victor! In the long run, he couldn't save any one of the people he loved, and he couldn't save himself. He'd lost everything but the desire for revenge.

And there was something else . . . He was haunted by a terrible dread that Victor Frankenstein had loosed upon the world the means for the destruction of the human race. In his nightmares Professor Krempe had told him that the name Frankenstein would forever after be a synonym for evil. Why had the Creature brandished the journal so mockingly? Could it be that he intended to use Victor's notes to create a mate for himself out of "materials," fresh materials that he butchered for their parts? Heaven only knew he had the intelligence, and what is more, he had the will. And after he had his mate, would he build others like himself? Would a race of monsters—without remorse, or faith, or pity or kindness—one day people the earth?

He mustn't let that happen. All of this was his fault, and he must correct it. Victor raced down the staircase, clear of the flames, and ran into Henry Clerval at the bottom. He headed for the front door of the mansion. Behind them, at the far end of the ballroom, a tower of flames erupted.

"Where are you going?" shouted Henry over the roar of the fire.

"To find him" Victor shouted back.

"Where?"

"Wherever, forever. However long it takes."

"Then you're a fool, Victor," Henry said bitterly.

Victor paused in the doorway. The madness had left him, and he seemed to be quite calm, although his face was grave. "You're right, Henry. You've always been right. You should have been my father's son. He'd have been so proud. God bless you, Henry."

"God forgive you, Victor," wept Henry. He knew

that he would never lay eyes on Victor Frankenstein again in this world.

Victor shook his head sadly. "He can't. He won't," he answered simply.

Victor left the house of his father and his forefathers, going out into the teeming rain outside and closing the door behind him.

Behind him, the Frankenstein mansion was now engulfed in flames. Nothing could save it from its total destruction.

18 Much Wisdom, Much Grief

Victor Frankenstein slumped down wearily onto the wooden bed in Captain Walton's cabin aboard the *Aleksandr Nevsky*. He was ravaged in body and mind, totally exhausted. The long telling of his strange tale had drained him of nearly all the small amount of life that was left to him because, just as he told it, so he relived it, moment by horrifying moment. The creation, the cruel deaths of everyone he held so dear, the ghastly finish to all his hopes and aspirations—with the retelling he experienced them all a second time. His madness was burned away, leaving him now only the worn-out shell of the Victor Frankenstein who used to be.

"And now that I have found him I know what I must do," he ended.

Victor lay back and closed his eyes, and to Walton it seemed that Frankenstein was no longer breathing.

Poor insane fellow! Better for everybody that he died here, and the end of nowhere. For he was too deranged and too tortured by his dementia to go on living. But what a tale! Robert Walton's blood ran cold just listening to it, and he had followed every word with fascination. Unbelievable, of course, made up of the whole cloth as it was woven in that pathetic demented imagination of Victor Frankenstein, yet all in all a mesmerizing narration of monstrous events. Well, it was all over now; the man was finally at peace. "Rest now," Walton told Frankenstein, and getting up he left the cabin. He emerged on deck, armed with his gun, to face down Grigori and his mutinous crew. The crew were waiting for some news, milling about and making threats, but when they saw Walton they quieted down.

"What is out there, sir? What does he say?" asked Grigori anxiously.

"He's dead. He died raving about some phantom . . . he told me a story that . . . it couldn't be true. He was mad . . . I think."

A light breeze caught the rigging. "A warming breeze." The captain nodded. "The ice will melt yet."

"And what then, sir?" Grigori wanted to know, and the crew made threatening noises behind him.

"We head north," Walton said firmly.

"No." The first mate was equally firm.

It was a moment of icy tension. The sailors exchanged uncomfortable glances. None of them wanted to be mutineers, but none of them wanted to continue north on their captain's insane quest for the Northeast Passage. Suddenly, the noise of a flapping door came from behind them. Somebody was in the ship, below. "You men come with me," ordered Walton and, his gun in his hand, he led some of the crew belowdecks, toward his cabin, in the direction of the noise.

Outside the captain's cabin, Walton silenced his men with a gesture. "Wait. Listen."

At the sounds coming from inside the men froze. They heard a soft weeping. Walton cocked his pistol hammer, and led his men inside the cabin. They eased silently forward to get a closer look at the bed. Victor was lying on it, eyes closed, very still. A dark figure was hunched and weeping at the bedside, holding a leather-bound journal limply in his fingers. Walton and the crew were stunned.

This pathetic weeping figure must be the Creature who tore an entire team of vigorous sled dogs into pieces with its bare hands. Although the crew had not been privy to Victor Frankenstein's story, they had a healthy enough respect for this being to keep their distance.

The captain took a brave step forward. "Who are you?" he demanded. The figure looked up, revealing its face in the dim light. It was hideously deformed, and crisscrossed by a patchwork of scars. The men took nervous steps back, each one crowding against the others to be closest to the door. There were gasps and a few of the crew crossed themselves to keep the Devil away.

"He never gave me a name," the Creature said simply.

The crew looked astonished. He spoke like a man! They trained their guns on the Creature but the Creature paid no attention to the men or their guns.

"Why do you weep?" asked Walton.

"He was my father."

Walton was staggered. So Frankenstein's story was true after all! It was incomprehensible, yet true!

This . . . thing . . . sitting here in his cabin was actually a reanimated man!

Captain Walton found himself very much moved. He felt a stab of pity for this unnamed, hideous, lonely Creature, even though—if Frankenstein's story were indeed to be believed—he'd committed monstrous and murderous acts. As for Frankenstein himself, Walton pitied him the most. The man's intentions were good, but their outcome was calamitous. He had lost everything—family, fortune, the love of a wonderful woman, a promising career, his hopes and his dreams. Possibly, his very soul.

"Give me the gun," a feeble voice said suddenly. It was Victor, raising himself up on his elbow, an inch or two from the bed. He was alive, but only just. He held his trembling hand out for the captain's pistol.

Walton didn't move; he was too startled. He'd been certain that Frankenstein was dead, and to hear him speak and see him move was unnerving.

"Give me the gun," Victor demanded again. And again, frighteningly loud, "The gun!"

Slowly, Robert Walton moved across the cabin and handed Victor his pistol. Victor took a firm grip on the butt of the gun and aimed the barrel at the Creature's head. The Creature didn't flinch or move away, he merely sat looking at Victor.

"This is the last thing I do," declared Frankenstein. It would end right here, in this cabin on a lonely, icebound ship at the top of the world.

What followed was a long moment when the creator and the Creature—father and son—looked deeply into each other's faces. Without a word, they both knew that their long, tangled story was coming to a finish, and that there had to be peace between them. This was the only son that Victor Frankenstein would ever have. He had never acknowledged his responsibility for the life of the Creature, but now, at the end of his own life, he did. The pistol wavered, then dangled limply from Victor's hand.

"I can't. . . ."

Slowly, he put the gun down. Without a word, the Creature handed over Victor's journal. Victor took the precious leather-bound journal into his frail hands, hugging it to him with a dying effort. He knew what the Creature, *his* Creature, was trying to tell him. It was over for both of them. There would be no more experiments.

Victor looked deeply into the Creature's eyes, seeing there for the first time a spark of divine humanity. How he regretted the way things had gone! If things had been different, if Victor had only lived up to his responsibilities, hadn't fled in fear back in Ingolstadt, but had stood his ground and tried to understand, had helped and nurtured the newborn being, then the Creature might perhaps have become a different person, filled with love and wisdom instead of hate and cunning. They might all be alive now—little Willie, poor Justine, his father, his beloved angel Elizabeth, and Heaven alone knew how many others. How could the Creature *not* have learned to hate? He had learned hatred when he learned the ways of Man. Men like the cowardly Victor Frankenstein had been his examples.

I meant no harm. I intended only good. It was a prayer; it was Victor's defense in front of his God; it was the last thought in his mind.

"Forgive me," Victor whispered. He slumped back onto the arm of the bed and died.

There was a moment of stillness, of honor. The Creature reached out his hand and touched the dead face of his father, Victor Frankenstein. And tears filled his eyes.

Walton gave the orders for an immediate funeral. Since they couldn't consign his body to the deep because of the ice, they decided to build a pyre and immolate him. Carrying Frankenstein out to the ice floe, they laid it on the ice, while three men chopped up the fallen mast for firewood. It was twilight, the long Arctic twilight that is neither night nor day, just as the Creature was neither animal nor man.

Very soon, the body of Victor Frankenstein was lying on an impressive bier of wood, stacked and lashed. His body was wrapped in rough canvas, his face as dead and white as the ice, his arms crossed on his breast, and a look of peace on his wind-roughened face. He seemed young again; it would be easy to believe now that this man was only twenty-five years of age.

Captain Robert Walton and his crew stood facing the bier; Walton felt that he was now a part of a much larger story, the full depth of which he might never comprehend. But it was fitting that Victor Frankenstein had met his end here, far from the haunts of man, because his plans for benefiting man had gone so sadly awry. The sailors listened gravely while their captain read aloud a passage from Ecclesiastes.

" 'And yea, I gave my heart to know wisdom and to know madness and folly: and I perceived that all is vanity and vexation of spirit. For in much wisdom is much grief: and he that increaseth knowledge, increaseth sorrow. For God shall bring every work and every secret thing into judgment whether it be good, or whether it be evil.' "

Oily black smoke from a small campfire drifted past. A little way off on the ice, the Creature stood, head back, wailing. At the inhuman sound of the howling, the men shifted uncomfortably, muttering among themselves. Walton and Grigori exchanged glances, and the captain nodded. It was time to light the pyre.

Grigori signaled to the other men. They ran forward and began dousing the pyre with a bucket of lamp oil, soaking the pyre and the body. Walton took the torch from his first mate and lit it at a pitch-pine flambeau.

The Creature was still howling, a forlorn, abandoned bestial sound, frightening enough to freeze the blood in a man's veins. Grigori, appalled by the sound, came up to Walton's elbow. "Captain—"

Walton shook his head, "It has a right to bear witness," he said firmly.

The first mate hesitated, then he nodded. Who were they to question a fellow Creature's grief? But he looked uneasy as he saw the Creature begin to move toward the ship. The crew grew more unsettled as it drew nearer. There was much frightened muttering, and some of the men started backing toward the ship. What could this Devil possibly want with them?

"Stand fast! All of you!" commanded the captain.

Reluctantly, the men obeyed orders, and came to a stop. The Creature stopped, too, some yards out. A silent tableau on the ice, with the apprehensive men facing the unpredictable Creature. What did he want? What was he going to do? Walton walked forward, holding the torch. The pyre was waiting for the kiss of the flame. He stared at the body of the dead man for a moment. The Creature only stood silent, watching.

Across the ice floe a large crack started to work its way in a zigzag toward the distant ship. A thunderous crack, like the crack of doom, split the silence. The men whipped their heads around to see a gigan-

tic plate of ice go spinning into the air some fifty
yards away, and come crashing back down again.
Like tectonic plates building pressure toward an
earthquake, it proceeded with terrifying speed and
force. The zigzag was coming straight at them.

Crack! Another eruption. Crack! And another.
CRACK! Ice burst skyward in giant chunks.

"Jesus, the bitchin' ice breakin' up! Captain, what
do we do?" cried one of the sailors.

CRACK!! The ice directly in front of Walton
erupted, sending him reeling. The torch went flying
out of his hands, to land on the floe. Walton was
thrown backward. The ice between the Creature and
the funeral pyre exploded, sending the Creature flying into the air, to land in the frigid water.

Most of the crew were on the run in full retreat,
scrambling for their lives. For miles around ice was
detonating as if pounded by artillery.

"Back to the ship!" shouted Walton as loudly as
he could. The crew scrambled to obey, but their
footing was no longer sure, and the moving ice made
it rough going.

The torch had landed on the ice just in front of
the captain, but as he leaned forward to get it, it was
pulled from his reach by the swift currents and
moved away from him on an iceberg. As he started to
go after it, his first mate yelled in his ear, pointing to
the widening crack at their feet, through which could
be seen the swift, angry current of the Arctic seas.

"Leave the damn torch! Come on!" The torch,
still flaming, continued to move away from them on
its iceberg.

With an enormous groan of timbers, the *Aleksandr
Nevsky* broke free of its prison of ice, heeling slowly
over, triggering massive eruptions in all directions. It
was pandemonium.

The crew running back toward the boat tried to clamber up the side of the ship, clinging on for dear life. Those men already on board leaned over the side, pulling their shipmates up onto the deck. Several men plummeted into the icy water as, slipping and sliding, they tumbled over the moving ice plates.

The bier carrying the corpse of Victor Frankenstein floated away from them all, spinning slowly through the currents. Suddenly, the Creature appeared from under the surface of the water. Seeing the torch floating away, he swam powerfully toward it, reaching the iceberg where the torch lay burning. He looked grimly back to Walton. The captain was standing there beckoning to him. *Come. Reach out and clasp my hand.* "Come with us," he called.

The Creature shook his head slowly. "I am done with Man," he said in a tone of finality. Taking hold of the torch he swam on toward the revolving bier.

Walton and Grigori slogged grimly on across the disintegrating ice, leaping a huge gap between the tipping icebergs. Around them, the few men not yet on board were panicking. A sailor fell into the water at their feet, and the two of them hauled him out and sent him on toward the ship. At last they reached the ship, which was heeling sharply as the ice broke up under it and the currents began to carry it forward. The men crowded around the deck rail to pull Grigori from the frigid Arctic ice and hoist him up the side of the ship.

The captain was the last man aboard, having made sure that every member of his crew was safe. Walton jumped for the ship, missed his footing and began to slide back down to the breaking ice and the frigid seas. His boots scrabbled on the side of the ship, and his hands were numb from clenching the rail. But at last, just as he was about to fall into the frigid seas, he regained his footing and climbed up on deck.

As soon as he was safe the captain lurched to the gunwale, looking for a glimpse of the Creature in the sea. The men crowded to his side. They strained their eyes in the Arctic twilight. Yes, there he was!

The Creature was swimming on, his head barely breaking the water, the torch held high to keep it burning. It was a grueling effort; these waters were frigid enough to kill, and the Creature's greatcoat must have weighed him down, but still he swam, relentlessly determined. Gasping and sinking beneath the surface, he would rise again like the phoenix in the myth.

At last the Creature's frozen fingers grasped the ice floe upon which lay Victor on his funeral pyre. He hauled himself from the water and slowly moved around to stand behind Victor's head on the bier, holding the torch aloft. Victor himself lay serene, his troubles behind him. The Creature turned his patchwork face to the sky, gulping air, and spread his arms wide in sublime triumph.

He glanced at the torch burning low in his outstretched hand. The pitch was almost gone, sputtering and trailing smoke. He looked down at his creator, wrapped in oil-soaked canvas.

Aboard the *Nevsky*, Walton and his crew looked on in horror. They knew suddenly just what the Creature's intentions were.

"Don't do it," whispered Grigori softly, and then, screaming, "For God's sake! Don't do it!"

But the Creature didn't hear him, or if he did, he didn't heed him. He turned his gaze one last time toward Heaven, finding in these last moments the sympathy he'd so long sought. He was content. He rammed the torch into the pyre beneath him. The kerosene ignited into a white-hot ball of flame. A massive ring of flame engulfed the bier, pushing a huge fiery fist into the sky. The flames went blossoming, roiling upward, reaching for Heaven with long red fingers.

The men of the *Aleksandr Nevsky* gazed in wonder and horror as the Creature, with Victor's head pressed against his body, took the torch and lit the journal, which burst into flames. Now he was cradling Victor in his arms. Their faces were pressed together through the flames. Father and son. Close at last. Peace at last. The Creature did not flinch as the flames began to eat at his flesh. They would be cremated together; it was what he wanted. Their ashes would be joined for eternity.

Robert Walton stood at the gunwale of his ship, watching the pyre burn far off, as the final act of this ghastly drama was played out to its inevitable conclusion. The aurora borealis danced mysteriously on the horizon. Distant slivers of lightning kissed the sky.

"Where to now, Captain?" a grim Grigori asked.

"Home," said Walton softly. "Let's go home." He'd had enough of obsession; he wanted peace now.

The flaming pyre, bearing the Modern Prometheus and his son, disappeared into the mist, borne away by the waves and lost to sight in darkness and distance. As for the journal of Victor Frankenstein, it was consumed in the blaze.

AFTERWORD

Frankenstein Reimagined

by Kenneth Branagh

Adapting a literary work—making it live in another medium in an interesting way, rather than just recording it—is something I've spent a lot of my limited film experience doing, particularly with Shakespeare. With *Mary Shelley's Frankenstein*, we wanted to follow the events of the novel as closely as practicable, to include as much of the story as possible, while tying everything to an overriding response to the material—that is, our interpretation of it.

For example, we wanted to use all the names correctly: in the 1931 film, Victor is called Henry Frankenstein, and they changed Henry's name to

Excerpted from *Mary Shelley's Frankenstein: A Classic Tale of Terror Reborn on Film*, published by Newmarket Press, 18 East 48th Street, New York, New York 10017. Introduction Copyright © 1994 Kenneth Branagh. Reprinted by permission.

Victor. And we've brought in such characters as Mrs. Moritz and Justine, who were left out of earlier versions. So I hope we can justify the title *Mary Shelley's Frankenstein* by finding a legitimate marriage between a desire to use excellent things in the book that hadn't been seen before, and our contemporary response to the novel and its meaning.

A Different Dr. Frankenstein

The first crucial departure for us was to render the character of Victor Frankenstein less of an hysteric—we believe Victor Frankenstein is not a mad scientist but a dangerously sane one. He is also a very romantic figure—there does seem to be much of Mary's beloved, Percy Bysshe Shelley, there. It was the dawn of the scientific age; Victor is someone ferociously interested in things of that nature. This was, as some have said, the last point in history when educated people could know virtually everything: have read every classic text, be aware of every experiment in physics, aware of medical developments, and so on. Victor, like Goethe, wanted to know more than he did, which was everything. Unlike Goethe, he discovers his limits tragically.

For me the lasting power of the story lay in its ability to dramatize a number of moral dilemmas. The most obvious one is whether brilliant men of science should interfere in the matters of life and death.

Today the newspapers are littered with such dilemmas—and they always bring up the word "Frankenstein"—for example, should parents choose the sex of their child? We can all see these developments taking place. It's now an imaginable step, to prevent people from dying. There's a place in the script where Victor says, "Listen, if we can replace one part of a person—a heart or a lung—then soon we will be able to replace every part. And if we can do that, we can design a life, a being that won't grow old, that won't sicken, a being that will be more intelligent than us, more civilized than us."

That element of Victor's philosophy is crucial. This is a sane, cultured, civilized man, one whose ambition, as he sees it, is to be a benefactor of mankind. Predominantly we wanted to depict a man who was trying to do the right thing. We hope audiences today may find parallels with Victor today in some amazing scientist who might be an inch away from curing AIDS or cancer, and needs to make some difficult decisions. Without this kind of investigative bravery, perhaps there wouldn't have been some of the advances we've had in the last hundred years—an argument Mary Shelley makes on Victor's behalf in the book.

There are weaknesses in his character. He's driven by an unyielding resistance to the way the world seems to be ordered, a resistance to the apparently arbitrary reclamation of good and kind and important people. In Victor's case—and this is most resonant in the book—his mother, someone whom he clearly adores. In his anger and grief he resists the most irresistible fact of all—Death.

He has a relationship with God that is annoyed and irritated. He says to Henry, "We're talking about research and work that may mean that people who love each other can be together forever." Victor is also tremendously romantic. He feels that the apparent natural balance—we all arrive and know we are going to die—is not necessarily a perfect one. The romantic idea of souls being together forever—and in the wake of this scientific knowledge, *literally* together forever—is something that appeals strongly to his visionary instincts.

This version also portrays Victor as someone a little more physical, earthy as well as intellectual. Rather than a neurotic aesthete, he's sort of a renaissance man, someone who could be anything he wanted to be. Someone whose future the audience can care about. If he's a powerful figure, he has more to lose. And Victor is far from perfect. He is an obsessive overreacher who fails out of what he believes to be the noblest of motives.

It's been said that, in part, the story of Frankenstein is an expression of the frustration men feel at being unable to have children on their own, and alongside that goes revulsion at the birthing process. For example, after the operatic fervor of the creation process, as this film depicts it, with the camera swinging and swooping across the lab and a great sense of power being embodied by Victor Frankenstein—the sarcophagus is suddenly thrown open and reveals this little stained burping thing which Victor is revolted by.

For anyone wishing to empathize with this character, perhaps the biggest difficulty of the book is the moment when Victor, having spent years researching and then building the Creature, is instantly repelled by it. It was one of the problems we felt we had to address: Why, after all this time, having seen what he was putting together, should he be so repelled and then be so frightened by it? We felt that if we did it exactly as the book does, it would be psychologically inconsistent with the Victor we were presenting.

The theme of parental abandonment is tremendously strong, and we tried to give Victor a moment when he is faced with what that means. "What have I done?" he says. Whether we find enough time to convince the audience that this shock has occurred—whether we believe that it would occur simply by seeing something that had been inanimate for a long time suddenly *be* there, and be so clearly and utterly dependent on him—remains to be seen. There have certainly been distressing cases in modern times, where mothers have found it difficult to hold or care for their offspring immediately after birth. We took some of these examples as our cue.

Reimagining the Creation . . .

The image I had in my mind for the birth sequence is of a child being born to parents who then walk out of the delivery room and leave this bloodstained, fluid-covered thing to just crawl around on its own. The whole issue of pregnancy and the birthing process is such an emotive one, and creates such powerful feelings in people. We tried to make it explicit in that sequence. Indeed, the entire conception/creation process is full of explicitly sexual imagery.

The Creature, once alive, is wiped down, and banged on the back and made to cough out the remaining fluid, taught how to stand and walk—far away from the old image of the pre-dressed, lumbering villain rising up from the slab. The birth image itself is one of the most striking in the film. There is a tremendously thrilling, sexual, musical sequence leading up to a moment that is without music—you hear just the shlurping of the fluid and this Thing, grunting and groaning. Suddenly, from the fever-ishly idealized imagination of Victor Frankenstein we go to the reality of a living thing—created in this abortive fashion, alive in this utterly confused way, with a set of different parts—born to a dysfunctional father.

Literary scholars often look to Mary Shelley's own life for the sources of all this: the horror of her own birth with her mother dying as a result, and Mary's own children dying in infancy.

The lack of specific information that Shelley provides about the creation process leaves filmmakers free to imagine it all sorts of ways. It's fascinating in itself, and texturally it's a good thing to have in the middle of a story like this—this rhythm of the first section leading up to this climax of creation. In the earlier Frankenstein films, of course, you had that great gothic laboratory and the body being hauled up into the storm. . . . It creates the sense of an epic struggle. Not unlike making a film, in fact. I sometimes feel there are uneasy parallels between Victor's obsessive desire to create his monster and what we've done in making a film of this size and scale. There is something compelling about watching a person in the grip of an obsession. People clearly enjoy watching other people go mad.

There is also a voyeuristic thrill to be had from watching the creation sequence. We feel as though we're behind closed doors. It's a secret. I hope the lonely and dangerous quality of this is something audiences will respond to.

. . . And the Creature

In portraying Frankenstein's Creature, we had the fundamental challenge of bringing to life in a different way a character that has already become universally familiar in another form. It began with certain decisions about the script—for example, that the Creature would learn to express himself eloquently, as he does in the book, rather than merely grunt. And of course Robert De Niro himself brought a great deal to the role.

We took as a departure point the ice cave scene in the book, where the Creature speaks so eloquently and articulately—using this to banish all comparison with the much less articulate Creature of earlier movies. (In the book, he and Frankenstein actually use a hut on the glacier, which we changed to a cave.) And again at the end, when speaking to Walton, the Creature reveals a level of sophistication, attained through the course of his education in the book, that we felt was important to achieve.

In the ice cave scene the Creature faces Victor Frankenstein with the questions that any such being might ask: What were you doing? What am I made of? Did you ever consider the consequences of your actions? You gave me emotions, you didn't tell me how to use them. Do I have a soul or is that a part you left out? The "son" questioning his father about being abandoned. That's certainly the meat of the role for an actor like De Niro, and he takes it with tremendous relish.

The Creature's rage is the product of clearly articulated confusions about where he's come from and what he's made of. It's not simply the violence of a great big tall Thing. We wanted him to be much more like an ordinary man. But one without a name or an identity.

We wanted to concentrate a lot on De Niro's

eyes—he has wonderful eyes—on trying to find the soul inside this collection of cuts and bruises and brain. That's what we want the audience to follow. There's a very strong image in Shelley's book of the Creature peering out between the boards of a pigsty, when he's crouched down and spying on the family. We reproduced that exactly, this image of the eyes as windows of his soul.

We felt that the physical silhouette of the Creature, abetted by his costumes, had to have a kind of mythic power. Something that conjured up images of Japanese warriors, or monks—that sort of dignified, noble, powerful type who represents something of what the Creature has achieved by the end of his very unsentimental education. An innocent, he learns very quickly that because of how he looks, he'll be rejected by mankind. As he says, "I think and speak and know the ways of man." We wanted him to have the tone of a philosopher, someone who's found a strange peace even if he still is tormented and frustrated by not having the companionship that humans most often need to be happy.

It was the interior, the heart and soul of the Creature, that De Niro and I were most concerned with, and the exterior had to support that. We always thought of him as a naturally gentle soul whose rage is produced when he's crossed by Frankenstein. He achieves articulacy very early on. He's a swift learner, not lumbering or slow, and not without humor. It may be confusing to some people who like their monsters a bit more "monstery." The story and the Creature in this performance remain frightening and horrific, but we wanted at all times to sympathize with him or at least understand him.

Insofar as he is a man, he embodies both the good

and evil in man and inherits the doubts and worries and concerns all human beings have. We see a child grow up before us and choose to dramatize those moments when this loss of innocence occurs.